HAPPY
Endings

HAPPY
Endings

A Novel

THIEN-KIM LAM

AVON
An Imprint of HarperCollinsPublishers

HAPPY ENDINGS. Copyright © 2021 by Thien-Kim Lam. All rights reserved. Printed in the United States of America. No part of this book may be used or reproduced in any manner whatsoever without written permission except in the case of brief quotations embodied in critical articles and reviews. For information, address HarperCollins Publishers, 195 Broadway, New York, NY 10007.

HarperCollins books may be purchased for educational, business, or sales promotional use. For information, please email the Special Markets Department at SPsales@harpercollins.com.

FIRST EDITION

Designed by Diahann Sturge

Library of Congress Cataloging-in-Publication Data has been applied for.

ISBN 978-0-06-304084-7

21 22 23 24 25   LSC   10 9 8 7 6 5 4 3 2 1

*To L.B., my happily ever after, who showed
me that love always wins*

ACKNOWLEDGMENTS

When I began my quest to write a romance that reflected my heritage and my experiences, I had no idea what I was getting into. Typing out the words to this story was a solitary endeavor, but this book would not have existed without my community.

Thank you, Erika Tsang, for taking a chance on my book and pushing me to take more risks. Tara Gelsomino, your guidance and tough love have been invaluable.

To the women of Binderhaus, you believed in me before reading a page I'd written. Lyssa Kay Adams, Jessica Cline, Jocelyn Cole, Tamara Lush, Gina Mitchican, Jennifer Seay, Amanda Trejbrowski, and Deborah Wilde, I hope we'll be able to have Hot Tub Plot Tub sessions in person soon.

Is it weird to thank Romancelandia? Many of you embraced me when I returned to romance after a long hiatus. You helped me find romances that reflected the inclusive world we live in, and I'm doing my best to tell as many people as I can about them. Gina, Tamara, Jessica, Amanda, and Adriana Herrera, your feedback on the early versions of this book helped me grow as a writer. My fellow authors Jasmine Silvera and Angelina Lopez, you lifted me up and pushed me to keep writing after a not-so-great experience.

Donyae Coles, you kept me sane throughout my revision process. You are the best hype woman!

My "oldest" friend, Jennifer Seneca, thank you for our late-night conversations and for sending me pens and notebooks to feed my addiction. It's rare that I go a day without chatting with my Boss Babes, Leticia Barr and Lisa Frame. Behind every great woman are great women replying to her texts in the middle of the night. Text me anytime, babes.

To my kids, S and J, who cheered me on and reminded me about my deadlines (multiple times), you're not allowed to read this yet! Infinite love and gratitude to my best friend and husband, L.B. For every crazy idea I've shared with you (including selling sex toys and writing this book), you've answered "Do it!" without hesitation. Thank you for believing in me.

CHAPTER 1

I s the glow-in-the-dark one leaning too hard to the left?"

Trixie Nguyen stepped back and cocked her head, taking in her artistic arrangement of vibrators, dildos, and lotions on the restaurant table. The bright purple cloth she'd tossed over two Formica tables pushed together gleamed next to the dark wood walls of Mama Hazel's, a soul-food restaurant whose worn tables and chairs had witnessed many secrets of its Northeast DC residents.

"No, he's leaning just the right amount. Your display looks perfect—like it does at all your shows," said Reina, who was coming back from the buffet line clutching two full plates. "Hurry up, I'm hungry," she added in her southern drawl.

Her best friend slid the heaping dishes of fried chicken, waffles, and collard greens onto their small round table. There were perks to holding a private pop-up shop for her bachelorette party guests inside a restaurant. For once, she didn't have customers hovering while she set up her display. Tonight, the bride-to-be and her thirty guests were spread out across several tables, each with her own plate of food. Though their feast didn't keep a few from pointing and giggling at the items on the display table.

"Wow, that smells amazing!" Trixie's stomach growled.

"You should see the buffet setup. I almost made myself two

plates, but I couldn't do that to you." Reina's wide smile was as bright as her red hair. "If the food tastes as good as it smells, I'm going back for seconds."

"Almost done." Trixie adjusted Glo-Man and placed a bottle of Unicorn Spit lube next to it. It was her first time doing a sales demo in a restaurant instead of a customer's home. "Everything needs to be perfect."

"Don't make me eat alone." Reina sat down and unrolled her silverware from the napkin. "This is totally worth fighting BW Parkway traffic across town on a Friday night during rush hour."

"Thanks again for the ride. My car will have a new transmission tomorrow, and I won't have to ask you and the rest of the Boss Babes for rides anymore."

The Boss Babes were her three brilliant, badass besties, and they'd kept her from falling apart when she left New Orleans to start over in DC two years ago. She'd known Reina the longest, after meeting her in New Orleans during undergrad.

"That sounds ex-peeeen-sive." Reina's drawl drew out the last and most cringeworthy word.

"At least I was able to book an extra show this week to pay for repairs." Her smile fell as she recalled her mechanic's estimate.

"I'm always happy to be your chauffeur. No way I'd let you take a rideshare carrying a suitcase of dildos. What if you got a creepy driver and the toys fell out of your bags?" Reina shook her head. "Hell, no. Boss Babes take care of Boss Babes."

"Thank you for—well, everything. For rescuing me from New Orleans and the longest self-pity party I've ever thrown. And giving me a job at your club until I got on my feet."

"Hush. You'd do the same for me. Besides, you were a terrible bartender," said Reina. "You're way better at slinging vibrators."

"It's easy to get distracted when there are hot guys performing burlesque onstage. Let's just say working at Lucky Stiff prepared me for this job." Trixie laughed and gestured at her display of vibrators.

She was relieved her bartending days were behind her. Tonight, Trixie was excited to explain how her table of arousal gels and battery-operated boyfriends would rock these women's worlds. The props currently on her demo table would make it an interactive experience that would hopefully lead to plenty of sales and referrals for more shows.

"This is sex on a plate," Reina moaned through bites of the crispy, juicy fried chicken. "I also ordered us a pitcher of margaritas."

"Ugh, no tequila for me." Trixie shuddered. "I need to stay sharp if I'm going to beat Betty Fairchild for sales rep of the year."

Not to mention snag the hefty bonus that came with winning. That money would bring her one step closer to opening her own sex toy boutique, where she could run things the way she wanted. After one more visual check of her display, Trixie pulled out the chair across from Reina and sat down.

"You're going to kick her ass this year!" Reina exclaimed before inhaling more food.

"I hope so." Trixie cleared her throat. "No, I *will* beat her and win the ten-thousand-dollar prize!"

"Keep saying it till you believe it."

"Yes, ma'am," Trixie replied with an exaggerated drawl. "Maybe it's not too late to change our drink order. A margarita might help my nerves right now, but it'll throw off my focus."

"Poor maligned tequila. Some of my best memories were created during a tequila haze in the French Quarter." Reina's eyes crinkled, and she winked at Trixie.

"Save your tales of debauchery for the next Boss Babes lunch!" Trixie laughed. She slid her fork out of the rolled napkin and immediately set it down. How could she be so rude? "Thanks for making me a plate, but I need to check in with Keisha first."

"Is that the woman wearing the colorful head wrap?" Reina looked over to the buffet. "She's the one who helped you organize this pop-up, right?"

Trixie followed Reina's gaze to a corner of the restaurant near the kitchen. Tables had been pushed together—much like her display table—and covered with white tablecloths to form a makeshift buffet line. It was easy to spot Keisha and her red floral head wrap, which barely contained her dark brown curls. Keisha chatted with a guest as she wiped spills and replaced serving spoons.

"Yes and yes. She's co-owner of the restaurant along with her brother." Trixie pushed back her chair. "I'll see if I can change our pitcher into one glass."

Trixie made her way across the full dining room, stopping to greet the bride-to-be and her maid of honor, who had organized tonight's bachelorette festivities. By the time she'd made it over to Keisha, a cloud of delicious scents had enveloped Trixie, and her stomach twisted in hunger. She regretted not tasting the food Reina had brought over.

"Trixie, your table looks, um, wow." Keisha giggled. "I don't think I've ever seen so many vibrators at one time."

"Oh, you get used to it." Trixie chuckled at herself. That was something she never thought she'd say about sex toys. But after working at Bedroom Frenzy for almost two years, this was her new normal. Her office showroom was overflowing with vibrators, and no one batted an eye unless a new product arrived.

"Did you make a plate yet?" Keisha stepped aside to give Trixie access to the steaming trays of food. "Or do you not eat before a show?"

"My friend Reina made me a plate, and it smells amazing. I wanted to thank you for letting us hold the bachelorette party here after the maid-of-honor's basement flooded. I'm sure you're usually swamped on weekends." Trixie hoped that tonight would be financially beneficial for both of them.

"You've kept me entertained for the past three months while we stuff hope purses together at the clinic. It's about time I saw you in action!" Keisha lowered her voice and added, "And I might need to add something new to my collection."

"I can definitely help you with that." Trixie winked. "Chatting with you makes filling the purses with pads and toiletries go faster." Trixie volunteered to teach sex-ed classes at a local women's clinic. When one of her classes was unexpectedly canceled, a bubbly woman invited Trixie to help sort toiletries and feminine hygiene donations for hope purses, which the clinic gave out to women in crisis. Three months later, they'd become friends. "Though I prefer hearing stories about your mom's food."

Keisha's smile wavered.

"I'm so sorry," Trixie blurted. "I didn't mean to make you sad."

"No, it's okay. Grief is weird. She's been gone for over a year now and it doesn't get any easier." Keisha squared her shoulders. "Do you need anything before you start your presentation? How about a cocktail?"

"No. I mean, Reina ordered a pitcher of margaritas and that's too much." Trixie turned to their shared table near her display area at the front of the restaurant. Reina was literally licking her plate.

Keisha followed her gaze and laughed. "It's not the first time an adult has licked their plate at Mama Hazel's."

"That's a good testimonial. If it's not too much of a hassle, can you change that to one margarita and a water?"

"How about I make it a half pitcher? On the house." Keisha put up a finger before Trixie could protest. "To thank you for introducing our place to some new folks."

Trixie nodded. "I'm going to sound like a broken record if I thank you again."

"Then don't. Go eat before your plate gets cold. I'll check on your drink order."

On the way back to Reina, party guests stopped her several times inquiring about different items on her display table. Trixie offered variations of "Wait and see" as she wove her way through the tables. Now that the guests' bellies were full, they were ready for Trixie's part of the party.

"Sorry that took so long." Trixie slid back into her chair.

"You know better than to leave me alone with good food. I almost ate yours," Reina teased. "Don't apologize for doing your job. You're a natural with your customers. Your boutique is going to help so many people."

"Once it's up and running, I can prove to my parents I'm not a failure. That I don't need to be a pharmacist or doctor or whatever else on the Viet parent–approved list." Not that Trixie hadn't tried. Memorizing names of meds and dosages bored her to death. She'd flunked her first semester of pharmacy classes.

"Sweetie, you're not a failure because you want to follow your heart."

"It's not like I planned on selling vibrators as a career," Trixie replied. "Who knew the beauty sales job was about beauty products for your lady bits?"

"That's what you get for answering 'help wanted' ads on Craigslist." Reina bit her lip to hold back her laughter. "You were in complete shock after that job interview."

"It was you and the rest of the Boss Babes who convinced me to take the job, remember?" Trixie was glad her friends had pushed her to try something new. But it turned out talking about sex wasn't that far outside her comfort zone. "I can't afford grad school to become a therapist, but I can help people be more comfortable with their sexuality."

"See? Following your heart."

"Not to mention, this is the best-paying job I've had ever. I've put a major dent in my student loans."

"I'm really proud of you," Reina said. "It's not easy going against your family's wishes and striking out on your own. You're a badass at this job and making enough to take care of yourself. That's success to me. Winning your company contest will be the cherry on top."

"Stop. You're going to make me cry right before I do my presentation." Trixie knew her friend was right, but it wasn't enough. She couldn't return to her family in New Orleans until she was her own boss.

"Fine. How about you try this chicken and cry about how good it is?" Reina mocked stabbing her fork into Trixie's food.

Relieved to change the subject, Trixie unrolled her paper napkin and tucked it into her teal blouse. Talking about the benefits of lube with a giant grease stain on her shirt would be distracting and unprofessional. She reached into her purse and grabbed a hair elastic. Her long, wavy black hair was overdue for a cut and style.

"Speaking of crying over something delicious, there's a tall drink of water working the bar tonight." Reina looked past Trixie and cocked her head. "Boy, am I thirsty."

"Reina," Trixie warned as she fought the urge to turn around. "I'm supposed to be working. Not checking out bartenders."

"Doesn't hurt to admire the scenery." Reina grinned. "Hot damn, his biceps are spectacular. I wanna lick every inch of his dark brown—"

Trixie couldn't stand it. She shot a glance behind her, trying not to be too obvious.

"Oh my God!" She turned back around. The hair elastic shot out of her hand and hula-hooped around the Glo-Man. She hunched over her plate of chicken and waffles, trying to make herself as small as possible.

"Trixie, are you all right? I'm sorry. I'm messing up your flow before your presentation." Reina gently touched Trixie's arm. "I'll behave."

"He's not just any bartender." Trixie's chest tightened and her heart raced. She'd never expected to see him again. Not after he ghosted her in New Orleans two years earlier.

"Hey, do you know him? Spill the beans."

"Andre," Trixie whispered. "That's Andre Walker."

"The jerk from New Orleans who dumped you with a Post-it note?"

"After almost two years together," Trixie scoffed. She wasn't just mad because of how he broke up with her. He'd left her after her family had kicked her out. He'd abandoned her when she had nowhere else to turn. When she needed his strength the most.

Wait, Keisha's last name was also Walker. She didn't talk about her sibling much except to say that he'd become a helicopter brother since their mother died. Her brother "Tre" must have been Andre. They had the same eyes. How could Trixie be so clueless?

"No one dumps a Boss Babe with a note. Especially a Post-it." Reina's green eyes flared with anger. She set down her fork and pushed back her chair. "I'm going to give him a piece of my mind."

"Don't cause a scene," Trixie hissed. "Please? I'm working."

She didn't need Reina to start an argument with the co-owner of the restaurant, especially when he was her ex-boyfriend. Trixie had bachelorette party guests to entertain and vibrators to sell.

"Fine. Once the party is over, I'm headed straight to the bar." Reina tilted her head. "Do you think knocking him in the head with the Glo-Man counts as assault with a deadly weapon?"

"You are not allowed to break him!" Trixie's lips pressed together as she snuck another glance at Andre, who looked even more handsome than she remembered. "Glo-Man's one of my top sellers."

CHAPTER 2

There are dildos on the table?" Andre glared at his sister.

"Ding, ding! My big bro is so smart." Keisha grinned. "I had no idea they came in so many colors. I mean, besides the obvious skin tones."

"Keisha," he growled, keeping his voice low so the customers couldn't hear him. "You said bachelorette party. Not . . . *sex* party!"

"Relax, Tre. It's a sex *toy* party. Any sex will happen off premises—after the party."

He grimaced.

"Sorry, I meant to say 'Andre.' I know you're not going by 'Tre' anymore."

"It's fine." Andre had given up on his sister and the neighborhood seeing him as anything besides little Tre, the third in his family to carry his name. What he didn't want to do was talk about sex with his sister. "A heads-up would have been nice."

"If I'd told you, would you have turned down thirty-five dollars a head plus a cash bar?" She waved her arm toward the thirty or so women sitting in the dining room.

Andre did the mental math. With the per-person rate and all the cocktails he had already served, they were going to pull in more than any recent Friday night service. Though their inheritance was the restaurant itself, his mom had left them with enough savings to reinvest into Mama Hazel's. Installing a bar and fighting the city's red tape for a liquor license had been worth the hassle.

He hated when his sister was right. At least it meant her accounting classes at the community college were paying off.

"Pay attention. Might learn a thing or two." Keisha picked up the tray of buttery nipple shots that he had made and stepped back from the bar.

Before he could respond, she walked off to deliver the drinks to table five. Andre wiped down the perfectly clean counter where Keisha had set down her serving tray. He wasn't naïve enough to think his sister didn't have sex. She was twenty-six and never lacked for a date. If only he could wipe the sex toy conversation from his brain. Which was not going to happen for the next two hours.

He turned back to the pile of tickets and resumed filling drink orders. Business had been slow. Very slow. It was now mid-August, so he couldn't blame the empty seats on the locals leaving town for summer vacations. There should be more customers due to the sweltering late-summer heat. People would rather eat out than heat up their own kitchen.

Being the only man in a room full of women waving vibrators around was going to be awkward as hell. But the restaurant needed every dollar it could get. Chain stores and hipster restaurants had practically taken over their neighborhood, and a small storefront like Mama Hazel's couldn't compete with the franchises and the dairy-free, gluten-free, *taste*-free eateries two blocks over.

The revolution had begun shortly after his mom passed away about eighteen months ago. He thought the newness would wear off and people would grow tired of trendy, overpriced restaurants at District Market. Suburbanites eagerly hopped the Red Line to show off their smoothie bowls and quinoa tacos on social media. District Market continued to draw foot traffic away from the businesses that had supported their community for years.

"Two pitchers of margaritas." Keisha shouted the order over her shoulder as she ran into the kitchen. His sister was doing double duty waitressing and keeping the buffet well stocked while their cook cranked out the food.

Andre smiled and pulled out two plastic pitchers. He could never be mad at his sister for long. She got a kick out of pushing his buttons, but she worked hard to help run their restaurant since their mother passed away. She was the only family he had left.

His sister had taken care of their mom while he'd spent two years finding himself in New Orleans. Instead of coming back to DC when his mom asked him to, he'd made excuses. After this bartending competition, he promised. Then there was another one. One more.

He should have been in DC to hold their hands when the doctor delivered the diagnosis that Mama had breast cancer. Instead, Keisha had to bear the burden. He'd let them down then.

Andre had dropped all his obligations in New Orleans and flown home. Mama's diagnosis was grim. Doctors had caught the cancer too late. The last six months of her life had not been enough to make up for his selfish two-year stint in the Deep South. So much time wasted.

Mama had built this restaurant from almost nothing while raising the two of them on her own. He'd do everything in his power to keep her hard work and passion alive. Like make margaritas at a private bachelorette party.

"Could you make one of those half a pitcher and take it to table three? I need to run back and grab more waffles." Keisha walked past the bar with a tray of fried chicken.

"Got it." He wiped his hands and picked up a pitcher. A quick glance at table three revealed two women happily tearing into his mom's secret chicken recipe. A woman with long black hair with her back to the bar and a white woman with red hair were leaning into each other in an intimate conversation.

Grabbing two glasses, he coated the rims with salt and set them on the serving tray with the pitcher. It was odd that bachelorette party guests would order only half a pitcher. He'd slung drinks enough for bachelorette parties in the Quarter to know that getting drunk was a highlight for the ladies. At least half of a pitcher was better for business than two glasses of water.

Instead of weaving through the full dining room, he swung around the side. Seeing a man walk through the crowd might make the guests feel uncomfortable. Better to disappear as much as he could.

This entire situation was getting more awkward by the minute. What would the neighbors say when they learned Mama Hazel's had turned into a private sex toy pop-up? He was pretty sure his little sister didn't even consider how this could hurt the restaurant's reputation. It was too late to worry about the consequences now. He would find another way to bring more people to the restaurant.

As he came closer to the table, something about the Asian woman seemed familiar. He shook away the feeling. Thinking about New Orleans and Mama had him out of sorts.

"Evening, ladies. My sister tells me you're thirsting for margaritas." Andre flashed a smile and set the pitcher on the table.

"Well, bless your heart." A southern drawl oozed out of the red-head's mouth as her green eyes flashed daggers at him. He'd lived in New Orleans long enough to know those words were meant as an insult.

"Reina!" a familiar voice rang out.

Andre froze. He closed his eyes. It couldn't be her. That woman just sounded like her because New Orleans had been on his mind.

Still, he could never forget that lilting voice. He opened his eyes and forced himself to turn toward her. Yes, it definitely was—

"Trixie."

She was more beautiful than ever. The black hair she usually wore in a ponytail cascaded in waves down her back. Her dark brown eyes bore into him, and her pink lips held a forced smile. Soft, full lips that he'd kissed almost every day for nearly two years. Until—he took a deep breath. An ache settled in his chest. Andre plastered on his neutral bartender smile.

This Friday night sucked.

"Long time no see, Andre Walker. Or should I say 'Tre'?" She did not sound happy to see him.

"What are you doing in DC?" he blurted. When her question registered, he replied, "I'm a third."

"Third?" Her brow furrowed.

"My full name is Andre Walker III, after my father and his father. Growing up everyone called me Tre."

When he'd moved to New Orleans four years ago, he needed to be his own person, not connected to his mom or the restaurant. He'd dropped his childhood nickname, Tre. With the city's French history, "Andre" fit right in. Going by it made him feel more grown-up. People automatically treated him like an adult.

Unlike people here, who couldn't see him as anyone but little Tre, Hazel's boy whose father died when he was young.

"You left bartending in New Orleans to tend bar in DC." Trixie pulled the napkin out of her shirt and stood up. "Guess you've moved on and up."

Behind him, Reina snorted.

Her short frame only reached his chin, but her verbal jab surprised him, and he took a step back. The Trixie he knew was quick-witted but didn't cut people down. Not even when people were unkind.

Not that she was meek. She had tried to see both sides. But this Trixie—she wanted to fight. Correction. She wanted to fight him. Which simultaneously put him on guard and turned him on. Nope, he shouldn't even go there.

"Mama Hazel's is—was our mother's restaurant. Keisha—she's my sister—and I run it." He nodded in the direction of their make-shift buffet area, where Keisha had—once again—replenished the fried chicken. He made a note to bump up their chicken order this week.

"Your mom owned a restaurant and you never told me?" Trixie waved her arm at the large dining room in disbelief. "*And* you have a sister?"

She looked toward his sister and back at him. Oh, she was pissed.

"Keisha is three years younger than me." Andre kept his face blank, but for the third time that evening, guilt flared. Even though they'd dated for two years, he'd been cryptic about his family whenever she asked.

When he arrived in New Orleans, he'd wanted a clean slate. A new name and no history to tie himself to anyone. Running away from his family, from DC—everything from his former life—had been so easy then. Now he was back in the neighborhood he grew up in, working at his mom's restaurant. As if nothing had ever changed.

"I can see the resemblance," Reina said.

"This is one of my best friends, Reina Guidroz." Trixie turned to her friend. "Reina, this is Andre Walker *the Third*, aka Tre, aka the asshole who walked out of my life and never looked back."

The bitterness in her voice stung.

"We agreed it was for the best." He knew the excuse was lame as soon as he said it.

"No, *we* didn't. You took that choice from me when you wrote that Post-it note."

Each word stabbed him like a knife, and he deserved every single cut that went right into his heart.

Unsure how to respond to her anger, he turned to acknowledge Reina. "Nice to meet you. I hope you're enjoying Mama Hazel's."

"The food is to die for! But the entertainment is even better." She poured herself a hefty serving of margarita then leaned back in her chair and sipped from her glass. "Carry on, you two. I want to see Trixie kick your ass."

"I thought we were in love. Instead, you ghosted me, and now I find out you have a sister and a restaurant?" Hurt replaced the anger in her eyes. "You lied to me about—everything. Was the Andre Walker I spent almost two years with even real?"

"Of course he—I was real." He might have used a new name during his four years in New Orleans, but he didn't pretend to be someone else.

"Did you even love me?" Trixie snapped, her breath hot against his neck. She locked eyes with him, refusing to stand down.

Andre opened his mouth but didn't know how to respond. He'd loved her to his core. She'd been his one regret when he left New Orleans. If he didn't love her, he wouldn't have left her the way he had.

Except he didn't know how to explain it to her. Even if they weren't standing in his restaurant next to a table full of dildos.

"I let you ruin my life then, but you're never going to hurt me again." Trixie's low voice didn't hide her scorn for him. "I hate you, Andre Walker the Third."

"Now, that's a bit harsh, let me ex—" Andre started.

Before he could reply, Reina stood up and stepped in between him and Trixie, forcing him to take a step back.

"You have a show to do." Reina rubbed Trixie's arms. "You can't win first place if you're upset."

He couldn't make out Trixie's response, but she sounded calmer.

"Now, you!" Reina spun around. Her wavy red hair flew with her and almost hit him in the face. He jerked his head back. With her three-inch heels, she was almost at eye level with him.

"You need to go to the bar and leave us alone." Reina spoke quietly, but the threat was clear in her voice. "Trixie has vibrators to sell."

Wait, Trixie was the sales rep? While he could easily imagine the redhead talking about vibrators and sex, the Trixie he used to know kept that topic to the bedroom . . . where she had been incredibly well versed. He didn't need to think about her dexterity in the bedroom right now.

He met Reina's gaze. "I can keep things professional."

Andre turned to Trixie. "I hope Keisha told you this was a one-time deal. We don't need to turn this place into a sex shop." He picked up their empty glasses and started back to the bar.

"You might have more customers if I turned it into one," Trixie said. "Keisha told me business has been nonexistent."

Ignoring her last words, he made his way back to the bar, where more drink orders waited for him. His body turned on autopilot as he mixed rum and Cokes plus more pitchers of margaritas. Trixie's words were true, but he didn't need her to remind him that Mama Hazel's was failing.

They needed this pop-up. He couldn't afford to turn away business or ruin the evening that Keisha had organized. All he needed to do was to keep his distance from Trixie. Even if he couldn't escape the memories of their time together in New Orleans. After tonight he wouldn't have to see or think about her again. For the second time.

CHAPTER 3

I saved the best for last." Trixie held up the purple vibrator that looked like a thumb and index finger held out. Except the thumb part had rabbit ears on the end. The demo for this toy was one of her favorite parts of her sales show. Everyone was hanging on her every word. "Meet Jack."

"Hi, Jack!" multiple voices rang out, as if they were vying for a red rose on *The Bachelor*.

"His full name is Jack of All Trades because"—she paused for extra suspense. The crowd leaned closer—"he does everything except take out the garbage and load your dishwasher."

More laughter. That joke was always a hit. When she took this job last year, she'd used the sales script provided by the company. She'd read about sex toys in erotica and romances but hadn't tried one out until she started this job. As she became more comfortable with the products and talking about them in front of strangers, Trixie came up with her own sales pitch.

"This bad boy is designed for both inner and outer play. The rabbit ears tuck around your clit, while the other part—let me show you." Without taking her eyes off the women, she pressed a button and the beads inside the toy's base began to rotate. Jack's shaft twirled clockwise, then, with the press of another button, twirled counterclockwise.

Everyone gasped in amazement.

"Hell, Jack can load me up anytime!" shouted out the tipsy bride-to-be. Giggles and murmurs of agreement erupted among her friends.

"There you have it. Our bride is adding Jack to her wish list. Don't forget you can purchase items from her list to help her build her passion trunk." Trixie winked at the bride. "I'll make sure everything arrives in time for the honeymoon."

Her friends cheered and encouraged the bride to add more items to her wish list. Turning the bachelorette shows into sex toy bridal showers had been such a hit, other reps at Bedroom Frenzy now incorporated this strategy into their shows.

A woman in the front made an impatient grabby hand motion, so Trixie passed Jack to her. She knew it would be her top seller tonight—just like it was at all her shows. Part of her job was to explain each item's features, but putting the toys into the customers' hands sold the toy. Once they felt the smooth silicone and wrapped their hand around the rumbly vibrations, they could imagine how it would feel on more intimate body parts.

As the final products made their way around the room and back up front to Trixie, she wrapped up the demo part of the show. "When you're ready, meet me in my office"—she pointed at the table she'd shared with Reina earlier—"and I'll process them. Everything you order is confidential, as are any questions you have about them. Your items will be shipped directly to you in the mail."

"What does the box look like?" asked the maid of honor.

"It's a plain brown box. The packaging won't say anything about sex toys on it," Trixie assured her guests.

"My delivery guy is hot," grabby hands lady said. "Can you put *Dick in a Box* on mine?"

The crowd roared, and Trixie joined them in laughter.

One by one, the women sat down with Trixie to place their orders. Here was the part she looked forward to. This private time with the guests was when she was truly able to help them. Even though she'd only met them a couple of hours before, they whispered their deepest fears to her.

A woman confessed that she'd never had an orgasm before and thought something was wrong with her until tonight's show. Another worried about emasculating her partner if she asked to use a toy during sex. Grabby hands lady was no longer interested in sex, but tonight made her want to give it another try.

Finally, it was the bride's turn.

"I can't wait to tell Wyatt about all the fun stuff we're getting!" Her friends had purchased everything on her wish list for her. Trixie only suggested the addition of lube and toy cleaner, which the bride happily added to her order. "I couldn't have had a better bachelorette party. Thank you!"

Once the bride was done, the bachelorette party moved their festivities over to the bar.

Trixie grinned as the intoxicated bride-to-be knocked back her buttery nipple shot and pumped her fist in the air. "Oh my God, I can't believe I'm getting married!" The rest of her friends followed suit and cheered along.

There was something about good food and frank discussions about sex that encouraged her customers to open their wallets. Though Trixie hadn't done all the math yet, tonight's show had been her most successful one this year. It wasn't just the income—she loved being able to help the women. Not just the ones who came in for the one-on-one "consultation" when they ordered, but the women who sat quietly in the back absorbing every second of her presentation.

When she first started this job a year ago, she was shocked by how little women knew about their bodies—herself included. Sex had been a taboo topic in her family, like in most Vietnamese families. Because of this, sex had felt serious and mysterious to her. Even when she became sexually active in college. She learned about sex from books and searching the Web. She had taken this job because she needed the work, but it was one of the best things to ever happen to her. Doing this helped her to realize how many misconceptions she'd had about pleasure and sexuality. Bedroom Frenzy taught her to embrace the fun of sex. Now it was her turn to teach others.

Behind the swarm of women at the bar, she could see a blur of tight black T-shirt and dark brown skin as Andre poured another round of shots. He seemed thinner, and she'd caught a glimpse of sadness in his eyes during their earlier exchange. He still kept his black hair in a short fade, but now he sported a light beard. She didn't care for beards on her men, but the tight coarse curls around his mouth and on his chin were sexy on Andre.

Seeing him again combined with the smell of fried chicken reminded her of their time together in New Orleans. He'd kissed her, clothes and hair exuding a mix of his masculine scent and Fleur de Lis, the bar where he worked. After he showered off the smells of fried food and spilled beer, she'd lain on his chest and inhaled his clean, woodsy scent while they watched cooking shows in bed. Thinking about the two of them in bed reminded her of the orgasmic high and musk of their post-sex bliss.

Now wasn't the time to rehash those memories. She wouldn't let their past ruin her sales-show high. Not even the unpleasant encounter when he'd brought the drinks to her table. Trixie was glad she wouldn't have to see him again after tonight.

She didn't need his restaurant to do her job. Most of her clients preferred buying sex toys in the privacy of their own home, surrounded by friends. This pop-up was a one-time event at Mama Hazel's. Trixie vowed to never see or speak to Andre ever again. This time it would be her decision. Not his.

"I love watching you in your element!" Reina handed her the stray order forms, catalogs, and penis pencil toppers that she'd picked up from the tables. "You're going to kick ass in Bedroom Frenzy's contest."

"I'd better. I've been stuck in third place all summer. And a new laptop is cool, but the money would be better." Trixie placed all the papers into her worn brown leather tote. "Thanks again for your help."

"If by helping you mean sitting here and eating the most amazing chicken and waffles I've ever put in my mouth, then you're welcome." Reina lowered her voice. "Andre may be a jerk, but he serves the best food I've had since I moved up here."

Trixie gave a half-hearted laugh. Her friend was right about the food. It was delicious. Like Trixie, Reina was a New Orleans native. A native who constantly moaned how Washington, DC, was not really the South—especially in the food department.

"Tonight was my best show this year!" Trixie resisted the urge to jump up and down as she changed the subject from Andre. "If I could have at least one like this every month for the rest of the year, I'm a shoo-in for first place."

"You can't go wrong with booze, good food, and battery-operated boyfriends," Reina said. "I think I just described my Friday night date!"

Reina waggled her eyebrows. Trixie laughed.

"Which boyfriend do you want? It's my gift to you for being my chauffeur and assistant tonight. I'll even toss in batteries." Her company never included batteries with any of their products. Sometimes Trixie would offer them free of charge to encourage customers who were on the fence. What was the point of buying a sex toy when they had to steal AAs out of their TV remotes?

"Now, that's friendship!" Reina chuckled. "Hanging out with you is the only gift I want. Though I'd like my own suction-cup, glow-in-the-dark dildo so I can play ring toss in my office."

"He's yours! I'll order you a brand-new Glo-Man."

"Oooh, a virgin."

"You are so bad!"

"I'm just being my fabulous self." Reina winked and tossed her red hair.

"Yes, you are." Trixie hugged Reina.

"Which reminds me. My offer is still good." Reina shot a look toward the bar. "Say the word and I'll kick his ass."

"I love that you have my back, but I don't want you arrested because of him. He's not worth it. I'm over him."

Except she wasn't. Seeing him again stirred up conflicting emotions. She wanted more closure than the note he'd left. And standing so close to his warm, muscular body had aroused her in ways a vibrator couldn't take care of.

Trixie needed to stay focused on her career. She wasn't about to give Andre Walker the chance to derail her dreams—or break her heart a second time.

CHAPTER 4

Two weeks later

"To the Bitchin' Boss Babes!" The four women clinked their glasses.

These weekly meetings were the highlight of Trixie's week.

At least once a week, she and her three best friends met for a business mastermind session, but the late lunches always became a combination of brainstorming business ideas and day drinking.

Without their help, Trixie would be aimlessly moving from job to job in DC, much like how she'd done in New Orleans after Andre dumped her. Reina had offered her a bartending job even though Trixie's main experience with cocktails was drinking them. Zoe literally opened her door to Trixie and let her move in rent free until she got on her feet. Then there was Josie Parks, the Boss Babes' leader, who helped Trixie set goals after she took the Bedroom Frenzy job.

"We made it another week, babes." Reina lifted her margarita and took another sip before anyone else lifted hers. "Too bad the zoning meeting I attended this week didn't serve cocktails. There would've been fewer stuffy dudes arguing."

Though Trixie was a latecomer to the group, she knew the origin story by heart. A few years ago, the three women attended a chamber of commerce happy hour only to be snubbed by all the suit-wearing, "serious" business owners there. They ended up huddling around a small cocktail table. Once they learned about each woman's "nontraditional" business, Boss Babes was formed.

Trixie sipped her cà phê sữa đá and leaned against the booth's high-backed seat. Phở-Ever 75 was one of the few places where they could commandeer a table for their long lunch meetings, and the dark roast espresso sweetened with condensed milk reminded her of home.

"Another toast to my parents, who don't mind that we spend hours at their restaurant and only buy a bowl of phở each." Zoe Tran, the best roommate Trixie could ever have, raised her glass.

"And for finding a parking space at Eden Center in less than five minutes."

Holding their weekly meetings among flourishing businesses run by scrappy Vietnamese refugees was fitting for the Boss Babes. The small strip mall in Falls Church was a hotspot frequented by the local Vietnamese American community and non-Viet people. Though the parking lot was huge, the center's popularity meant driving in circles and following people to find a parking spot.

"Cheers to Auntie Trinh and Uncle Van!" Trixie was a frequent visitor to Eden Center, not just for food but when attending Tết for fireworks and lion dancing to celebrate the New Year. Spending time with Zoe's family during festivals helped Trixie feel a little less homesick for her family.

She found comfort in the sameness of phở restaurants, no matter where they were located. Utilitarian metal chairs with cheap vinyl cushions that scraped the linoleum floor when you pulled them from under the table. Photos of idyllic prewar Vietnam hung on the walls. Depending on the owner's religion, there may be a small ancestral shrine that held burnt incense sticks and an offering of fresh fruit. Oh, and there was always a small South Vietnamese flag somewhere in the restaurant, the golden yellow rectangle with three proud red horizontal stripes in the middle.

Trixie pulled a paper napkin from its holder and wiped where the small coffee filter had dripped onto the red gingham vinyl tablecloth. She grabbed a pair of melamine chopsticks from the tray in the middle of the table, next to a plate filled with fresh herbs, bean sprouts, jalapeños, and limes waiting to be dunked into steaming bowls of beef noodle soup. She'd eaten this almost every Sunday at her parents' home. It was her ultimate comfort food.

"Now that my cranberry and vodka and I are reacquainted, let's go around the table and update us on your business. Reina has already shared one of hers. Trixie, what are your wins for the week?" Josie ran a boudoir photography business. Not only was she a talented artist, but she was brilliant with numbers. With her warm brown skin and tall Afro, she could have easily been a model. Instead, she chose to stay behind the camera to capture her clients' sensuality.

"No wins this week. The huge bachelorette party earlier this month put me at second place, but since then my sales have flatlined. Wedding season is mostly over, so no bachelorette shows for a while." Trixie sighed. "Not only that, I've dropped back to third place."

"Your win is that you kicked ass at the show," Reina said. "That's thirty more women who know how to pleasure themselves."

"That show was pretty good," Trixie admitted. But only if she didn't count running into Andre there. "A few women texted me some fireworks emojis after their packages arrived."

"I say happy customers are a win." Reina was always the cheerleader of their group. "You have to celebrate the small accomplishments, too."

Growing up with overachieving siblings made it hard for Trixie to embrace minor achievements. No matter what she'd accomplished, her brother and sister got better grades and won more awards. Even chose the right careers. But hanging out with the Boss Babes never felt like a competition. They supported her when she was down and pushed her out of her comfort zone when she needed it. Like today.

"Are you on track to meet your sales goal this month?" Josie was a whiz at business planning and projecting sales. Her photography business was in such high demand, she had a two-month-long wait list.

"I'm far behind, based on the spreadsheet you helped me put together." Trixie rubbed her forehead. "I'm running out of ideas on how to find new show hosts."

"We could hold another event at Lucky Stiff." Reina waggled her eyebrows. Her club had been voted DC's top all-male burlesque club two years running.

"That was some night," Zoe's soft voice chimed in. With her short, sleek bob, she was the most stylish of the Boss Babes. That was no surprise, since she owned a boutique where she designed and sold plus-size lingerie.

They all laughed.

"Sweet Jesus." Reina whistled. "My guys had a blast dressing up and serving cosmos to those wild women."

"Girl, I couldn't believe how many Jack of All Trades you sold!" Josie said. "Those were some happy ladies."

"Mmm-hmm," Reina agreed. "She sold a ton of those at Mama Hazel's, too." There were a few seconds of silence while each woman recalled her own experience with the rabbit vibe's rumbly ears and rotating beads.

"When I'm trying to figure out why one negligee sells ten times better than another design, I look at customer reviews and what I did differently with it," said Zoe, who designed a majority of the intimates in her boutique, Something Cheeky. "What happened at Lucky Stiff and Mama Hazel's that was different from your other shows?"

"Let's see—"

"Booze," Reina interrupted Trixie. "My club has the best bartenders, but the margarita from Mama Hazel's was perfect. Those gals were in great moods by the time Trixie started her presentation."

"At the bachelorette parties I do in people's homes, the maid of honor usually has a table set up with wine bottles and a few liquors for DIY cocktails," Trixie added. "Not having to make your own drinks probably made the evening feel more special."

"Don't forget the food," Reina added. "There was an all-you-can-eat soul food spread that was so to die for."

"Good food always brings people together." Zoe gestured to their table in her family's restaurant. "And puts them in a good mood."

"What if you re-created that big show? No bride-to-be needed," Josie suggested. "Like a pop-up shop for your best customers?"

Zoe nodded. "Maybe you could do another one at—"

"No!" Trixie's voice echoed in the mostly empty restaurant.

Meeting after the lunch rush had yet another perk. No diners to disturb when she accidentally raised her voice. "I'm not going back there."

"Back to Lucky Stiff?" Zoe's face scrunched in confusion.

"No, the restaurant where the bachelorette party was held." Trixie swallowed the panic in her throat. She didn't want to see Andre ever again.

"I didn't say you had to go back to that restaurant." Josie eyed Trixie, then looked over at Reina. "What didn't you tell us?"

Trixie and Reina made eye contact and quickly looked away from each other. Josie crossed her arms and stared them down.

"The co-owner of Mama Hazel's is Trixie's ex," Reina blurted out. "I'm sorry, Trixie, but they should know who that jerk is."

"You never told us you had an ex-boyfriend who lived in the DMV." Zoe sounded hurt.

"I had no idea he came back to the metro area," she replied. She realized how little she knew about Andre outside of their time in New Orleans. It wasn't for lack of trying. She'd been so absorbed with her family troubles that she hadn't pushed him for more. "He ghosted me, remember?"

"You never did tell us what happened with him," Josie said. "All I knew was that you had a bad breakup in New Orleans and came here to start over."

"Even though he dumped me two years ago, it's still hard to talk about." Trixie owed them the full story. "He's the reason my parents kicked me out. I'd flunked out of my first semester of pharmacy school and he'd convinced me to tell my parents I wanted to become a therapist instead." Trixie turned to Zoe. "You know Vietnamese parents don't believe in therapy. It's not on the approved list of medical careers."

"Only medical doctors, dentists, and pharmacists." Zoe ticked off the list on her fingers. "But never therapists because that's not 'real' doctoring."

"Some Black folks don't believe in it either." Josie sighed. "But back to what happened in New Orleans."

"My parents were furious with my decision and kicked me out, so I moved in with Andre. A couple of months after that, he dumped me with a Post-it note stuck to the fridge. It read *It's over. You deserve better.*"

Zoe gasped. Josie growled.

"At least he had the decency to cover three months' rent. I—" Trixie's voice cracked. "I never heard from him again."

"Oh, Trixie." Zoe reached over and hugged her. She and Zoe had grown close as roommates. Both were daughters of Vietnamese immigrants, and they understood the pressure their parents put on them to be successful. Too bad Trixie's parents weren't as understanding as Zoe's parents when it came to nontraditional career choices.

"I'm sorry." Josie touched Trixie's hand. "It must have been terrible to see him after all that time."

"It's in the past. Right now, I'm focused on the future. I'm going to set up shop after I win first place. Once it's open, my parents will see that I made the right career choice for me. Not for them. I'm not giving up."

CHAPTER 5

Monday

"Fuck!"

Andre resisted the urge to slam the phone down after hearing the voicemail that his bank loan application had been denied. Duct tape barely kept the battery from popping out, and the base garbled any messages it managed to record. Mama Hazel's had moved to a digital voicemail system while he'd been in New Orleans, and the phone still worked, so why replace it?

If he was honest with himself, he wanted to keep the relic because Mama had been so excited when she'd "upgraded" the restaurant's phones. Sometimes if he stood in the doorway of this office and looked hard enough, he could see Mama sitting in this same worn chair with the phone cradled in the crook of her neck and shoulder.

With no bank to bail them out, he had to figure out how to move the money around to replace the fryer. He dug through the stacks of bills for a scrap piece of paper but settled on using the back of an envelope from their produce vendor.

"Hey, what's going on?" Keisha popped her head into the office. "I thought I heard a yell."

"I thought you were in class." Andre grabbed the unopened bills and flipped them over so she couldn't see who they were from. "Sorry I disturbed you."

"We had a test and I finished early." Keisha brushed imaginary lint off her shoulder and grinned. "Your sister is a whiz at numbers, you know."

He nodded.

"You're supposed to say, 'Keisha, you're the smartest person I know,'" teased Keisha.

"If you already know it, why should I say it?" he tossed back.

She stuck her tongue out at him before throwing herself onto the futon they used for naps in between meal services.

"Now spill it." She crossed her arms. "Or show me those bills you're trying to hide from me."

He wanted to tell her after he'd come up with some solutions, but she was dead serious about going through everything on his desk.

"We didn't get the loan."

Keisha's face fell. She walked over to him.

"Andre, we'll figure something out." She leaned over and wrapped her arms around him before he could stand up. "We always have. Just like Mama did."

His sister was the more optimistic one in their family. Figuring out a life without Mama had been hard. Keisha had missed too many classes when Mama was diagnosed with breast cancer. Since she'd passed, Andre had tried to shoulder as much responsibility as he could so Keisha could focus on school.

"It needs to be soon. The fryers are working for now, but one is going to break again. We can't afford to lose a fryer." Seeing the worry in his sister's hazel eyes, he forced a smile. "It'll be fine, Keisha."

"It's not that." She sniffed and blinked rapidly, as if she was holding back tears. "I don't want anything to happen to Fred."

Who the hell was Fr— He'd forgotten she'd named their double fryers after the Weasley twins from her favorite childhood books. Before he could respond, she broke out in laughter.

"Oh my God, you should have seen your face, Andre!" Keisha doubled over. "Why do you think I named him Fred and not George? That one has always been on the fritz."

"You're such a nerd." He pulled one of her curls and let it spring back up.

"Stop it. Mama thought it was clever." She pushed some papers aside and pulled herself onto the desk. "I miss Mama so much. Some days, I'm minding my own business, then *bam*. I hear someone talking and it sounds almost like her voice, but not quite."

"I know." He sighed. "Like I don't want to replace this sorry excuse for a phone because she asked Santa to buy her a fancy cordless one knowing full well—"

"We were supposed to buy it for her." Keisha finished his sentence. "She hinted about it for weeks!"

"Even though she could have bought it for herself. She worked so hard to provide for us." And now he was trying his best to pick up where she left off.

"You know it was easier for her to help others than it was to treat herself. Like serving community dinner every Monday," said Keisha.

Mama had been cooking a community dinner every Monday night since she opened the restaurant twenty-three years ago. Back then the neighborhood moved at a slower pace, and many folks hit hard times. She couldn't bear to let folks go hungry. Anyone who walked through that door on Monday was served. No questions asked.

"People thought she was crazy for giving out meals every week. I was only six years old then, but even I could sense the judgment behind the gossip. You know what she said, when I asked her about it?"

Keisha had heard this story many times over, especially since Mama passed. But she gestured for him to continue.

"Mama said, 'When people break bread together, they break down their walls and talk to each other. Never forget, Andre—'"

"Food is family," they finished together, and smiled at each other.

Keisha's eyes were glossy with tears. She pushed off the desk. "Speaking of food, have you had lunch?"

He shook his head.

"We can't brainstorm ideas to save the restaurant on an empty stomach."

"I made some shrimp etouffee this morning." Andre had been so nervous about the call with the bank, he'd rummaged around in the walk-in fridge for something to cook. Chopping and stirring helped keep his mind off things he couldn't control. "Want some?"

"Yes! What did you do to it this time?" Keisha pulled him out of the chair.

"Why do you always ask if I did something to my cooking, like I messed up Mama's recipes?"

"I said it that way because I'm excited! You need to spend more time there instead of at the bar." She pushed him out of the office and into the restaurant kitchen. "I like your twist on her food."

"She didn't." He spoke quietly, trying to hide his disappointment. All his life, Mama had groomed him to take over for whenever she was ready to retire. After he graduated high school, he joined Mama full time at the restaurant. He thought he could add his own touch to the menu, but she was adamant about keeping it the same.

"I'm sorry she couldn't see how creative your recipes are." Keisha bit her lip. "I'm also sorry you felt you had to leave DC in order to be yourself. I should have spoken up for you."

"It's all in the past, Keisha." When Mama was sick, none of that had mattered anymore. If he changed her menu now, he'd disrespect her memory and hard work. "Besides, people love her food. Why change it?"

"When I'm not starving, I'll tell you why we should change things up. But right now, I want to hear about your etouffee."

Andre breathed a sigh of relief when she didn't push about changing the menu. It was easier to let Luis do all the cooking. Their cook had worked alongside his mom for years and knew her recipes by heart. If Andre were in the kitchen, he'd be tempted to try new ingredients or techniques. Instead, he wrote them in his notebook and only made these dishes for himself. And Keisha.

She tapped impatiently while he reheated the stew and rice. He'd gotten the idea to serve the rich, buttery stew over scorched rice. Technically it was the scorched rice at the bottom of the pot. Normally he'd scoop out the steamed rice and dump the scorched part. Until he went over for dinner at Trixie's house.

When her mom scooped the scorched crust into a bowl and filled it with a vegetable soup, he was curious. Trixie taught him how to eat it. Once Andre had tasted the crunchy, nutty rice mixed with the flavorful broth, he was hooked.

He'd forgotten about the scorched rice, but this morning, the idea came to him. Seeing Trixie again was bringing back too many memories. At least he could channel some of it into his cooking.

"Usually shrimp etouffee over steamed rice is too mushy— texturally," he explained as he set the bowl in front of Keisha. "So I'm serving it over scorched rice."

"Shut up and let me taste it." Keisha grabbed her spoon and dug in. "Oh my God, that's—" She stuffed another spoonful into her mouth.

"I guess you like it." He chuckled.

Keisha held up a finger to quiet him while she scarfed down the rest of the bowl.

"That was so fun to eat." She wiped her mouth. "Where did you get this idea?"

"Um, I—" He wasn't ready to tell her about Trixie. Then he'd have to tell Keisha how badly he'd mangled their breakup.

"Never mind, I don't care where you got it, we need to serve this in the restaurant. Maybe invite some food bloggers to try it." Keisha was practically bouncing. "We need a catchy name for it."

"We can't serve it. It's not Mama's recipe." He couldn't change her legacy. If they put it on the menu and it became popular, he'd have to go back into the kitchen to change even more of her recipes.

"How about Crispy Etouffee? Or Etouffee Surprise? No that sounds too much like Tuna Casserole Surprise."

"Keisha, stop." Andre grabbed her arm to quiet her. "This is just for fun. Not for public consumption."

"But think of all the bougie people who would come for this!"

"I'll think of another way to bring in more business. One that doesn't blaspheme Mama's food. You should concentrate on school.

I'm the head of the family now. I'll figure out how to save the restaurant."

"I wish you'd stop being such a man!" Keisha smacked his
shoulder.

"Hey! What was that for?" He grimaced and rubbed his shoulder. That really hurt.

"Stop treating me like a kid! I'm twenty-six and I want to be
an equal partner in this restaurant," Keisha demanded, hands on
her hips.

"You are an equal partner. Mama left the restaurant to both
of us."

"Waiting tables and helping Luis in the kitchen doesn't count,"
she huffed. "I can help you with the management and accounting and still get my classwork done. The experience will be good
for me."

His sister had a point. She'd been taking business classes at the
community college. Some real-life experience would be good for
her. But he wanted her to focus on her degree first, without the
burden of past-due invoices.

"After you finish your accounting class this semester, you can
help me with the books," he conceded.

Keisha's face lit up with a huge grin. Her eyes glittered. He
knew that look. She had some kind of scheme up her sleeve.

"Spill it, Keisha."

"Let's hold another bachelorette party," she blurted. "Look at
how much money we made last—"

"NO!" His voice boomed in their small kitchen.

Keisha jumped, and her face fell.

"You didn't have to yell at me."

"I'm sorry," he said, his voice softened. "We're a family restaurant.

On a block with a used bookstore, a hair salon, and other businesses who don't sell sex toys. What would everyone around us think?"

"They'd be excited for the foot traffic. Didn't you say if the hipsters would walk a few blocks past District Market, we'd make more money?"

Andre pressed his lips together. He hated when his sister was right.

"Besides, if you'd ever sat in the hair salon, you'd know all those ladies talk about is sex." Her eyes narrowed. "You men don't talk about that in the barbershop?"

"Maybe." Why the hell was he talking about sex with his sister? Again.

"It's not just about selling sex toys, you know. Trixie is helping people." Keisha rummaged around in the fridge. "Especially at the clinic."

His sister was right. Trixie seemed to love what she did. Based on what he'd seen that evening, she was good at it, too. How long had Keisha known his ex-girlfriend? Andre didn't realize the two of them had crossed paths at their neighborhood clinic.

"How come you never told me about Trixie? When did you meet at the women's clinic?"

Keisha shrugged. "You've been in your broody cloud, worrying about the restaurant. I didn't think you wanted to hear about my volunteer work."

"I always want to know what you're doing." Being a good brother was yet another thing he was failing at. Though he and Keisha saw each other most of the day, they didn't seem to have much downtime to check in with each other lately. Whenever she wasn't at the restaurant, she was in class or studying. As for him, he was always at the restaurant.

"Hey, broody brother! You still here?" She snapped her fingers in front of his face.

"Yeah, I'm here." He leaned in closer. "Tell me about the clinic."

"As I was about to say before you started daydreaming, Trixie and I met a few months ago when one of her classes canceled at the last minute. She offered to help me pack hope purses, and we hit it off. She has a good heart. She helps people."

"Helping people in the bedroom isn't exactly changing the world." Andre shrugged.

"Men." Keisha scoffed. "It's more than that. She teaches sex ed to seniors, both the high school and the older adult variety."

This conversation was going all sorts of sideways. Now he had images of elderly people having sex in his head.

He must have grimaced because Keisha laughed at him.

"You're such a prude, Andre."

"Am not." He cleared his throat. "Folks can do whatever they want. But I don't need to know about it."

"Whatever."

"Want another bowl?" Andre picked up their empty bowls.

"I'm stuffed. That was exactly what I needed before my exam on tax liabilities. Even if you won't cook at the restaurant, you should experiment at home. My stomach will thank you." Keisha patted said stomach.

"It's silly for me to cook when we can just bring home the leftovers from the restaurant. I'd rather work the bar. I'm infusing coffee-and-orange bitters for a new cocktail recipe."

Since New Orleans, he'd dived into the art of craft cocktails. Mama Hazel's wasn't the right place to serve cocktails like a Sazerac with house-made bitters. Their food was too homey and comforting to serve with fancy craft cocktails. No way their clientele would pay for the fancy drinks, but he enjoyed the creative outlet.

"Now back to my idea," Keisha said. "Let's invite Trixie to hold another bachelorette party at the restaurant. Her customers are exactly the new blood we need. Then they'll tell their friends about us, who'll tell their friends, and so on."

His sister had a point. Maybe they'd come back for lunch service, then visit the bookstore next door. They could even create some kind of incentive to get people to visit all the stores on their block. The foot traffic would benefit everyone, not just Mama Hazel's.

"But it's August. Wedding season is almost over." At least it had been in New Orleans when he tended bar. "She's probably done with those."

"So it doesn't have to be a bachelorette party. How about a pop-up?"

He sighed.

"You said we made more money that night than we did the rest of the month! Let's try, please?"

Keisha was so annoying when she was right. She flashed puppy dog eyes at him.

"Wait, is it because you don't like Trixie?"

"Why do you think I don't like her?" For a moment, he worried his sister had overheard his impromptu reunion with Trixie. In fact, he hadn't shared much about his life in New Orleans. There hadn't been time.

When he came home for good, the two of them had been too busy driving their mom to doctor appointments and chemo sessions, there was no time to nurse his broken heart. Taking care of his mom had made it easier to forget Trixie and the mistakes he'd made.

"After you dropped off the margaritas, you didn't go back over there. Even though I saw you looking their way."

"It's not that." He avoided Keisha's eyes. "I'm worried that Mrs. Harris and the rest of the neighborhood will be scandalized to hear that we're selling vibrators in Mama's restaurant."

The restaurant was a safe place for their neighbors. How could he sully his mother's legacy that way? There had to be another option. One that didn't involve Trixie. He thought about the pile of receipts on his desk. Keisha wasn't a kid anymore, but he still wanted to protect her. Underneath those receipts were piles of invoices, including their mother's medical bills. Who knew dying was so expensive? Keisha would panic or try some crazy scheme to get more customers in the door. She didn't need that kind of stress while she was finishing college.

"Fine. Be hard-headed."

He shuffled his napkin and fork to avoid the disappointed look on her face.

"In the meantime, I'm calling Trixie."

Andre's head snapped up. "Keisha, let's talk before we make any drastic decisions."

"Nope. I gave you a chance and you didn't offer any other ideas. I inherited half of this restaurant, and I'm making an executive decision. I have to run out to the clinic anyway. I can catch Trixie before her class. Be back to help with community dinner."

Keisha walked out of the kitchen.

Andre banged his head on the table. He never thought he would see Trixie again after New Orleans. Now she was here. In his hometown. Selling fucking vibrators. And changing the world, according to his sister.

Trixie looked as sexy as the last time he saw her. No. Sexier.

Something was different about her. She had looked taller. No—felt taller. Her confidence had grown.

Back in New Orleans, Trixie didn't like being the center of attention. When she'd walked into Fleur de Lis on her twenty-first birthday, she went straight to the bar and nursed a rum and Coke while her girlfriends monopolized the dance floor. She struck up a conversation with the bartender—him.

Most women flirted with him because they wanted stronger pours or free drinks. Trixie seemed so unhappy. Which was a shame since it was a milestone birthday. He did his best to cheer her up and ended up with her phone number.

Two weeks ago at Mama Hazel's, she commandeered a roomful of drunk women with poise and humor. He knew from his French Quarter bartending days that closing a bar full of drunk bachelorettes was like herding cats. Yet those women hung on her every word and practically begged to see each toy by the time she'd gone over its features.

He hadn't handled the surprise of seeing her very well. It had been hard not to touch her arm, hug her, kiss her on the cheek—hell, anything besides their terse exchange.

Seeing her again had cracked open the box where he'd crammed all his feelings for her. The ones he'd had to set aside when they broke—when he'd left her. He'd loved her. But not enough to be the splinter between her and her parents. Leaving her was one of the hardest decisions he'd ever made.

He was glad that she'd found a career she loved. It was impressive how effortlessly she spoke about lube and orgasms. She practically glowed during her presentation.

Trixie was happy.

The realization hit him in the gut. After all she'd gone through with her career and family, she was finally happy. Without him.

Trixie didn't need him after all. Sadness swept through him, but wasn't that what he wanted? For her to find her life's calling and patch things up with Mr. and Mrs. Nguyen?

There was his proof that leaving her had been the right decision. If he'd given her an inkling that they could have worked things out, she wouldn't have fixed things with her family. No matter how he'd felt about her, she'd moved on and that was a good thing. He couldn't let his feelings for Trixie distract him from saving his family. He had a restaurant to keep afloat and a neighborhood to feed. People depended on him.

Keisha depended on him.

CHAPTER 6

Keisha!" Trixie exclaimed in surprise as her friend walked into the clinic. "What are you doing here? I thought you couldn't come on Mondays."

When Trixie began volunteering at the clinic three months ago, her schedule didn't overlap with Keisha's. Ever since that first night when Keisha found her alone in the meeting room, Trixie tried to come in to help her friend whenever she had the chance.

Now that she knew Keisha was Andre's sister, the family resemblance was obvious. Keisha's eyes were hazel, and Andre's were brown, but the sparkle in them and the way they crinkled when they smiled? Exactly the same. How could she have been so oblivious?

Right. She'd missed the connection because she had no intention of seeing him again after he walked out of her life. It's not as if she moved to the DMV hoping to run into him. She came because Reina helped to give her a fresh start.

"I'm sorry I can't stay," Keisha apologized. "I'm picking up some purses for our neighborhood dinner tonight."

"Good timing. I just finished assembling the most recent donations." Trixie waved at the table in the back of the room. "Tess told me you hadn't picked up this week's supplies, so I wanted them to be ready when you stopped by."

The used purses were more than unwanted handbags. Inside were sanitary pads, tampons, deodorant, and other feminine products. One of Trixie's volunteer duties at the clinic was collecting the purses and donations, then assembling them. She even filled some tote bags with supplies for those who didn't want or need a purse.

"Thank you!" Keisha threw her arms around Trixie and gave her a bear hug. "Oooh, is that a Kate Spade? Mrs. Harris will be fighting the others for that one!"

Trixie laughed and returned the embrace. Time always passed faster at the clinic with Keisha's happy vibes. "I'm sorry they were late this week. My car went back into the shop for a new transmission. I bailed it out this morning and picked up the donations."

"Sorry about your car. My car isn't fancy, but if you need a ride, let me know."

"I might take you up on that." Trixie looked at her watch. "Don't you need to get back to Mama Hazel's soon? Let me help you put the purses in your car."

"Actually, I'm here to talk to you about Mama Hazel's. And Tre. I mean Andre."

"Your brother goes by Andre now?" He'd kept so much about his life in DC from Trixie, she wondered how much of their history he'd told his sister.

"Yeah, when he came back from New Orleans, he wanted everyone to call him Andre. But folks are set in their ways. They've only known him as Tre."

"That's why I've never heard you call him Andre before," said

Trixie. Otherwise, Trixie might have made the connection between the siblings sooner.

"I'm trying so hard, but I forget, too." Keisha groaned. "He's right, though. He's not the neighborhood's little Tre anymore."

"What did you want to ask me about the restaurant and Andre?" Trixie twisted a strand of her hair. She wasn't trying to fish for information. Not really. "He was very surprised to see me and my products there."

"Don't worry, it wasn't you." Keisha waved her hand. "He's just broody. And feeling weirded out about being the only man there."

It *had* been Trixie. Which meant he didn't tell Keisha about their past. She couldn't keep such a big secret from Keisha. After volunteering together for the past few months, they'd become friends. If he didn't tell his sister soon, she'd tell her.

"Of course. I can see that."

"Thanks again for suggesting our restaurant to the maid of honor. It was fun and, uh, I—we—Andre and I, we want you to come back."

Trixie's eyes widened. Andre had made it very clear that she was not welcome at the restaurant.

"Andre said that?"

"Well, not in so many words." Keisha bit her lip. "I own half the restaurant, so it's my decision. I want you back."

"I don't know if that's a good idea. He didn't seem happy to have a table full of vibrators in the restaurant."

"He'd be happier if he had a girlfriend who could show him the joys of sex toys!" Keisha shuddered. "Forget I said that. Eww. I did not need that picture in my head."

Trixie didn't need a picture of naked Andre in her head either.

His hard chest. Muscular arms. He must be lifting a lot of boxes to have that kind of muscle tone. She recalled the wiry black hairs sprinkled across his dark brown chest. Taut abdomen and the hollows next to them that converged into a sharp V—

"Good idea," Trixie squeaked. She cleared her throat. "No matter how he feels about my products, I got the impression he didn't care for the arrangement."

"It doesn't matter if he cares or not. We need new people at those tables eating our food and drinking his cocktails." Keisha leaned closer to Trixie. "Business has been slow. Too slow."

"How can that be? Your food is amazing! My girlfriend has been begging to come back for your fried chicken."

"I know we serve the best soul food in DC. Our regulars love us, but we need new customers." Keisha frowned. "The new hipster joints are stealing away all the new business."

"I thought the developers were revitalizing the neighborhood."

"More like gentrifying." Keisha snorted. "They're drawing in new people, but only to those fast-casual faux-ethnic chains. I mean, only white folks could come up with cauliflower fried 'rice.'"

"How bad is it?" Trixie ignored the ache growing in her chest. "Surely people will get bored of the other places soon."

"Andre says we'll manage, but I can tell he's worried. Which is why I want you to partner with Mama Hazel's."

"I'm not sure if that's a good idea." A partnership would help her sales, but she wasn't sure she should see Andre again. Or be in the same room with a man who didn't respect her enough to break up with her properly.

Her body reacted to his in ways she hadn't felt since she moved to DC. Just being near him electrified her body, filling her with a low hum, like one of the vibrators with a fresh set of AAs.

"Didn't you say you were trying to win a sales contest? You bring in the fresh blood, and we'll serve them margaritas to help loosen up their wallets."

"That's one way to go about it." Trixie laughed. "I'm not complaining! That was my best show last month."

"Perfect! Come by tonight and we can hash out the details."

"I can't tonight. Mondays, remember?" Trixie was relieved to have a good excuse not to return to the restaurant.

"That's right." Keisha's face fell. "Your sex-ed classes."

Twice a month, Trixie sat in a room with women old enough to be her mother and talked to them about sex. The evening usually began with contraception and STIs, but sometimes veered into orgasms. She could never have such a frank conversation about sex with her mother. Yet her students taught her as much as she taught them.

She'd love to expand the classes, but it wasn't practical. The clinic had limited space, and another evening there meant one less night she could hold her shows. Maybe holding pop-ups at Mama Hazel's would help her reach more women and win sales rep of the year.

"Please," Keisha begged. "Come over so we can at least talk about it?"

It was hard to say no to her friend's eager and expectant smile. Trixie sighed. "How about I come after class is over? Ten-ish?"

"Yes, perfect! Andre thinks I'm mad at him, so I'm going to use his guilt to my advantage. We have to strike while the iron is hot!"

Trixie smiled. Younger siblings always knew how to push their older siblings' buttons. As the youngest of three, she knew how to rile up her brother and sister. Going to Mama Hazel's again meant running into Andre. Which was a bad idea considering the jabs they tossed at each other during the bachelorette party. But the Boss Babes were right about one thing. Delicious food and great cocktails loosened her customers' inhibitions and wallets. She should hear Keisha out.

After Keisha drove off, Trixie rearranged the chairs to form a circle. She placed pamphlets on each chair. Her Monday-night routine couldn't distract her from the conflicting feelings inside her.

Partnering with Mama Hazel's could be the push she needed to win the ten grand. She'd be able to book more shows if the hostess didn't always have to worry about food and drinks. Or cleanup. Throw in a presentation about clit gel and vibrators, and they had the ultimate girls' night out.

But then there was Andre. She tried not to blame him for the rift between her and her parents, but—that fight had put her in a bad place. Then he left her with no warning. Only a stupid note.

Trixie shook her head and blew out a deep breath. Time to focus on the present. She was in a much better place now thanks to the Boss Babes.

If partnering with Andre could make her dream happen, she would, as Reina would say, put on her big-girl panties. If she kept things purely professional, what could go wrong?

CHAPTER 7

The bell hanging over the front door rang. Was it that late already? Andre looked up from the piles of receipts on the bar.

"Xavier, what's up, bro!" A smile broke out on his face. "Tell me you found us a sugar mama to take care of all our bills."

"Andre, my man!" Xavier walked across the restaurant. The two bumped their fists in greeting. "I did, but she didn't want your ugly mug."

They laughed. Shooting the breeze with his best friend always lightened his mood.

"Guess I better keep slinging drinks." Andre picked up his papers and set them under the bar. He and Xavier had grown up in this very neighborhood together. Both had gone away to pursue their dreams, but home called them back.

"You're done with your delivery shift, right?" Andre asked. He glanced at his watch. "Want a beer? It's after five."

"Nah. Don't want to be tipsy in the kitchen. Last time I did that, I burned a whole pot of greens." He whistled. "I thought Keisha was going to beat me with a frying pan."

Xavier volunteered at Mama Hazel's every Monday night. He'd started coming by when Andre's mother got sick and couldn't work in the kitchen anymore. Mama couldn't relax during her chemo because she worried about him and Keisha doing all the cooking for family dinners. Xavier was able to convince her that he'd make the perfect sous chef.

"Dude, how do you burn collard greens? Wait, it's best if I don't know." Andre chuckled. Only Xavier could forget about something simmering for so long, the pot liquor cooked off. He often got sidetracked when inspiration for a poem hit. His best friend had become a poet while he'd been away.

"I'll get you a Coke?" Andre picked up a glass and filled it with ice before his friend could answer. They had the same conversation every week, give or take a few kitchen horror stories. Poking fun at Xavier made it easier for Andre to take his mind off Trixie tonight.

"What's on Keisha's menu?" Xavier took a long, deep drink from the glass.

"Gumbo."

Xavier nodded. "Cornbread, too?"

"Can't have gumbo without cornbread. I'd never hear the end of it." Especially from Mrs. Harris, who lived across the street from him.

"I had to make sure you didn't go hipster on me and serve some sort of vegan, gluten-free shit."

"You'll have to go two blocks up for that." Andre nodded his head in the direction of District Market. "Keisha put you on cornbread duty, so you're welcome to make it however you want."

"Hell no. Keisha would kick my ass if I changed the recipe." His best friend shuddered. "As long as I don't have to stand over the stove for an hour and stir a vat of roux, I'm good."

"Nope." A mixture of fat and flour, roux took patience and constant stirring until the flour turned dark and a nutty smell filled the air. His mom's gumbo called for a deep-brown roux. "I'll let you in on a secret. We make it in bulk every week and freeze it."

"Seriously? How come Keisha threatens to put me on roux duty when I don't do as she says?" Xavier pursed his lips. "In that case, I got time for another Coke."

"You got it." Andre would do anything for his childhood friend, not just fill him up with free drinks. Having Xavier in the kitchen was a godsend. No matter what happened, Andre vowed to continue Monday dinners for as long as he could.

"Thanks, man." Andre's voice cracked. "I appreciate you."

"You all right?" Xavier studied Andre. "Pile of bills looks bigger than usual."

"They keep coming." Andre sighed. "Keisha wants to try something new to compete with the new restaurants . . ."

"I sense a *but* here."

"She wants Mama Hazel's to host a sex toy pop-up shop."
Xavier choked on his soda. He coughed and sputtered. Andre stifled a laugh and smacked his friend on the back.

"That was my reaction, too. But she's got a point."
Xavier raised an eyebrow, still unable to talk.

"I meant about the 'something new' part." While his friend recovered from inhaling his soda, Andre recounted the bachelorette party they'd held last month. The wild women doing shots and raving about fried chicken. How Mama Hazel's had made more that one night than they had the previous two weeks.

"You're leaving out the most important part, Andre."

"What do you mean? I just told you it was the best night we'd had in a while."

"The toys, man." Xavier shook his head. "You had a restaurant full of inebriated women talking about vibrators and you didn't call me?"

"Girls only. Me and Luis were the only guys here."

"You're killing me." Xavier groaned.

Andre shrugged. He'd barely noticed any of the women that night. Except for Trixie, once they had their "reunion" and he realized she was a vibrator rep. Watching her stand in front of all those women and confidently talk about sex—fuck, it was a huge turn-on. No matter what had happened between them, his body missed her.

"Whoa, Andre—" Xavier snapped his fingers in front of Andre's face. "Did you get laid that night? Because you have a shit-eating grin on your face."

Andre immediately scowled.

"Don't keep me hangin', bro. Please tell me you finally got laid."

"Even if I did, I don't kiss and tell." He held up the soda nozzle. "Another soda?"

"Fine. I thought we were friends." Xavier held out his glass for a refill. "Was the woman selling sex toys hot at least? Were you like, yeah, baby, let me tap that—hey!"

Andre tipped the nozzle up. Soda sprayed all over his clean bar and Xavier. "Shit, sorry, man. I didn't mean to—"

Xavier sputtered and grabbed a stack of bar napkins to wipe the Coke off his face and neck. "You got a problem with me appreciating the female form? I'm in a delivery truck all day. Let me live vicariously through you."

"Right. As if you don't have women opening their door wearing nothing but a towel when your brown truck pulls up to their house."

"You got me." Xavier held up his hands. "You win. Now, what's

the deal with this woman? The last time you got pissy was when—"
Xavier stopped and gaped at him.

Andre grabbed a towel and wiped the soda from the bar. He
could feel the heat of his best friend's stare.

"Hold up, are you telling me that the woman selling vibrators
in your mama's restaurant was—"

"Trixie Nguyen. My ex."

"Damn." Xavier drew out the word then laughed. "After what
happened in New Orleans, I hope you didn't hook up with her."

"Can you stop talking about my sex life?"

"What sex life?!" Xavier guffawed at his own joke. He quieted
when Andre didn't respond. "You all right, bro?"

"How the hell do you think I felt seeing her again?" Andre
poured himself a tonic, wishing he could add gin to it, but dinner
service started in an hour. "It was shitty."

"Look, Miss Hazel was sick, and you had to come home to
take care of your mama. If she couldn't understand that, then she
wasn't right for you."

"I never told her why I left." Andre cringed. It sounded worse
when he said it out loud. "I left her a note."

"Aw, man. That's not cool." Xavier held up his finger as if he had
something more to say. He took a deep swallow of his soda. "But
it's the past, bro. Life ain't *Groundhog Day*."

"I left because I couldn't do to her what my father did to my
mom." Andre closed his eyes, remembering how he'd tracked
down his father's old friends so he could learn more about the
man, know more about where he came from, and the disappointment that came with it. "I didn't want to keep her from her dreams
the way my dad did to Mama."

"What the hell are you talking about, Andre? I thought your

father died in a car crash when you were just a little kid." Xavier tilted his head in confusion.

"He did. But they had a fight before he died." Andre leaned in, even though they were the only ones in the dining area. "Mama wanted to open a small restaurant in New Orleans. Use some of their savings. He flat-out refused. Said he didn't want any wife of his cooking for strange men."

Xavier whistled. "That's some old-school shit."

Andre nodded. "She tried to bring it up again, but he refused to even listen to her business plan. You know Mama had a good head for business."

"She sure did. Miss Hazel was a tough lady."

"Mama was going to make an ultimatum. Half her share of their savings or a divorce. The car accident happened before she could do it." Andre wiped down the bar again. "That's when she packed everything she owned and moved us here. Fresh start."

"You learned all that while you were in New Orleans?" Xavier looked incredulous.

"Yup." Andre nodded again.

"What does that have to do with Trixie?"

"Trixie." Andre sighed. "Her parents gave her an ultimatum. Keep studying to be a pharmacist or they'd cut her off. When she chose to become a therapist, her parents blamed it on me. The American Black boy from DC with his big-city ideas."

"They didn't like that you're Black?"

"No, not like that. Apparently Vietnamese people don't believe in therapy. At least her folks didn't. To them, I was an outsider who didn't understand how things worked in Vietnamese families. Too American, they told her. They really cut her off, too. I thought that stuff only happened in movies."

"Damn, bro." Xavier shook his head. "So why did you leave her?"

"She and her family were tight. Being cut off messed her up. I met my dad's family and realized what I missed out on. I didn't want that to happen to her." Andre thought about the cousins he'd never met. He made a mental note to email them.

"How come you never told me this?"

"I don't know. It was so personal. I hadn't even talked to Mama about my father before . . ." He didn't need to complete the sentence. Looking back, he saw the bad decision for what it was.

"Let me guess. You told her it was you and not her."

Andre hung his head.

"Oh, snap. I bet she wanted to beat your ass."

"I don't blame her for still hating me."

"But?"

"Damn, Xay, she looked good. Not just her curves, but the way she carried herself. Confident and sassy. Like what happened between us never affected her. As if . . ."

"As if she's over you?"

Andre inhaled sharply. He dumped the ice out of his glass and began washing it. His best friend was right.

"Are you over her?"

"Yes," Andre replied too quickly.

Xavier raised his eyebrows. "Yeah, sure."

"I sort of told her the pop-up was a one-time thing."

"That was stupid. Especially since you need more paying customers."

Andre threw the bar towel at Xavier.

"I've moved on, and so has she. I do not have time for drama or a relationship of any kind right now."

"Relax, bro. I'm not telling you what to do." Xavier raised his hands up, then grinned. "Just don't do anything I wouldn't do."

"That leaves the door wide open."

The two men laughed. The door to the kitchen flung open, and Keisha's head popped into view.

"You two gonna sit there like lumps of lard or help me load in these purses? I need to get back to the greens. I don't want Mrs. Harris to complain that hers are better. For the hundredth time!" Without waiting for a response, she disappeared behind the door, leaving it swinging.

"Cornbread Captain, reporting for duty!" Xavier stood up and saluted.

Keisha's middle finger shot out from behind the door.

Xavier laughed. He threw back the last of his soda and slid off the barstool. He looked at Andre. "If Keisha wants your ex to do pop-ups, she's going to be here. You need to own up to the truth sooner or later."

That's exactly what Andre was afraid of.

CHAPTER 8

Trixie pushed open the door to Mama Hazel's. The aromas inside teased her with memories of New Orleans. Her stomach grumbled. She'd been so engrossed at the clinic that she'd forgotten to eat dinner. Again. They were extremely understaffed, so she tried to do as much as she could on her one day there.

"Hello?" Trixie called out.

She followed her nose past the hostess stand and into the dining room. Was that the smell of gumbo? Not just any gumbo, but the real deal from home?

The lights were still on, but the restaurant was empty. She half expected to see Andre behind the bar washing glasses. Why was she so disappointed? She was here to talk business with Keisha, not see her ex.

The temporary buffet area and her display table from the bachelorette party were gone, broken back down into their original seating. Tables were still littered with dirty dishes, crumpled napkins, and straw wrappers. Whatever had been on the menu must have been delicious. Most of the plates and bowls were empty.

"Trixie?"

Trixie yelped. She turned toward the voice and found Andre

behind the bar. How had she missed him when she came in? Maybe he had been under the bar doing whatever bartenders do.

"What are you doing here?" His voice was hard, and his eyes bore into her.

"Keisha asked me to come by after ten." She met his gaze, daring him to challenge her.

"She's in the back, cleaning."

"Where's everyone else?"

"There is no everyone else. Our cook Luis went home early to spend time with his kids. Xavier gets up early for his delivery route in the morning. Just me and Keisha now."

"Oh." Trixie connected the dots. Keisha had mentioned her mother—*their* mother—dying after a too-short battle with cancer. Which meant she died not too long after he'd ditched her in New Orleans. "I'm so sorry about your mom, Andre. Keisha told me some wonderful stories about her. She was an amazing woman."

"Everyone loved Mama." He swallowed hard. "Which is why I'm doing my best to keep this place going."

Why hadn't he told her about his mom when they were together? All he'd said was that she was a talented cook and then changed the subject. He hadn't lied to her, but he hadn't been forthcoming about his past either. Trixie swallowed the anger and sadness welling up inside her.

"You must miss her terribly." She thought about her parents, whom she hadn't seen since moving to DC last year. Even though she offered to fly home to visit, her mom told her to wait for her dad to cool down. A year later, he was still mad at her.

"Every day." Sadness flashed across his face before he smoothed his features. He pointed to a booth in the back. "You can wait for Keisha over there."

Trixie bit her lip. Yep. Still the same Andre. The stoic man who never talked about his feelings. Sure, he shared when he was happy or if someone at work made him mad. When it came to deeper emotions, he'd rather run away from them—from her—than deal with them. The funny, sensitive brother Keisha talked about during their volunteer work did not sound like the Andre she'd known.

No, Trixie had deserved better from him. Tonight there were no customers and no Reina to keep her from giving Andre the treatment he deserved. From telling him exactly how he ruined her life in New Orleans. Even better, how she survived—no, thrived without him.

She took a step toward the booth. Suddenly her head spun, and black spots covered her vision. Her hands flew out to grab on to the nearest steady thing. Which turned out to be something not so steady. The chair slid under her hand and bumped into a table. Her vision cleared in time to see a plate and utensils crash onto the floor.

Strong hands grabbed her shoulders as she swayed. Andre. His warm, spicy scent was comforting. She leaned back into him and closed her eyes. Maybe if she waited, the room would stop spinning.

"Are you okay?"

His breath warmed the nape of her neck, causing a ripple of chills across her body. Her nipples tightened under her blouse. Her shoulders relaxed against his firm chest. Heat bloomed across her torso. Her body responded automatically to his, even though it had been two years since they'd touched.

"Trixie." He inhaled sharply.

Clearly his body remembered hers, too.

"Fine," she whispered. "I—I'm fine."

If *fine* meant that she was dizzy and turned on at the same time.

Bang. They jumped. Something big and metal had fallen in the kitchen. Trixie pulled herself away from him, but he slid his hands to her upper arms as if she'd keel over any minute.

"If you're fine, why do you have a death grip on my chair?"

She let go of the chair as if it were on fire. The room started spinning again. She swayed, but only a little, thanks to Andre's hold on her.

"I forgot to eat today," she confessed. "The clinic was swamped so I jumped in to help."

Andre sighed. He eased the grip on her arms and rubbed them. His hand shifted to the small of her back, searing her skin through her shirt. Trixie ignored the heat simmering below her belly. He guided her over to a nearby table that had already been cleaned. Pulling out a chair, he eased her into it.

"Don't move. I'll make you a plate."

As if she could move with the room spinning around her. He strode into the kitchen, leaving her with a view of his gorgeous backside. Even through her dizziness, she could appreciate his well-sculpted ass. Memories flashed through her brain. Her hands on his buttocks as he thrusted into her. Nails digging into his skin as they both exploded together.

The spinning slowed down as her body began to buzz. A low vibration that gently swept over her as heat spread through her body. Sex had never been a challenge in their relationship. They couldn't keep their hands off each other. Being so close to him and feeling the heat of his voice in her ear. Their physical attraction was always fully charged. Even if their relationship had run out of batteries.

Trixie inhaled deeply to clear her mind and ease the spinning. She vowed to stay focused. She couldn't afford to let him distract her again. Not like last time, when she crashed and burned. At first, she'd blamed him for the rift between her and her parents. He'd been the one who convinced her to go against their wishes and change careers. Even though he promised to support her, he'd left her all alone in New Orleans to deal with the aftermath.

After many late-night conversations with Zoe about their very different Vietnamese upbringing, Trixie realized that she'd already made up her mind deep down. But he'd pushed her to tell her parents before she was ready.

Past Trixie had learned her lesson. She would never again let someone else push her to make life-changing decisions. Present Trixie knew what she wanted and had a time line to achieve it. Lust would not derail her tonight.

Andre flew through the swinging kitchen door, expertly juggling several plates. One was piled high with cornbread. Another held a bowl of collard greens. The third was a large soup bowl, steam still rising from it. With practiced hands, he slid them in front of her and pulled a set of silverware out of his pocket.

"Eat," he commanded. "I'll get you some water. And a Diet Coke with lime. Keisha will be out in a bit."

"Thanks," Trixie said weakly. He still remembered her favorite drink.

She surveyed the food while he walked to the bar. Trixie closed her eyes and inhaled deeply. A deep nutty and savory scent filled her nose. Her stomach twisted. Not just from hunger but homesickness. The deep-brown stew reminded her of New Orleans almost as much as her mother's pork egg rolls. Flunking out of school. The rift with her parents. The good times she and Andre had.

Coming home to that final note.

"I lied," said Andre as he slid into the chair next to her. "I poured a glass of orange juice instead. You need the sugar right now."

She opened her mouth, but he interrupted.

"Don't argue with me." His tone was warm. Worried even. It was the opposite of when she first walked in. He pushed the glass closer. "Drink."

Trixie nodded. She gulped the cold juice, ignoring the straw he set next to it. She was grateful as the sweet tang of citrus slid down her throat and cooled off her body.

"Easy now! There's more where that came from." Andre eased the glass from her hands. "Sugar works faster, but you still need real food."

Trixie unwrapped the thin paper napkin from the utensils. Grabbing the spoon, she dipped it into the gumbo and stirred the rice into the thick, brown stew. Outside a big bowl of phở, gumbo was one of her favorite comfort foods. This version had chicken, sausage, and okra. The scent was intoxicating. Or maybe it was Andre's nearness.

"This smells"—Trixie leaned over the bowl and breathed deeply—"like home."

"Because it is. Mama is from New Orleans. Her recipe calls for hand-stirred roux in a cast-iron skillet. After the roux is the color of dark chocolate, we caramelize the onions in it." Andre's eyes got a faraway look and his shoulders relaxed.

"Sorry," she whispered to her stomach. "I'll feed you right now."

He chuckled.

"Do you have any—"

"Louisiana hot sauce, your favorite." He handed her a tall, narrow bottle, its red-orange cap already unscrewed.

Where had he been hiding that bottle? There were no pockets on his snug shirt. The jeans pocket he fished the silverware out of barely had room for a bottle of hot sauce.

Was he fucking with her on purpose? Remembering all her favorite drinks and brand of hot sauce? Acting like he still cared about her when he made it seem last time that he never wanted to see her again? Whatever he was up to—this super-nice-guy act—she wasn't going to fall for it.

"You happened to have this around?" She grabbed the bottle from him and shook the hot sauce over her gumbo, which had a generous sprinkle of filé powder on it. No gumbo was complete without a dash or two of dried ground sassafras leaves. "This brand isn't a common staple around here. There's only one store in my neighborhood that sells it."

"It grew on me during my time in New Orleans. Probably because you left a bottle at my apartment to put it on everything. Now stop talking and eat." He pushed the plate of cornbread and greens closer to her. "Let me clean up those broken plates before someone steps on them." He didn't have to tell her again. The gumbo was an explosion of spices and flavor in her mouth.

ANDRE WALKED TO the wait station and grabbed a broom and dustpan. Seeing Trixie in his restaurant again stirred up too many conflicting feelings. It was his decision to walk out on her. Even if his intentions had been good, he'd broken up with her in the most cowardly way. He'd convinced himself that he was over her. But watching her walk through that door again had made his heart leap.

When she almost passed out, what else could he do but rush over and help her? He was falling back into his old role. Trixie, so driven and focused on her to-do list that she forgot to eat or brush her teeth. She was always doing things for others, putting their happiness before hers. So he made sure she ate, brushed her teeth, and went after the career she wanted.

What if he wasn't over Trixie?

No. He couldn't entertain that thought. Andre had the restaurant to worry about. He walked over to the broken plates and began sweeping them onto the dustpan. Normally, each month he'd order another set to replace the ones that broke, but that wasn't an option right now. All funds leftover after payroll, food, and operations went into replacing the fryer. It wasn't as if there were lines out the door these days. They had more dishware than they could use at one dinner service.

Behind him, he heard metal scraping against ceramic.

"Oh my God," Trixie moaned. She set down the spoon with a soft clatter. "I haven't had gumbo this good since I moved to DC."

"Mama's gumbo is the best in the DMV." Andre's chest puffed with pride. Some restaurants in New Orleans had come close, but never as good as his mother's. Mama drew on her roots for this recipe. Andre was grateful that Keisha had written down as many of Mama's recipes as she could before—

"I'm sorry I never got to meet her," Trixie replied softy.

"Want another?" Ignoring her condolences, he dumped the dustpan's contents into the trash. The broken ceramic dishes clanged as they fell into the bin, the sound echoing in the open dining room.

"No, thank you. Everything was perfect. Glad to see you're cooking your greens with smoked ham hocks," she said as she rubbed her belly with satisfaction.

"Mama insisted on it. You should have seen the look on her face when Mrs. Harris suggested using smoked turkey necks to make her greens healthier." Andre chuckled at the memory. "We have plenty in the back if you want more."

"I couldn't eat another bite," she said brightly. Trixie stopped mid-smile and her face fell. "I'll just wait for Keisha. You don't have to be nice to me."

"Seriously?" He dropped the broom and dustpan into the corner of the service station. "You think I'm that petty?"

"What am I supposed to think after our last conversation? You can't even look at me."

Andre forced himself to look at her. *She's so hot when she's mad at me.* Where the hell did that come from? He didn't need to get involved with her again.

"You'd rather avoid the problem than face it head on," she continued. "You hate confrontation so much it's easier to walk out."

Andre spun around and strode over to her table.

"Yes, I walked out on you," he said, his jaw clenched. "It was for the best."

"What happened to standing behind me no matter what happens?"

He did promise her that. And broke that promise in the worst way possible. If he told her the real reason, he'd break her heart again. She didn't need to know about the talk between him and her father.

"After all we'd been through with my parents." Trixie pressed her lips together, and her nostrils flared with anger. Her eyes told a different story. Those deep, thoughtful brown eyes held back tears. "You were the one who pushed me to tell them I didn't want to be a pharmacist. That I wanted to become a therapist. How could you give up on us after they gave up on me?"

"Fuck, Trixie. I—I didn't give up on us." He sighed and rubbed the back of his neck. Andre grabbed a chair from the nearest table and sat down. The booth had space for four but sitting side by side that way felt too intimate. He needed space between them, so he could think.

"Then explain." She crossed her arms over her chest.

The movement pushed her full breasts up higher, and his eyes followed their movement before he caught himself.

"My eyes are up here, Andre." She tossed her napkin on the table. "You haven't changed. I can't even have a serious conversation with you. You spend all night discussing the best way to mix an old-fashioned, but when it comes to emotions, you bail."

"I do not."

Not anymore anyway. That was the old Andre whose world revolved around his New Orleans bartending job. Everything changed when he got the phone call about his mom's cancer. He grew up. Something he should have done after he graduated high school and worked at the restaurant full time instead of running off. Now his family needed him, and he had no plans on bailing. This restaurant was all he and Keisha had left of his mother, and he wasn't going to give up on it.

"Okay, maybe I wasn't so great at talking about my feelings. But I've changed in the last two years." Losing Mama had changed his priorities. No more partying and sowing wild oats in other states. He had responsibilities now.

She scoffed, not backing down.

"Host another show at Mama Hazel's." The words flew out of his mouth. Where the hell did that come from? This was Keisha's idea. He didn't want to spend any more time near Trixie than was necessary. But it was too late. He couldn't take back his offer without looking like an asshole. Correction: more of an asshole than he already was.

"Excuse me?" She leaned forward and looked him over, tilting her head left, then to the right. "Where is Andre Walker, and what have you done with him?"

"I'm serious." Maybe if they did spend time together, she could see that he was different now. More mature.

"Why should I? I'm doing fine without you."

Ouch. He had a feeling she wasn't talking only about her job.

"Maybe you are, but you could be doing better if we team up."

"Keep going." She uncrossed her arms and leaned forward.

"Look, things have been tight around here since District Market opened. We need something different to draw in new customers. You'll introduce your clients to Mama Hazel's by holding your shows here. They fall in love with us and come back with their friends for dinner."

"Now you want sex toys in your restaurant? What happened to 'We don't need to turn this place into a sex shop'?" She deepened her voice as she tossed his words back at him.

She caught his eye, and he burst out laughing. Trixie glared at him, but a smile finally broke out. A deep, throaty laugh escaped her mouth. How he missed that sound. There hadn't been much laughing between them their last few months together.

"Wow, you still suck at impressions," he said. The laughter melted away the tension between them.

"Shut up." Her voice was stern, but her eyes were still laughing. "Actually, that's what I was going to talk to Keisha about. This is my year to win the company sales contest, but I have to do things differently if I want that ten-thousand-dollar bonus."

He whistled. "What are you going to do with all that cash?"

"I'm opening my own boutique. No more working for the man."

Andre grinned. There was his Trixie. Determined, ambitious, and fucking sexy as hell. She'd always had big dreams. Bigger than his. He knew he was destined to come back to Mama Hazel's and take over. He thought he'd had more time to travel and play around. Until Mama got sick.

"I can see it now: Trixie's Sex Emporium." He waved his hands at an imaginary sign.

"Who even says *emporium* anymore? It sounds like a brothel when you say it that way." She beamed. "I was planning on calling the shop Happy Endings."

"Of course you are." He put out his hand. "So, partners? We provide food and cocktails while you sell your products?"

"As long as we keep things professional. We can't let our past get in the way."

"I can do that, but what about you?" he asked, referring to her angry words earlier. The last thing he wanted to do was to dredge up the past with her, even if they had more good moments than bad ones. He had put aside his feelings to keep Mama Hazel's alive. His sister depended on him. The neighborhood depended on their weekly dinners. They couldn't afford to lose the community his mother had nurtured. Those people were his extended family. People who had helped his mom start over after leaving New Orleans.

"I will do whatever it takes to win this contest." She sat up straight and took his hand.

Electricity ran up his arm as she shook his hand. He inhaled sharply and ignored how the pads of her fingers seared his skin.

"I'm so sorry, Trixie." Keisha's voice boomed as the kitchen door swung open. She spotted them in the back booth. "Oh, baby. What do we have here?"

Andre and Trixie froze, their hands still clasped together. He was never going to hear the end of this. He let go of Trixie and stood up.

"Trixie has agreed to partner with Mama Hazel's."

Keisha squealed. She ran over to hug Trixie. As the two women embraced, his sister shot him a *What the hell happened out here?* look. He shrugged, pretending he didn't understand her.

"Now that my brother has beaten me to the punch, you and I have lots of planning to do." Keisha was practically vibrating with excitement.

Trixie's face fell, but she quickly smiled. Keisha hadn't seen it, but Andre recognized the disappointment that flashed across his ex-girlfriend's face. As if Trixie was disappointed that he wasn't on the planning committee.

"Great. The sooner we get started, the sooner we can both make money." Trixie pulled out her phone. "I'm usually free in the mornings. How about Wednesday?"

Keisha swiped through the calendar on her phone.

"This week is not good. I have a big project due for school next week. It's a group project." She rolled her eyes. "I know! Why don't you and Tre meet without me? He can fill me in after."

"What?" Andre whipped his head around. "Keisha, this was your idea. You said you wanted more responsibility here."

She responded with a mischievous grin. If he didn't know better, he thought Keisha was playing matchmaker. He really had to tell her about his history with Trixie and explain how complicated things were between them. But not tonight. Keisha would have a million questions, and he wasn't ready to rehash the past again.

"Let me check my calendar." He walked over to the bar where he kept his phone.

"As if you have a life, big bro. You live and breathe this place," Keisha called to his back. She turned to Trixie. "He's totally free. Come by around nine o'clock on Wednesday. That should give you plenty of time before Luis comes in to start lunch service."

Andre glared at his baby sister. He, too, had a life. If you considered balancing spreadsheets and shuffling money around to pay bills a life. Someone had to take care of the business side of running Mama Hazel's.

"Thanks, Keisha." Trixie was holding back a smirk. With two older siblings who liked to tease her, she should empathize with him. Not laugh at him.

"Ha, ha, not funny." He turned his nose up at his sister.

"I should go," Trixie said, ignoring him. "It was a long day at the clinic."

"You work too hard!" Keisha grabbed Trixie's arm. "Can I make you a to-go box? We have plenty of leftovers."

"You Walkers are food pushers," Trixie exclaimed. "You're not going to stop until I say yes, are you?"

"You know it!" Keisha laughed. "It's not right to send people home empty-handed."

"Can you make a couple of boxes for the Kims while you're back there?" Andre interjected. "They were shorthanded tonight at the convenience store, and Mrs. Kim wasn't feeling well, so Mr. Kim stayed to run it."

His sister nodded, then guided his ex-girlfriend into the kitchen. What the hell just happened? Keisha and Trixie were closer than he realized. If he told Keisha what he'd done to Trixie, his sister would feel obligated to choose sides. He couldn't put her in that position.

Maybe this was his chance to right things between them. Partnering with Trixie meant spending more time together. He'd have more chances to show her that he had changed. That he wasn't the villain she'd made him out to be. Andre didn't know how he was going to do it, but right now he had a dining room to clean and prep for tomorrow's lunch service. He picked up a plastic bin and got back to busing the tables.

Hopefully partnering with Trixie wasn't a mistake.

CHAPTER 9

"Why are you throwing your life away selling those things? People who love each other don't need that stuff."

Trixie cringed as her mom's shrill voice blasted through the phone. She held it away from her ear, which didn't soften her mom's tone. Was it just her mom, or did all Asian moms speak at full volume on the phone?

"What am I supposed to tell my friends at church? Auntie Janie will be horrified. Then I'll have to listen to her brag about that spoiled son of hers. The one who graduated from Yale and is a big-shot lawyer at some prestigious firm in New York." Her mom scoffed. "He's probably in charge of getting all those rich white men coffee."

"Má!" Trixie rubbed her forehead, hoping this conversation wouldn't give her a headache. Her mom's rapid-fire Vietnamese hit too many different issues to confront all at once. Trixie responded in Vietnamese. "You don't have to tell them anything. And yes, Trevor probably is picking up coffee for his bosses. He's a first-year."

"You know she's rubbing Yale in my face because you dropped out of school. You need to go back! Finish what you started."

Trixie sighed loudly, but her mother ignored her as she usually did.

"Go back to pharmacy school. Or law school like Trevor. More respectable than being a"—her mother paused, then said in English—"therapist."

Here she goes again. Trixie was convinced her mom knew the Viet word for *therapist* but chose to say it in English to alienate it. She didn't have the energy to argue with her mom today.

"How will you make a living listening to people talk all day?" she asked in Vietnamese. "I can do that for free on my porch."

"Má, I need to go. Get ready for work. Tell Ba that I love him."

Her mother went quiet at the mention of her father. He hadn't spoken to her since she flunked out of school. She was too embarrassed to tell them she wasn't smart enough for pharmacy school. They only knew that she had quit.

"He already knows that," her mother said softly. "You know he only wants the best for you, right?"

"I know, Má. How's he doing? Is he taking his meds?"

"I don't want you to worry, but he's going in for some tests. Doctor said his cholesterol and blood pressure are too high. Medication is not helping."

"How bad is it?" She couldn't tell by her mom's voice. Trixie sat up straighter. "Do I need to come home and help translate during his doctor appointments?"

"No! Don't waste money on a plane ticket. Your sister can come and explain everything to us."

Of course, Lucy, her lawyer sister. Rubbing in the fact that both her older siblings were dutiful kids who had parent-approved careers.

"He still doesn't want to see me?" Her shoulders slumped.

"You know how stubborn he is. But he'll come around. I'll work on it."

"Okay. I love you, Má." Trixie blinked away the tears that came to her eyes.

"Good talk. Make sure you eat." Her mother hung up.

Her mother never said, "I love you," but Trixie made sure to tell her every time they talked. Declarations of love and displays of affection made her parents uncomfortable. Love was expressed through giant bowls of phở and making sure her car got oil changes every three thousand miles. Maybe it was too American of her to wish for it, but one day her mom would say those three words back to her.

Trixie released the death grip on her phone. Talking to her family was more stressful than not talking to them. Were all Vietnamese mothers this masterful at guilt trips?

No, Zoe's parents were more laid-back. They always seemed happy with Zoe's career choice as a plus-size lingerie designer. They even let the Boss Babes hog a table at their restaurant for the weekly lunches. Sometimes they even hung out with the Boss Babes and asked them about their businesses.

All her mom ever asked about her job was when Trixie would quit Bedroom Frenzy. Trixie didn't know how much mom guilt she'd be subjected to and if she would be given a chance to defend her decision for the umpteenth time. Every phone call left her emotionally spent.

For as long as Trixie could remember, though, nothing she'd done had been good enough for her parents. They constantly bragged about her two older siblings. Binh was a chemical engineer for one of the biochem companies in New Orleans while Lucy owned a law practice and did pro bono work for Vietnamese fishermen who were still fighting for their share of the reparations after the oil spill.

In college, Trixie had tried to take the recommended classes for pharmacy majors. Medicine and other sciences bored her to death, but pharmacy required less school than being a doctor. She could have chosen another parent-approved career, like computer science, but hated the idea of sitting at a desk all day. It didn't matter which of those disciplines she chose, her grades were never going to be good enough. After jumping from major to major, she'd graduated with a liberal arts degree. How was she supposed to keep up with her siblings or the other smart Viet kids in their social circle? According to her aunties, liberal arts degrees were only good for finding husbands. Trixie didn't manage to do that either. Flunking out of pharmacy school had been the ultimate failure.

After her parents cut her off and Andre dumped her, Trixie cobbled together work at retail shops. She didn't love those jobs, but they paid the bills. Plus, she didn't have to sit in Andre's apartment all alone any more than necessary.

As much as she disliked working retail, she became great at sales. Through trial and error, she learned how to read people's body language and facial expressions to sell expensive perfumes and makeup during her stint at Canal Place. The upscale mall in New Orleans' historic district catered both to tourists and locals.

Selling sex toys wasn't that much different from pitching beauty products. She honed in on a customer's problem and found the right product at the right price point for them. With vibrators, she was helping women on a deeper level, unlike pushing wrinkle cream for women who barely had any.

Trixie would show her parents that success didn't mean picking from a list of Viet-parent-approved careers. This was her year. With the support of her Boss Babes, she'd win the contest.

The first official pop-up had been two weeks ago, a thirtieth birthday party for one of her regular customers. The party was originally at the hostess's home, but Trixie had bribed her with bonus toys in order to move it to Mama Hazel's. The per person fee was more than worth it. Who wouldn't want to hold a party where they didn't have to cook or clean afterward? By holding the show at the restaurant, her customers could invite even more friends.

The first time had gone well both for her customers and Andre. Trixie had stayed up front by her happy and horny clients while Andre kept to the bar. Keisha was the only one who dared step into their unspoken demilitarized zone.

As long as they barely spoke to each other, Trixie could keep things professional. No personal conversations. Business didn't rely on emotion to succeed. Making sales required emotion, but not partnerships. She didn't need to be friends with Andre to win her company's sales competition.

That realization made her heart drop. Seeing his easy smile and how he charmed his customers at the bar brought her back to the first time they'd met. Her girlfriends had dragged her out to the Quarter for her twenty-first birthday party, when all she'd wanted was to have a quiet dinner with friends. She hated the Quarter at night. Too many drunk tourists who heckled every woman who walked by to show their boobs. As if a set of plastic beads would convince a reasonable woman to flash a crowd holding cell-phone cameras.

While her friends went crazy on the dance floor, she nursed a drink at the bar. All the men there must have sensed her dark mood, because they left her alone. Except for the bartender, Andre. She resisted his smile for as long as she could. But his dark brown eyes were kind, and he was so easy to talk to. Not once that night did he hit on her. So she hit on him instead.

He turned out to be as easy to talk to outside of a bar setting. It didn't take long for them to be inseparable. Part of her missed having someone she could share intimate thoughts with. Another less cerebral part of her missed all the great sex she used to have.

Her body always hummed when they shared space. The low vibration that swept through her made concentrating on her sales demo challenging. Every time she spoke about a clit cream or bullet vibrator, she could imagine the two of them naked in bed trying out the products together. They had never used much more than water-based lube when they were dating. She'd been curious to try toys but had been too embarrassed to bring up the topic. Now she'd toss her favorite vibe on the bed and demand to use it together. What a long way she'd come!

But sex with Andre was a horrible idea right now. No, she needed to focus on winning. However, she couldn't erase the image of the two of them playing with vibrators together. She needed to do something about it. Before she saw him in person.

Trixie reached into her nightstand and pulled out her Jack of All Trades. She'd bought herself one as a reward after her first successful sales show, though at the time she declared it was for *research purposes.*

Jack of All Trades was her top-selling product, even though it had been more than twenty years since *Sex and the City* made it popular. For good reason. She uncapped the base and slid two rechargeable batteries in. Batteries should never be left inside when they were not being used. They could leak and ruin a favorite toy.

Trixie hiked up her dress and sat in the armchair in her bedroom. Tucking the throw pillow behind her, she slid low into the chair. Her hips relaxed, she opened her legs wide and planted her feet on the carpet. She set Jack—as she liked to call it—on her lap. For now.

Closing her eyes, she caressed her breasts through the fabric of her dress. Shocks rippled down her stomach as her fingers skated over her nipples.

Trixie bit her lip as she pretended it was Andre touching her. A sigh fell from her lips as she imagined his soulful eyes looking deep into hers as his fingers skimmed her breasts, stomach, and thighs. Teasing her until her hips bucked. Beckoning him to touch the throbbing sensitive parts right where her thighs parted.

Picturing the dark brown of his hands on her tan thighs, she parted her outer lips. Her body shuddered as her fingers circled the most sensitive part of her. She gasped at how wet she already was. The light touch quickened as she pressed harder on her clit.

She slipped two fingers inside herself and pressed the larger pad of her thumb on her clit. Her breaths were shallow as jolts of pleasure shot through her body.

"Yes." She sighed through her clenched teeth as the waves grew bigger and bigger. Now was the time for her toy.

Without opening her eyes, she picked up the toy from her lap. Deft fingers pressed the button. One, two, three times to her favorite vibrating setting: a pulsating buzz that grew faster into a crescendo, then repeated. Another press on a different button activated the pearls embedded in the lower part of the shaft, which also vibrated.

A deep moan escaped her throat as she imagined Andre's hands sliding the shaft into her pussy. She guided his hand so the extension—shaped like a rabbit's ears—wrapped around her throbbing clit.

Yes, babe. She heard his voice in her head. *Come for me. You are so beautiful when you come.*

She nodded weakly as Jack of All Trades stroked her. Slowly at first, so she could feel the beads rotate around her sensitive opening. Then deeper as she needed more. She tilted the base of the toy up slightly to press the rabbit ears harder against her clit. Her thumb fumbled as she pressed more buttons, turning up the intensity of the vibrations.

You're so close. She imagined his hot breath on her ear. *Wrap your hand around mine, and we can make you come together.*

Trixie gripped the toy, imagining his hand under hers, and let her body take over. Stroking and vibrating. Her clit taking as much pleasure as the toy could give while the beads spun inside her. Her hips bucked as her body tensed—right on the edge.

Fuck, you are so hot right now, the pretend Andre spoke.

"Yes!" she screamed, as his hoarse voice pushed her over the edge. Her muscles clenched around the toy as wave after wave of pleasure rippled through her. The powerful orgasm rocked her body and left her gasping for breath.

After a while, the still-vibrating toy became too much stimulation. She slid the toy out. Turning it off, she gently dropped it on the carpet.

Now that she was working for Bedroom Frenzy, she was no stranger to using toys on herself. But this time was different. She hadn't fantasized about Andre in that way since they were dating. On the nights he worked late tending bar in the French Quarter, she'd get herself off. Then jump him when he walked in, skin and hair smelling of cigarette smoke and hurricanes.

Once her legs felt steady, she reassembled her clothes. Practicing what she preached, she removed the batteries from her Jack of All Trades and cleaned it off before returning it to her nightstand. The orgasm had left her more relaxed and ready for tonight's pop-up.

No matter how good fantasy Andre was for her orgasms, she couldn't afford to tangle with him again. She had an arsenal of vibrators to stave off any need for a hookup. She had to keep her eyes on the prize, and Andre was not that prize.

Trixie had finally found something she was good at, and she was determined to be the very best at it. Once that bonus check was in her hand, she could strike out on her own. Prove to her parents that she didn't need multiple degrees to be successful.

Andre and his restaurant were just a means to an end, she reminded herself. They both knew what they were getting into with this partnership. All business. No feelings. Feelings just complicated things and made failure imminent. The last thing she wanted to do was admit to her parents that they were right. She couldn't afford to fail this time.

Because if she did, Trixie had no idea what she'd do next.

CHAPTER 10

Andre pushed the four-tops together for the buffet line. He stacked the chairs from those tables and pushed them into a corner next to the service station before grabbing tablecloths. Their makeshift buffet area was turning into a semipermanent one.

So far, he and Trixie had kept their interactions professional. Their planning meeting—that Keisha scheduled for him—was short. In fifteen minutes, Trixie explained why her customers wanted private spaces for their parties. He shared what Mama Hazel's could provide and the minimum number of guests for the pop-ups to be profitable for him. After that meeting, Keisha handled scheduling.

Their first official partnership had been for her customer's thirtieth birthday. It was extremely successful with more than forty guests. They didn't order as many drinks as the bachelorette party, but this crowd had been generous tippers. Some had even left them five-star reviews online.

Tonight was the second pop-up with Trixie in just as many weeks. He'd never heard of a divorce party. None of his close friends were married, and most of the couples his mother's age were still married. It made sense to throw a party to celebrate the end of something. Or was it the beginning? Keisha assured him it was a thing.

Since the partnership had originally been her idea, it made more sense for her to run it. It also meant that he didn't spend as much time with Trixie as he wanted. They barely spoke at the first pop-up. Part of him wished he could make things right with her. Show her that he wasn't the horrible person she remembered him to be. How would he convince her that he'd changed if they didn't have to talk to each other?

He looked at his phone. An hour to kill before Keisha and Luis returned from their afternoon break. An hour after that, Trixie would arrive to set up. Andre had enough time to make last-minute tweaks to his shrimp etouffee dish that Keisha raved about. At first he wasn't sure about serving it tonight, but his sister convinced him that being part of the buffet would be a low-pressure way to test it. If tonight's crowd enjoyed it, he could add it as a daily special.

Before he could step into the kitchen, there was a knock at the front door. He opened it to find Trixie. What was she doing here two hours early? She was breathing hard, as if she'd run all the way there from—well, he had no idea where she lived. Two heavy bags hung from her left shoulder and she towed a purple suitcase, which he recognized by now as her bag of vibrators. Demo kit, as she called it.

A citrus scent drifted into his nostrils. She always smelled so sweet. Their bodies were almost pressed together, separated by just a thin layer of crisp fall air. That layer heated up quickly. Andre fought the urge to swallow the air between their lips and kiss her. He cleared his throat.

"You're here early."

"It's an emergency. I didn't know where else to go, but I couldn't stay home. My friends are all busy, and I didn't want to be alone.

Can I come in early to set up?" She held his gaze and didn't budge from the doorframe.

He wasn't her first choice in an emergency, but at least she was thinking about him.

"What kind of emergency can there be with sex toys?" He paused. "Don't answer that."

"It's—it's—my dad is in the hospital," she blurted. "My brain was taking me to horrible places and I needed to get out of my apartment."

Trixie's face crumpled. Her shoulders fell, and the bags slid onto the ground with a thunk.

"Oh, no. Come in and tell me what happened." He stepped back to let her in. "I'll pour you a Diet Coke."

She nodded and dragged her suitcase over to the bar. He picked up her bags and closed and locked the front door so they couldn't be disturbed. Andre set the very bright purple bags on the stool next to her.

"My mom and I talk every week. When we spoke yesterday, my dad was fine. Then an hour ago—" Trixie leaned on the bar and closed her eyes.

Andre walked behind the bar to pour them both drinks.

Trixie gulped down half her glass in the time it took for him to sip his tonic. He refilled her glass and waited. When they first started dating, he'd tried to fix her problems right away, which made her even more upset. After a few big fights over minor things, he learned to give her time to process her feelings and think things through. He hated not being able to fix things right away, but Trixie wouldn't let herself be helped until she was ready.

She opened her bag and flipped through the papers inside, counting under her breath. He couldn't make out the numbers, but she looked better already. Color had come back to her cheeks, and her breathing was back to normal.

"Order forms, index cards, penis pencil toppers. Crap, I forgot to pack another box of pens."

"I have extras in the back office." There was the Trixie he knew. Worrying about all the practical aspects so she didn't have to deal with what was truly bothering her. "Trixie, want to talk about your dad?"

"Can we reserve that back booth for ordering? There's more privacy than doing it by the display table." She pointed to the booth they'd sat in a couple of weeks ago when she'd almost passed out. "I think I'll play orgasm bingo instead of Glo-Man ring toss."

"Slow down, babe." He cringed. The endearment fell from his lips too easily. So much for keeping things business only. "What's going on?"

She ignored the question and riffled through a side pocket of her bag.

"Trixie!" He reached over the bar and stilled her hand. "Talk to me. Why is your dad in the hospital?"

Her eyes closed, and she bit her lip. Was she going to cry?

He'd met her father only a couple of times. Mr. Nguyen was a quiet yet stern-looking man who clocked eighty-hour weeks to take care of his family. The last time Andre had seen him, he seemed strong and healthy.

Trixie placed her hand on top of his, sandwiching it with her other hand. Her light-tan skin contrasted against his dark hand. He missed seeing their skin next to each other.

"My mom called in a panic while I was packing for the pop-up."

He nodded and squeezed her hand, encouraging her to continue.

"He had a minor heart attack. He was in the doctor's office getting tests done when it happened. I can be grateful for that. He's been transferred to the hospital for observation."

"Thank God." Andre breathed a sigh of relief. "We can reschedule tonight's pop-up if you need to fly home."

"No." Trixie shook her head. "My mom told me to stay put and save the money. Besides, he doesn't want to see me."

"Of course he does. Why wouldn't he?"

"He refuses to see or talk to me since I quit pharmacy school." Her voice cracked. "I'm a failure to my dad."

"You're not a failure." He meant it. She was good at her job. Not everyone could stand in front of strangers and talk about the benefits of water-based versus silicone lube. "I take it he doesn't approve of what you're doing now?"

She laughed bitterly. "Good Vietnamese girls don't talk about sex. Ever."

"Maybe if you explained—"

"No way. Did you ever talk to your mom about vibrators?"

His expression turned to horror. Trixie laughed.

"You have a point."

"He also didn't want me to move to DC, but after you—what happened—I needed a fresh start."

There it was again. His fucking breakup note to remind him of what a horrible person he'd been.

"Right after I moved here, my car broke down and I had to ask my parents for money to get it fixed. My mom unleashed a string of I-told-you-so's while my dad gave me his usual disapproving look. Gotta love the wonders of Skype. I can see every frown and wrinkle reminding me what a disappointment I am."

"Trixie, they don't think you're a disappointment. They love you." He meant it. She wouldn't fail, because she always picked herself back up again. Besides his mom and Keisha, he'd never seen someone work so hard to get what they wanted.

"I keep hoping he'll come around, but he won't even talk to me on the phone." Trixie shook her head. "You must think this is so stupid. I should be able to separate what I want from what my parents want me to do, but I can't."

Despite the sacrifice he'd made by leaving her, she and her parents were still at odds. He'd hurt her deeply for nothing. What an ass he was. To both Trixie and his mom. He'd left both of them when they needed him. Andre had to make things right between him and Trixie. But how? He walked around to where she sat. She turned so they were now face-to-face. Andre tipped her chin up so he could meet her deep-brown eyes.

"Look at all you've accomplished in a brand-new city where you barely knew anyone. You're a smart, successful woman." In fact, she reminded him of his mother. He had not fully appreciated what Mama had done until after he left DC. Not until he learned how his father squashed his mother's dreams of opening a restaurant. He was grateful his mother had been stubborn. With a jolt, he realized that all the women in his life were stubborn. Mama, Keisha, and now Trixie, who was back in his life. Her eyes widened.

"You think I'm successful?"

Andre nodded, afraid he'd said too much. Seeing her like this—so vulnerable underneath her surface strength. It reminded him how much he cared for her. How much she trusted him to reveal this side of her. Trixie despised vulnerability. She hated looking weak. He missed being able to take care of her. Missed when she let him in. When she let him help her.

Suddenly, she slid off her stool and threw her arms around him in a tight hug.

Muscle memory took over and he wrapped his arms around her. She tucked her head into his chest and forearm. Andre leaned down and inhaled her familiar sweet scent. It felt good to hold her like this again. The past couple years had been all business for him, taking care of his sister, the restaurant, and their neighbors. There had been no time for anyone or anything else. No fuck buddies. Definitely no romantic relationships.

As they stood there in the empty restaurant, arms wrapped around each other, more sensual memories kicked in. The feel of her round breasts pressed against his body woke up other parts of him. Parts below the belt. His cock twitched and tried to stand at attention inside his jeans.

He inched his hips away from Trixie while keeping his arms wrapped around her. No need to ruin a perfectly tender moment with a hard-on. This was supposed to be a professional partnership.

"I'm sorry." Trixie looked up at him. "You probably have a ton of prep work for tonight, and I'm keeping you from it."

She didn't let him go.

"It won't take me long." He kept his arms around her, not wanting to be the first to break the embrace. "This isn't my first rodeo."

Trixie's hands slid down his back. Andre inhaled sharply when she stopped right above his ass. Her fingers twitched as if waiting for permission to move lower.

"I'm not sure this is a good idea—"

Andre's words vanished as Trixie stretched up on tiptoe and covered his mouth with her lips.

CHAPTER 11

Trixie only meant to give him a quick kiss, but instinct took over. A shock rippled through her body upon contact. Standing so close to him had been distracting. His scent was familiar. Comforting.

The way things had been in New Orleans before her life imploded. He knew when she needed a self-esteem boost and reminded her how strong she was. She came to him when she needed more courage to take risks.

Like kissing him again when it was probably a bad idea.

Her body started its low hum again.

Andre's lips were soft yet firm. She'd caught him midsentence, so his lips were slightly open. Her lips opened to match his, and her tongue caressed his mouth, inviting his to dance with hers.

His mouth opened wider to deepen the kiss. His hands wrapped around her head. Fingers intertwining with her long hair. His tongue was hot. Insistent. No—demanding as he tasted her. Pulling back just enough to make her miss him before coming back to mingle with hers. Andre's warm, spicy scent filled her nose, and she breathed him in as best she could.

She loved it. This dance between them felt familiar yet different. Andre's lips were no stranger to hers, yet he seemed more forceful. He knew what he wanted, and it was her. A heat flashed through her body.

Trixie's head swirled as she relaxed into his hold. Somewhere in the haze, she heard a moan. Hers.

Andre pulled away. She whimpered, missing the heat of his lips. He bent his head and kissed her neck right behind her ear.

She sucked in air, trying to find her footing after their kiss. Her brain told her to stop and that this would complicate things between them. Trixie pushed the thoughts aside with each kiss he left on her neck. She gasped at the contrasting sensations of searing heat from his lips and the tender bites against her skin. The heat spread into her chest, down into her belly.

"Are you sure this is a good idea?"

"No." It was the truth. Her brain screamed at her to back away. Not to trust this man again. Her body wanted comfort, no, *needed* comfort from him.

He froze.

"But I've missed this. Us." She wasn't sure if she meant sex or something more.

"I've missed you."

She searched his eyes. He was telling the truth.

"Kiss me again," she demanded. Trixie needed to get him out of her system. If they had sex one last time, that would be the closure she needed. She'd set the terms this time, not him.

"Just remember who started it."

Impatient, she drew his head down. Once their lips reunited, she bit him.

"Ouch."

She heard no pain in his voice, so she bit him again. Not hard. Playful, but hungry for more. A deep growl escaped him as he claimed her mouth, opening her lips for a deep, searing kiss.

This had been their game. Fighting for control. Giving in and immediately seizing it back. Hell, that had been their relationship toward the end.

In and out of bed.

She missed it. Missed him. The way his support gave her the strength to follow her dreams. To trust that she knew what was best for herself.

Trixie shivered as his hands slid down her back. Gasped as he cupped her ass and pulled her even closer. His hardness pressed against her stomach. Somewhere, faraway, she heard herself moan.

"I need you," she groaned against his lips. "Inside me."

"Are you sure?" Andre pulled back and looked into her eyes. He was so damned beautiful.

"Yes," she said, her voice hoarse with arousal. She ran her hands over his hair—soft, tiny curls he kept short—and kissed him. "Touch me. All of me."

"Fuck, Trixie," he moaned as his hips rubbed his cock against her. The heat of his erection stoked a different heat deep within her body. She wrapped her arms around his waist and pulled him closer. So close, but not what she needed.

"I have condoms in my bag," she uttered in between gasps. He'd returned to her neck. Kissing and biting his way to her nape.

"There're some behind the bar." He shifted his upper body and palmed her breast. "You left some behind after the last pop-up. I stuck them there until your next pop-up."

"Oh, the party favors, mm-hmmm." Concentrating on his words became more difficult.

Her body stiffened as he ran his thumb over her left nipple. Each flick sent shocks down to her core. The soft pad brushed her again. And again. Three times and her nipple hardened, straining against her bra.

"Yes," he whispered into her ear. "I love how eager your body is. So fucking hot."

"Andre—" Unable to express her needs through words, she pulled open the front of her wrap dress, revealing a black plunge bra. She pulled down the left side of her bra to reveal a darkened, very hard nipple.

"Impatient, aren't we?" He chuckled.

She grumbled but pulled down her bra to reveal her other breast. Andre stepped back to admire the view. Trixie caressed the outer curves of her breasts. Her fingers traced a large circle. Goose bumps exploded on her sensitive skin.

"I can always take care of myself." She grinned. "In fact, I got up close and personal with my Jack of All Trades yesterday."

"Fuck, Trixie," he growled. "Don't tell me things like that unless you want me to sink my cock inside of you and make you scream with pleasure."

He loved watching her pleasure herself. But he could never stay hands-off for long. Andre's pupils were so big, his eyes looked black. He shifted his legs, trying to ease the bulge in his pants.

Eyes still on his, she pinched her nipple and inhaled sharply at the pleasure-pain-pleasure. Her breathing deepened as her other hand reached up to the other breast. She swirled the pads of her fingers around the outside of her breasts, making the circles smaller and smaller until she reached the most sensitive part.

Before she could tug on her left nipple, he leaned in to her chest. Finally. She closed her eyes and arched her back, so her breasts could meet his mouth, but she met only air. She whimpered.

That was the signal he'd been waiting for. His hot mouth

crashed onto her breast. A tongue circled her nipple, making it bead even tighter. She held his head against her body. Waves of pleasure pulsed with each orbit around her nipple.

She wanted nothing more than to rip his clothes off and touch him, but he shifted attention to her other breast. Heat surrounded her nipple as he wrapped his lips around it. He alternated sucking and licking until her body shook.

"Andre—now!" Her hips pushed her mound against his hardness. She needed more.

He kissed her hard and deep—until they were both gasping for air.

"One sec." He ran behind the bar and grabbed something from underneath.

"A bit overconfident, aren't we?" she teased, glancing at the handful of condoms he dropped onto the bar.

"Remember the night after the Endymion Parade?" He raised an eyebrow.

"Mardi Gras carries good memories." Trixie closed her eyes. Images of their torrid all-nighter wearing nothing but the beads they'd caught at the parade flashed in her mind. Her pussy throbbed. Apparently, that part of her remembered, too.

She curled her finger and called him back to her. No argument from him now. As soon as he was close enough, she reached for his belt loops. Making quick work of the button and zipper, she slipped her hands inside his boxer briefs.

They both gasped as her skin made contact with his cock. Her hand curled around his hardness. She felt the veins pulsing around his girth. Fingers danced down the length of him, until she reached the head. He inhaled sharply when her thumb grazed the tip and found him wet. For her.

With one hand still in his pants, she reached for one of the condoms on the bar.

"You're not going to make me wait any longer, are you?"

"No more waiting." His voice hoarse as her thumb circled his most sensitive part the same way his tongue had circled her nipples. He tugged at his boxers to free his erection.

She released him to tear open the condom.

Suddenly they heard a clang. They froze, the condom hovering over his cock. A quick glance around showed that they were the only ones in the front of house.

"I thought we were alone," she whispered.

"We were." He cocked his head toward the kitchen. "Sounds like Luis is here early to prep for the pop-up. It's okay. Let's go to my office." He touched her cheek and pulled her in for another kiss. "Let's finish what we started."

Dishes clattered in the kitchen, and the fog in her head dissolved. What the hell was she doing? They were falling right into old habits. She'd been down this road and had been disappointed. In the end, Andre gave up on them. She couldn't go through it again. Not if she wanted to win this contest and open her boutique. Not if she wanted to finally pay back her parents and prove to them she wasn't a washout.

"I'm sorry, I can't do this." Trixie pulled away. Grabbing a napkin from the bar, she wrapped it around the unused condom. She ignored her heavy breathing and the wetness between her legs. Her bra and wrap dress quickly returned to their original positions.

"What the hell, Trixie?" Andre's chest rose and dipped as he tried to catch his breath. His face scrunched as he gingerly tucked himself back into his jeans.

She looked away to avoid the hurt in his eyes. Too bad her eyes dropped right onto his cock standing at full attention. A bead of arousal glistened on the tip before disappearing into his shorts.

"I broke our rule. We're supposed to keep things professional." She smoothed out her hair. "It won't happen again."

Trixie moved to grab her bags. Andre touched her arm, and she jerked away. When she saw the hurt in his eyes, she immediately regretted it.

"If that's what you really want." He nodded and backed away to give her space. Andre straightened his clothes.

"It's what I want."

He frowned. "Okay. I respect that. Actually, I'm glad we stopped."

"Wait, what?"

"We can't keep avoiding the conversation about how I left things in New Orleans. Between us. We—I need to tell you what happened. Can we talk after the pop-up?"

His hands rubbed the stubble on his chin.

"No," she whispered. She couldn't dredge up old feelings right before her show. She didn't need to remember how it felt to flunk out of the pharmacy program. Or the disappointment in her parents' faces when she told them. Or how she came home to his stupid, stupid note.

"Trix—"

"No!" she blurted, and dashed to her bags. "It's all in the past, and we can't change it. No point in bringing it up again."

"I can't promise you that. We can't pretend the past doesn't affect us."

"If you really believed that, you would have told your sister about me. She had no idea you even had a girlfriend in New Orleans, did she?"

He cringed as her jab hit. Her old self-defense mechanism was to hurt someone before they hurt her. She hadn't told Keisha about them either, but he'd had more time to tell her the truth. He'd been home for months before she moved to DC.

"I need to set up for tonight." She glanced over at the table up front. Keisha and Andre had created a stage of sorts for her demos.

Before Andre could respond, they heard the jingle of keys in the front door. Keisha walked in. Trixie had literally been saved by the bell.

"Trixie, you're here early! I'm so excited about tonight," Keisha said. "I always learn something new during your shows. Did you bring anything new to demo?"

"Of course! Let me freshen up before I unpack everything." Trixie's cheerful voice felt false, but she allowed Keisha to help carry her bags to the table. "Wait until you see the newest couples toy."

She walked into the bathroom, ignoring the heat of Andre's gaze on her back. Once again, she had failed. Failed at staying focused on her professional goals.

She had only a few years before she turned thirty. No more wasting time. She'd vowed that by the time she turned thirty, she would prove to her parents that she didn't need to be a lawyer or a pharmacist to be successful. That she could take care of them when they retired, like the dutiful Vietnamese daughter she was.

Now was not the time to deviate from her plan. Nothing could stop her, not even Andre. No matter how good he made her feel when he touched her.

CHAPTER 12

It wasn't hard to keep his distance from Trixie for the rest of the evening. He had drink orders to fill, and she had customers to greet. If they didn't have to interact for the rest of their partnership, everything would be fine. Keep emotions out of business. Those types of things only complicated the path to success—according to Trixie anyway.

She was wrong about that. Growing up, he'd seen his mother's acts of kindness over and over. She wouldn't call it kindness. Just the right thing to do. Opening her restaurant up to others who needed a helping hand, like their head chef, Luis. He'd knocked on their door and asked if she could teach him how to cook. Instead of asking why a Guatemalan American wanted to learn how to cook soul food, she hired him. They worked side by side for years, becoming part of Luis's family. He and Keisha attended Luis's wedding and grew up with his kids.

Family wasn't all about blood. All the neighbors watched out for each other—especially the kids. Andre couldn't kick a trash can without someone telling his mom. She'd made him take out the entire block's trash for a week for disrespecting the neighborhood. Andre had felt suffocated. A teenager was supposed to be able to make his own mistakes. Not here, though. Every move he made was scrutinized by church ladies who sat on their stoop all day. Even Mrs. Harris was always watching him after he was old enough to take care of himself.

That's why he left for New Orleans. He'd needed to live in a town where no one knew him. Better yet, where no one knew his mother, where he could be more than just Mama Hazel's boy.

And his mom had stoically let him go. "If that's what you need right now, go."

Now he was back in DC with a new perspective. His neighbors came from different backgrounds, but they helped each other out. As cheesy as it sounded, this neighborhood was a family. One he didn't appreciate until he navigated New Orleans without one.

He wasn't sure if running Mama Hazel's was his life's passion, but his community depended on him. Keisha was excited that he'd made his etouffee for tonight, but he was nervous. Mama had never let him change anything on the menu. No one outside of family had tasted his twists on Mama's recipes. He promised his sister if the dish went over well, they could put it on the menu. Knowing his Keisha, she probably wanted to revamp the entire menu. They agreed to start with just a couple of dishes as to not upset the regulars. And maybe a small craft cocktail menu while they were at it.

"Andre, you still here, bro?" Xavier waved a hand in front of Andre's face.

"Sorry." He picked up the towel and wiped down the bar. "Keisha let you out of the kitchen?"

"Yeah. She figured since it's a coed pop-up, no one would feel uncomfortable with a male waiter."

"She's got a point." The dining room was completely full. And loud. The energy from the mixed crowd was livelier than the previous pop-ups. "Thanks for coming in on late notice. We'll pay you for your time."

"No way! I've always wanted to be a fly on the wall at one of these things." He nodded at Trixie's table up front. "Maybe I should write a poetry collection about sex toys. I'll use my experience tonight as research." Xavier waved at the crowded room.

"You sure I can't pay you for tonight? It wouldn't feel right."

"Being here is more than enough payment for me. That and tips. I'm happy not to be banished to the kitchen with your bossy sister."

Xavier normally helped on community-dinner nights but mostly in the kitchen. Having him serve paying customers in the dining room meant more of his trash talk every time he walked up to give drink orders. Andre didn't mind. He looked forward to watching his best friend's reaction to all the toys on the table.

"Be cool. Don't embarrass me tonight," Andre reminded his best friend. Xavier was a lady's man. Once Trixie began passing her vibrators around, the toys wouldn't be the only things buzzing. Everyone would be excited and ready for action. "No hookups with future customers."

"I'm hurt." Xavier held his chest as if Andre had shot him. "You think I can't stay cool?"

Andre threw him a skeptical look.

"All right, I'll be extra good tonight. I'd never hit on one of your customers. At least not while I'm on the job." Xavier looked back at the dining room. "Can I flirt at least? I'm saving my tips for a new laptop. For my poetry."

"Fine. What do you need?"

Xavier rattled off several drink orders before a guest waved at him. The brunette wore a body-hugging dress that accentuated her breasts. Xavier's face broke into a grin. "I'll be right back. Have orders to take."

Andre chuckled. Xavier was in his element. No doubt he'd get great tips tonight. He returned his attention to the glasses on the bar. Two rum and Cokes, a gin and tonic, and four glasses of house red.

Plus, an appletini for Trixie. Maybe her favorite cocktail would help her nerves. He could tell she was still shaken up from their earlier . . . well, *encounter* wasn't the right word, but he didn't know how else to describe it. Not without getting another hard-on.

She hadn't settled down after all the guests arrived and piled their plates full of food. Instead, she paced around her demo table, straightening and adjusting her products. Next, she shuffled and stacked her order forms and counted the pens.

"That her?" Xavier reappeared and moved the drinks to his tray.

"Who?"

"Don't play dumb with me, man. You've been watching her all night." He picked up the appletini. "I didn't order this. Either you're off your game or it's for her."

"Fine. It's for Trixie."

"Finally! A face for the infamous Trixie." Xavier whistled. "I can see why you think about her 24/7."

"I do not think about her all the time."

"Oh, shit! You want her back! You still got it bad."

Andre remained silent.

"Andre, I'm just teasing. Having a little fun. We cool?"

"She was upset earlier—before everyone else got here. So I

talked to her. Let her cry on my shoulder. I'd forgotten how good things were between us. Then she kissed me, I kissed her back, and one thing led to another. Then Luis interrupted us."

"He walked in on the two of you?!"

Andre scowled. That would have made the situation much worse.

"Hold up. Let me drop off these drinks. That woman in red has been making eyes at me all night." Xavier whisked the tray off the bar and strode away.

Andre watched as he charmed every lady—hell, even the one guy—sitting at table seven. If they ever had enough money, he'd hire Xavier to run his front of house and publicity. That brother oozed charmed. People fell over themselves to earn one smile from him.

On the other hand, Andre couldn't even get Trixie to make eye contact with him tonight.

Xavier zoomed back to the bar. "Talk. I have five minutes before lady in red downs her rum and Coke."

"No one walked in on us. There was a crash in the kitchen. Ruined the moment." Andre shrugged. "It didn't mean anything."

"Sure. That's why you've been moping behind the bar all night. Frowning at highball glasses and using your soda gun as if it were a weapon."

"I have not."

"Your tip jar is proof you've been scowling all night."

The jar was empty, except for the fiver he'd stuck in there earlier.

"That's because all the tips are going to you tonight."

"I thought you were going to keep things cool between you. Profesh," Xavier reminded him.

"We are."

Xavier snorted.

"I am. Starting now."

"I'm not the stay-professional police. Do what you want, but don't sit on the fence. It's not good for anyone."

"We have unfinished business. The way I left New Orleans—it wasn't cool. I need to explain what happened."

"Are you doing this for you or for her? Because if you're only doing it to ease whatever unfounded guilt you got, that's the wrong reason."

He hated when Xavier knew him better than he knew himself. Andre came home because his family needed him. But how he left was cowardly. Maybe it was better to keep things in the past. That's what Trixie wanted.

"Crap," Xavier said through a forced smile. "Lady in red is waving again."

She was waving wildly and grinning at Xavier. Andre reached for the rum.

"That woman has grabby hands. Let's hope all she wants is a rum and Coke this time." Xavier placed the drink on his tray. "If you want to patch things up with Trixie because you still have a boner for her, do it. But don't force things because you feel guilty about leaving her to come home to take care of Miss Hazel."

The truth was, Andre wasn't sure how he felt about Trixie. She didn't want to talk to him, so his feelings wouldn't make a difference anyway. But he had to patch things up with her. What did he have to lose if she already hated him?

CHAPTER 13

"Wasn't that the best fried chicken you've ever had?" Trixie said to the forty people who were eagerly watching her. "Now that you're done licking chicken from your fingers, let's talk about licking other things."

A smattering of laughter rippled through the crowd. Though she was still worried about her dad, the large group's responsiveness helped her focus on her semi-scripted sales show.

"I'm Trixie Nguyen, your new sex toy pusher." She winked. "You may be wondering what the heck do I know about all the things on the table behind me. I thought the same thing when I was recruited for the job. You should have seen me try to put batteries into my first toy. Not an easy feat when they only come with IKEA-style instructions."

Some of the women nodded knowingly.

"Good thing you have me! Tonight I'll show you Bedroom Frenzy's most popular products and ways to use them you won't find on an insert. Ready?"

A smattering of yeses rang out.

"Earlier, I handed everyone a five-by-seven index card. This is where size really does matter, because it's your wish list. Write down all the items that strike your fancy."

"The bigger the better!" a woman wearing a body-hugging red dress exclaimed. A few people around her murmured in agreement, while others chuckled.

"As you'll see tonight, it's not always about the size, but the motion of the ocean."

Trixie smiled, making a mental note to keep an eye on the woman. Some guests drank too fast because sex talk made them nervous. Sometimes they got rowdy and heckled, which was not good for her sales. After a summary of how the show worked, she jumped right into her sales presentation. *Darn it.* She realized a few minutes into the sales demo that she'd forgotten to play orgasm bingo. The game usually helped the nervous people relax and become more comfortable with her. It was also fun and hilarious with larger crowds.

Trixie always ran her show the same way. Icebreaker game, brain equals foreplay, physical foreplay, and then all the toys. Just like a date. You couldn't jump right into the battery-operated equipment before getting in the mood.

The schedule had always worked for her, but she couldn't go back and play a game now. People were already making their wish lists. Stopping the flow to play the game would take them out of the buying mood. As much as she loved telling her customers how amazing the clitoris is, she needed sales. Lots and lots of sales to pull her out of third place.

Guests scribbled on their index cards as she talked about how their brains were their biggest sex organ. Things like flirting and dirty talk could get the blood flowing in more than their brains. How intimacy—talking and sharing feelings—connected them to their partners and increased arousal.

Which was exactly why Trixie had found herself kissing Andre earlier. His arm around her, comforting her, talking her through the worry about her dad and their estrangement. She'd only spoken with Zoe in depth about her parents' disapproval. Zoe understood the cultural nuances and didn't try to vilify her dad like Reina had.

Andre made her feel safe. Kissing him felt so natural at that moment. Of course things had heated up quickly. Sexual chemistry was never an issue for them. Thank goodness they'd been interrupted before they had gone any further. She didn't want to get back together with him. They'd gotten carried away, but she wouldn't let it happen again.

"This is boring! Get to the sex toys already!" the woman in red yelled. Her face was flushed. Clearly, she'd had too much to drink. Her friends shushed her, but she waved them away. "My boyfriend doesn't want any of this body lotion crap."

"I'm a fan of quickies, too, but I promise it'll be worth the wait." Trixie pulled her face into what she hoped was an encouraging smile.

"Better be," she huffed, and waved for another drink. Keisha brought her a glass of water. The woman frowned and pushed it away.

"What's your name, miss?" Trixie asked. Hecklers don't like being the center of attention, so attention she'd get.

"Jessica."

"Jessica, can you come up and help me with the next product?" Trixie held up a bottle of warming massage lotion. "Unless you're worried it won't work."

"I've tried that stuff before. It doesn't work." Jessica crossed her arms and glared at Trixie. "I thought this was supposed to be fun. You suck at this."

Trixie froze. Her mother's voice ran through her head. *Why are you throwing your life away?* Maybe she wasn't any good at this. She'd been stuck at third place in her company for months. Tonight's pop-up was already going off the rails.

"I'll try it," a deep voice called out.

Andre. Did he volunteer himself?

"Yeah, Andre!" Xavier hooted. Apparently, he and Andre were childhood friends. The waiter had introduced himself earlier when he dropped off her appletini.

The guests joined in and cheered, except for Jessica.

Andre walked up to her front table and handed her a Diet Coke with a perfectly cut lime wedge.

"Relax," he whispered. "You've got this."

"Thanks," she whispered. She gulped the cold, bubbly soda, eyes widening when the taste of rum hit her taste buds. Taking a deep breath, she mentally found her place in her presentation.

"Now that your brain is in the mood, let's get the rest of you revving. A massage is a good way to ease into the physical part of intimacy. The Blow Me massage oil will heat things up."

The crowd smiled.

"Here's how you activate it. Andre, can you roll up your sleeve and hold out your arm?"

Are you sure? she mouthed to Andre. He pushed up his sleeve. Her throat went dry. The dark brown curves of his muscles were very well defined. The same strong arms that had wrapped around her body as their tongues danced. She cleared her throat.

"Blow Me massage oil comes in several flavors, but Wicked Juicy Apple is one of the most popular." She opened the bottle and squeezed several drops on his arm. "Like any massage oil, it helps hands glide over your body so you can work out tight muscles."

Setting the bottle down, Trixie held his upper forearm with both hands. Using the pads of her thumbs to apply light pressure, she pulled gently toward his wrist. His toned muscles rippled under her touch.

A quick glance showed Andre's eyes shining, a half smile on his face.

"That feels, uh, nice."

The men in the room chuckled nervously. No doubt worried she'd ask them to help model the merchandise, too.

Andre shifted his feet, as if suddenly aware that forty pairs of eyes were on him.

"Doesn't the massage oil smell good?"

"I do love apples. Smells like Mama Hazel's apple cobbler," he added. "Which is our special dessert on Friday nights."

Who was this man? Charming the audience while marketing his restaurant at the same time.

"That's not the best part." Trixie leaned over his arm and blew on it.

"Whoa! It's getting hot," Andre exclaimed in surprise. He deepened his voice. "Hot in a good way, if you catch my drift."

The women in the front row swooned. Damn, he was good at this.

"Once your massage starts to heat up, you'll want to nibble and kiss each other." Trixie turned to Andre. "Lick your arm."

"What? Oh, I mean, of course." Andre's eyes were shining as he pulled his arm up to his mouth. "Should we taste it together?"

"I already know what it tastes like," Trixie stuttered. Did he suggest she lick him in front of forty strangers?

But the guests cheered and hooted, egging them on. This pop-up was not going the way she'd planned. However, tonight's focus was on couples, per her newly divorced hostess's request. After leaving a bad marriage, her hostess had found a partner who treated her like the queen she was. What better way to show how couples—especially those with reluctant partners—could enjoy the products together?

Trixie took a deep breath and exhaled slowly. Eyes on the prize. Nothing was going to keep her from first place.

"Okay, okay," Trixie called out to the crowd. "I'll taste it, but Andre has to go first."

ANDRE'S MOUTH FELL open. He didn't think she would go through with it. Time to play along.

"This isn't enough for both of us to taste. I need more." He gestured at the bottle. "If you'll do me the pleasure."

Trixie shot him a hard look, but her smile didn't waver. *Uh-oh.* He was in deep trouble. She did not like it when people imposed on her schedule. He'd be safe until everyone left, though. Trixie was too much of a professional to tell him off in front of her guests.

At least, that's what he hoped.

"That's what I'm talking about!" a deep voice bellowed from a big hipster guy who likely spent more time on his beard than Keisha did on her hair.

Andre gave the hipster a mock salute. Maybe this guy would tell all his friends about Mama Hazel's after tonight. Bring in some new customers. He looked like the type that left good Yelp reviews.

"What if we mixed two flavors?" Trixie held up two bottles. The crowd applauded in approval. She looked to Andre. "You are the mixologist here, so let's create a sensual cocktail."

He swallowed hard. One of the bottles had red flames on it.

Filled with bright-red massage oil. An evil grin was plastered on Trixie's face. What had he gotten himself into? He didn't think things through when he volunteered himself. All he'd thought of was the drunk woman derailing Trixie's show and ruining her sales. Now he was a guinea pig for massage lotion—in front of people he'd hoped would return to Mama Hazel's. Xavier was not going to let him forget this.

"How about I create a special *cock*tail for this evening?" he asked the crowd. More cheers. "Can you tell everyone what the flavors are? So our guests can add them to their wish lists?"

Trixie rattled off the different flavors as the guests wrote furiously. She threw him an appreciative look. Perhaps she'd forget about that fiery bottle she was about to douse his arm with.

"Tonight's special is the Pants-on-Fire Cinnamon."

Damn.

"What drink would you pair it with?" She turned to him, bottle open and ready to pour on his skin.

"Cinnamon and apple go well together. Let's try that." He cleared his throat. How hot could this massage oil be?

"Wicked Juicy Apple it is." She picked up the bottle with the apples on the label. Turned both bottles upside down over his arm and squeezed. Whoa, this was more than the few drops she'd put on his other arm.

"Dear Trixie, can you massage my arms? I like my cinnamon apple rubbed, not stirred."

The crowd chuckled. They were loving this. He wondered if she'd ever had a partner during her sales presentations before.

"My pleasure," she replied too cheerily. She glared at him but wrapped her hands around his wrist. She squeezed, much harder than the first time. His eyes widened as she tightened her grip and "massaged" his arm.

"Now that our cocktail is well mixed." He cleared his throat and pulled his arm out of her grasp. "Tasting time."

The room was silent, everyone on the edge of their seats.

Andre closed his eyes and opened his mouth. He lifted his arm to his mouth.

"Wait, you have to blow to activate—" Trixie leaned forward to blow on his arm.

A warmth spread over his arm before his mouth reached it. The warmth quickly grew hot. He jerked his arm away as a fiery heat spread across it. He opened his eyes in time to see Trixie's pursed lips coming at his face.

Cheers erupted as her lips landed on his. His eyes met her panicked ones. She quickly pulled away, face turning red.

He didn't have time to absorb their accidental kiss. He waved his arm furiously, trying to cool it down. Except waving made it worse. What did she say about the oil? Blowing on it made it hotter. That's why they named it Blow Me!

"It should be activated now," Trixie squeaked as she tried to hold back her laughter.

The crowd didn't hold back. Out of the corner of his eye he saw Xavier laughing.

"Right." Andre stopped flailing his arm. He stood up straight, breathing through his mouth. "That was a demonstration on how *not* to use it. Start with just a little."

More laughter. They thought this was part of the presentation!

Trixie walked over with a wet wipe for his arm. He held a hand up to stop her. Time to get this over with. He squeezed his eyes shut and brought his arm up to his mouth again. He took a quick swipe with his tongue. It tasted pretty good. He opened his mouth wider and licked again. The oil warmed his tongue. Cinnamon filled his nose as the sweet yet tart apple filled his mouth.

"Wow, this is delicious." He looked over at Trixie in surprise. "Tastes like our apple cobbler. But not as hot."

The crowd chuckled again. He saw more people writing on their wish list.

She nodded in agreement, pleased with his reaction.

"There you have it, ladies and gents. Turn your lover into apple cobbler, which is the Friday-night special here! Let's give a hand to our helper and proprietor of Mama Hazel's, Andre Walker!"

Andre bowed as everyone in the room applauded and cheered. Even Xavier and Keisha were cheering for him.

"In honor of this pairing, tonight's special cocktail will be Pants-on-Fire appletini!" He looked over at Xavier, who nodded.

"Who wants a Pants-on-Fire?" Xavier asked. Hands flew up. His friend ran out into the crowd to take orders.

While the crowd was distracted, Andre accepted a wet wipe from Trixie.

"Thanks," she whispered. Her eyes gleamed. "Sorry about the, uh, kiss."

"That was fun, but nerve-racking. You are really good at this— heckler and all. I don't think I could stand in front of a crowd for an hour like you do." He pretended not to hear her comment about the kiss. He was not sorry about feeling her soft lips on his. "Trixie, you're pretty amazing. I hope you know that."

He kissed her cheek and walked back to the bar before she could reply.

Andre spent the rest of the evening mixing drinks, many of

which were Pants-on-Fire appletinis. From now on, they needed to create a special cocktail for every pop-up. Something fun and tied into one—or two—of Trixie's products. He made a mental note to talk to her about this perfect pairing of their talents.

As for the woman in red, Jessica, she kept quiet after their massage-oil demonstration. Good thing he volunteered early, before Trixie pulled out the toys. He didn't think he could stand in front of strangers and talk about vibrators. Whew. Saved by the lady in red.

For the first time since his mother died, Andre felt truly alive. His blood hummed through his body as he mixed drinks, while Trixie shot her electric smile at him in between her product demos. It had started when she kissed him and practically jumped him. Each kiss they'd shared had given him energy. Like recharging his batteries. Batteries he thought had faded when his mother died, and he had to focus on keeping Mama Hazel's solvent.

Tonight reminded him that he and Trixie had been great together. Not just sexually. They played off each other during the massage-oil demonstration like they'd been doing it for years! He hated being the center of attention normally, but showing everyone how Blow Me worked had been fun.

And it had been fun because he was doing it with Trixie. Even the previous pop-ups had made running the bar less like work and more fun—simply because she had been in the room. Though they had unfinished business to discuss, he could see himself licking fiery but sweet/tart massage oil from her body as he rubbed her all over.

Andre wanted Trixie back in his life as more than a business partner.

He wanted her back. Not just in his bed. But as his girlfriend.

CHAPTER 14

"Not counting my very first sales show, this was one of the hardest." Trixie dropped into the nearest chair. She kicked off her pumps and propped her feet up on another chair. Her feet ached after standing for almost two hours.

The customers had dragged their full, happy stomachs home for the evening. Almost everyone left with a bag of samples to tide them over until their orders arrived. She typed a note into her calendar app to email everyone in two weeks to see how they liked their products.

"You were on fire tonight!" Keisha reset the tables for tomorrow's lunch service. "Who knew Andre had it in him?"

"I'm glad he was a good sport about the cinnamon massage oil. I didn't expect him to volunteer." Once again, he'd surprised her. Not only had he been brave, he'd charmed the pants off the crowd. He'd even done Trixie a favor by diffusing the situation with that heckler.

"Maybe he can be your assistant if his day job doesn't work out," said Keisha.

"I heard that." Andre popped up from under the bar and shook his head at Keisha, as if telling her to be quiet. "My day job isn't going anywhere."

"You okay closing up?" Keisha looked at her phone. "I need to go home and study for my accounting exam."

"Go," Andre replied. "I can handle it. School is important."

"Hey, Xavier! Wanna walk me home?" Keisha called into the kitchen. The swinging door was propped open so cleanup could move more quickly.

"Sure. Give me five minutes," Xavier's muffled voice called back.

"Night, big bro." Keisha kissed his cheek and hugged him. She glanced at Trixie and grinned. "Don't do anything I wouldn't do."

"What are you—" Andre started, but Keisha ran into the kitchen, giggling. She kicked the doorstop and let the door swing closed.

He shook his head at his sister, but he didn't look upset. There was so much love between them. Trixie wished she was that close with her own siblings.

"Want another drink while I finish up? A Pants-on-Fire appletini maybe?"

"Very funny. Just water. Maybe that will help with my ankles."

He squinted in confusion. She pointed to her swollen feet.

"Your ankles look normal to me." He shrugged and quickly returned with a glass of ice water.

"Thank you," she said softly after he handed her the drink. "For earlier. My sister texted that my dad is stable. They're keeping him overnight."

"That's great news!"

They fell silent. Trixie replayed how she'd found comfort in his arms. She gulped the water to cool off her suddenly flushed body. She forced herself to focus on their business partnership.

"If you ever want a second career, you should join Bedroom

Frenzy." Trixie chuckled. "I've dealt with hecklers before, but that woman was something else. I would have crashed and burned if you hadn't come to my rescue."

"I couldn't stand how that woman was treating you. We should have stopped serving her alcohol sooner." He picked up her feet and sat down on the chair they'd just occupied. Andre put her feet on his lap.

"What are you doing?" Trixie tried to sit up, but he held fast to her feet.

"Returning the favor from earlier." He grasped her right foot and pressed the ball with his fingers. Then he ran his thumb firmly down her arch.

"Is that a threat—oh, wow." She slid farther down in the chair, her head leaning back. "That feels so good."

He switched to her left foot and gave it the same treatment as her right one.

"I could have handled her, you know." She held back a groan as his thumb rubbed insistently over her arch. "I get hecklers all the time. Usually it means they're intimidated by the products, or their partner—usually a guy—didn't want them to attend the show."

"She was rude to you, and I couldn't stand it anymore." His voice was soft, as if he didn't want to wake her from the reverie of her foot massage.

Trixie heard herself murmur in agreement. She couldn't remember the last time anyone besides her nail technician touched her feet. Andre's hands felt ten times better. After a long, stressful day, the massage was almost as relaxing as a glass of merlot and her vibrator.

"I said it earlier tonight, but I'm saying it again. You're really good at this."

"You're just saying that because I'm bringing customers to your restaurant."

His hands stopped for a second then continued their firm pressure on her foot. Was it her imagination or did he stiffen when she said that? Why did she have to ruin one of the few moments where they weren't bickering?

When he didn't respond, she pulled her feet away and sat up. His eyes were sad and far away.

"Andre." She touched his hand. "Is Mama Hazel's doing okay? How bad is it?"

"Bad." He sighed. "We're barely hanging on. One of our fryers has been acting up. Keisha's tuition for next semester will be due soon."

"I had no idea. When you said things were tight, I didn't think they were this bad." Trixie scooted her chair closer to him and held his hand. "How can I help?"

"You can help by not telling Keisha. I don't want her to worry."

"But she's your family. You two are so close."

"Look what happened when you told your family the truth," he shot back. "Sometimes it's better to keep family in the dark."

Trixie dropped his hand and looked away.

"I'm sorry." He grabbed her hand. "That was uncalled for."

She remained silent but didn't pull her hand away.

"Trixie." He took her other hand and held both in his own.

His fingers caressed the back of her hands. Suddenly the room felt very warm. Trixie inhaled deeply to clear her mind, but only Andre's scent filled her nose.

"You underestimate yourself. You're one of the most talented, badass women I've ever known."

"Did you just give me a compliment?" she shot back a little too quickly. "I'm only here because of Keisha."

"I'm tired of fighting with you," he said, his eyes wide and hopeful. "Can we start over—on a friendlier note?"

Could they really be friends? All their arguing wore her out, too. It took a lot of energy to stand her ground with him and not let down her guard. Waiting for his next barb to hit her.

She nodded, eyes glued to his.

"Hi, Trixie, it's been a long time. I've missed you," he whispered. His strong, warm hands were still wrapped around hers.

"I—I—I've missed you, too." She leaned forward and laid her head on his chest. "You smell good."

Like that, the wall between them broke. He wrapped his arms around her and held her tight. Trixie exhaled in relief. For this one moment, everything felt right between them.

ANDRE CUPPED HER head and pressed his forehead to Trixie's. Relief flowed through him. Though she didn't want to talk about the past, she was opening up to him now. Here was his chance for a do-over.

"I want to kiss you. Do you want me to?"

She held her breath. Exhaled and nodded. "Kiss me."

That was all he needed to hear. Andre's lips crashed into hers. She wrapped her arms around him, pulling him tighter. The arousal that she'd doused earlier that evening rekindled. The need to touch her—claim her—overwhelmed him.

If she wasn't ready to talk, then he would show her how he felt. He pulled her onto his lap and kissed her again and again. A soft kiss to apologize for how he walked out on her. A deep, longing kiss to welcome her back into his life. Andre was determined to make up for the last two years apart from her.

Trixie broke away from him, panting. He claimed her mouth again, and she eagerly returned the kiss.

"Maybe we should go to your office now," she blurted in between their kisses.

"Are you sure?" He searched her eyes, terrified she would change her mind like she had earlier that night. "This isn't part of our professional agreement."

"I'm willing to make an exception if you are," she said, nibbling his earlobe.

She sucked his earlobe before running kisses down his neck. He groaned. The tingles on his neck went straight to his hard cock, still aching from their interrupted moment earlier that afternoon.

"Fuck, Trixie. Don't play with me. I can't keep things professional between us if you keep kissing me like that."

"Let's call it research. A case study of arousal and pleasure."

She shimmied on his lap, wiggling her eyebrows as her ass pressed against him. His hips instinctively pushed against hers, increasing the pressure against his throbbing cock. Electricity shot through his body. He groaned.

None of this made any sense to Andre, but right now his brain wasn't in charge. His body was. He'd given her plenty of opportunities to turn him down, but she still wanted him. Yes, she wanted him.

"I have a better idea." Trixie's eyes gleamed.

"What?" He knew that look. Whatever idea had popped into her head was going to get them into trouble. The good kind of trouble.

"Let's have sex on the bar. I'm always telling my customers to change things up."

"That's definitely not up to code." When had she become so . . . daring?

She kissed his neck before gently nibbling the sensitive spot below his ear.

He inhaled sharply. Then leaned his head back, letting her mouth leave a trail of goose bumps on his neck.

"Please? For my sex bucket list?" Her hot tongue swirled around the edge of his earlobe before traveling down to his collarbone.

"You have a sex bucket list?" It was getting harder to think straight. When he was a teen, he'd fantasized about having sex on the bar. Now that he was the one cleaning it every night, the fantasy had lost its charm. Until now.

"Mmm," she replied into his neck. She'd turned her attention to the other side.

"All right, but you have to do what I say."

"I've always liked this demanding side of you." She slipped her hands under his shirt and found his nipples.

"I don't want you to fall off and twist an ankle. Too much paperwork." His eyelids drifted closed as her fingers drew circles. She still remembered how to make him ache with need. He forced his eyes open. *Focus, Andre.* He grabbed her wrists and pulled them to her side.

"I've missed you so much, Trixie."

Damn, she looked so hot. Her light-tan face was flushed with arousal. Pupils wide, lips swollen from his kisses. He should take her right now. Bury himself deep inside her until they both screamed out in pleasure.

"Me too." She gyrated. "Can we go to the bar now, Mr. Walker?" Andre didn't know what tomorrow would be like between them, but dammit, he'd take her and make her come over and over.

"Only if you do what I say."

CHAPTER 15

Trixie dragged herself off his lap, body shaking in excitement. Andre's firm voice went straight to her core. Heat flashed between her legs. Her heart pounded.

Maybe giving in to her lust was a bad decision. But tonight was just a one-time thing. Didn't she tell her customers that sex was a great way to release tension? She hadn't had sex with anyone since she moved to DC. Unless she counted her vibrators, which paled in comparison next to Andre.

Sex with Andre would be a stress reliever and research at the same time. For work. One final fuck and she'd get him out of her system for good.

"What?" Patience had never been her friend. Not when orgasms were involved.

"Grab the Blow Me from your bag. The cinnamon one." He leaned back in his chair, legs spread out.

Trixie licked her lips as her eyes dropped to the erection bulging under his jeans. Her fingers twitched, remembering his silky hardness from earlier.

"Time for some payback." He reached up and slipped his hand into the neckline of her dress. When his fingers found her nipple, he lightly pinched it.

She gasped, but the pain quickly turned into pleasure as he rolled her beaded nipple between his fingers. As soon as she began to moan, he let go.

"Bring the bottle to the bar when you have it."

She wanted to rip open her wrap dress and offer her breasts to him, but she didn't. His eyes were dark and intense. If Andre really wanted the massage oil, she'd get it for him. Part of her was excited to put the oil to good use beside at a sales demo.

They'd never used anything more than lube when they were dating. Trying something new with him thrilled her and turned her on more than ever before.

Trixie nodded. She'd play along. No matter which massage oil he wanted to try, it meant the night would end with him buried inside her.

She sashayed across the dining room to her purple bags, making sure to exaggerate the movements of her hips. Behind her, Andre grunted in appreciation. Trixie smiled and bent over her bag to dig out the bottle of Pants-on-Fire Cinnamon.

"What a lovely view," Andre called from his chair as she passed him on the way to the bar.

"Place the bottle on the bar," he called when she reached the barstools lined across the front of the bar. "Boost yourself up onto the bar—but take your panties off first."

What did he have planned? She'd expected a quickie from him. Especially since she'd put a halt to their earlier activity. Trixie reached under her dress and pulled down her black lace panties. She balled them up and tossed them at him.

Andre caught the panties midair. "A souvenir, Ms. Nguyen? Why, thank you."

"I—I—you can't have those!" she stammered. "They're one of my favorite pairs."

"Hop on up." He stuffed her panties in the front pocket of his jeans. "Need a hand?"

Trixie turned to the bar. Reaching almost her chest, it was higher than she thought. Maybe having sex on the bar wasn't a good idea. She couldn't afford to get hurt. That would put her out of commission.

"Um, maybe we can go to your office instead." She bit her lip, embarrassed.

"What about your sex bucket list?"

"I wrote it. I can change it." She shrugged. Trixie had lied about her bucket list, but after tonight she'd write one.

"Come on." Andre grabbed her waist. "On the count of three, hop and I'll help you up."

"I'm too heavy," she protested. "We can—"

"Three!"

With some effort, he picked her up and set her on his bar. Trixie gasped and looked down. The ground seemed very far away. Cool air flowed under her dress as her legs swung.

"I like this," she said breathily.

Andre looked at her and smiled. "You're about to like it even more."

With his eyes still locked on hers, he placed his right hand on her left knee. The warm hand slid up her thigh, under her dress. His left hand repeated the action on her right knee. He pushed her knees apart. She adjusted her butt on the bar to open herself to him.

He gathered the silky fabric of her skirt and pushed it up behind her hips. She inhaled sharply as the cool air caressed her outer lips. His large warm hands caressed her sensitive inner thighs.

Trixie's breathing quickened, and her head fell back. His touch was familiar, even if the situation between them wasn't. That newness charged the air around them. Part of her wanted to ride him until they both came, but she also wanted to savor this moment between them. Explore the new people they'd become.

Sitting up on the bar with her legs splayed and her pussy bared to him turned her on even more. She shifted to spread her legs farther apart so he could see the wetness of her arousal. His gaze fell down between her legs.

"Damn, woman. You're so wet." His voice was low and hoarse. "I'd like nothing more than to bury myself inside you."

"Why don't you?" she whispered at the tight curls on his head. "Take me."

"It's been two years since I've been with anyone." He shook his head. "I'm taking my time and enjoying every second."

Two years? She did quick math in her head. This meant he hadn't slept with anyone since they'd broken up. Based on the amount of flirting happening at his bar, she was shocked that he hadn't found comfort in someone.

"Ready for your payback?" he asked, holding up the bottle of Blow Me.

Before she could respond, he squeezed some of the warming massage oil onto her thighs. She gasped. The oil was cold on her skin. The cold was replaced by his warm hands as he rubbed the oil into her thighs. The sweet, spicy cinnamon scent filled the air.

His hands caressed her, moving higher and higher up her thighs. She tensed and braced herself, waiting for him to reach the ache between her thighs. But he pulled back each time. Leaving her on the edge.

She forced herself to breathe through her nose in order to tamp down the desire to stand up and pleasure herself. With almost two years' experience becoming an expert on an entire collection of vibrators and dildos, self-pleasuring had become her art form.

Though the urge to touch herself was strong, she needed to feel Andre's hands on her body. Much like her fantasy with him as she pleasured herself with Jack of All Trades. Except now she didn't have to fantasize. He was right in front of her.

"Not much of a payback," she teased, hoping lighthearted ribbing would convince him to touch the heat between her outer lips.

"Always in such a hurry, Ms. Nguyen." Andre grabbed some napkins from behind her and wiped his hands. He bent his head closer to her thighs.

Finally.

And he blew. Her already warm thighs flared as the massage oil heated her skin.

Trixie gasped. Pants-on-Fire felt nothing like how it felt on her arm. There it was a pleasant warmness that made her skin tingle. On her thighs, the fire spread across her body and converged at her pussy.

"Oh my God!" she whispered. She closed her eyes and let the warm waves pass through her body.

"I'll be right back." Andre stepped quickly away from her, causing air to rush over her thighs. Another wave of heat and pleasure rolled across her.

"Where are you going?" she gasped.

"Need to lock up."

He ambled to the front door and turned the dead bolt. Trixie was glad Keisha had closed all the blinds before she left. Instead of walking to the bar, he circled the room. Straightening chairs. Turning off lights. She willed him to move faster and return to the bar.

"Seriously, Andre?" she called. Her body was screaming for his touch. How could he leave her sitting here as fire raged in her? She needed him to stoke the fire and bring her over the edge.

He flipped a switch, leaving them in darkness. Slivers of light from streetlamps peeked through small cracks in the blinds. She blinked quickly to adjust to the darkness.

"Do you know how beautiful you look right now?"

She shook her head. He returned to his position between her legs.

"Unbelievably sexy. So fuckable."

"Well then, fuck me," she gasped. Trixie breathed faster. "Touch me. I don't care how."

Andre hooked his hands behind her knees. She held her breath as his mouth opened. He kissed her thigh. Trixie shuddered. She couldn't believe she was so wound up, she might come from him just licking her thigh.

"Tastes even better on you," he murmured. He licked his way up her thigh until he reached her folds. Then turned his attention to the other side. "So sweet, but spicy. Just like you."

She groaned and grabbed his head with her right hand. Her left was still gripping the edge of the bar. There was no way she'd forget how high up she was.

Not giving in to Trixie, he kept his attention on her thighs. When she finally let go of his head, his hot tongue dipped between her outer lips. Her hips bucked, and she gasped.

"So sweet," he whispered. "And wet."

He pulled his head back. She moaned, missing his warmth on her skin.

Dipping his fingers between her lips, he kissed her thigh. Nipped the tender skin. She moaned when his fingers found her clit. They circled her sensitive bud. First slow, then faster and faster until she was gasping for breath.

"I love hearing you moan. Let's see if I can make you moan louder."

The fingers disappeared. Trixie felt her blood pounding through her clit, which felt tight and demanded more attention.

"More?" He leaned in until his face was right in front of her pussy. What was left of the massage oil heated up her skin as his breath hit her thighs.

She nodded, unable to speak. Her body was on the precipice of pleasure. Was he going to eat her out in this position? Her brain was overwhelmed by the thought.

"Hold on to the bar, okay? I don't want you to fall off."

She nodded as he spread her knees apart with his hands and dove into her. He kissed her outer lips, then traced his tongue in between them. Sighing, Trixie closed her eyes. His tongue darted between her folds, dipping in to find her clit before tracing her cleft once more.

Warm hands touched her thighs. Fingers traced her skin and spread open her folds as his tongue found her innermost place.

She shivered. Tingles spread through her body. She whimpered when his tongue pulled away, leaving her tightening around air.

Soft lips wrapped around her clit and sucked. Andre's tongue swirled around and around. A guttural moan escaped her mouth. She could no longer think. Trixie let the pleasure radiate through her body. He lapped at her clit in broad strokes. Her legs trembled.

His tongue was relentless. Dancing across her most sensitive nerves. Suddenly her body tensed, as if the pleasure was all too much. His mouth covered her clit again and sucked. Hard.

Trixie cried out and the world around her exploded. All she could do was hold on to Andre as her orgasm rocked through her body.

CHAPTER 16

How I've missed hearing her come. Andre lapped until the tremors in her body subsided, his hands holding her steady on top of his bar. Each gentle touch elicited a delicious gasp or moan.

Watching and feeling her body trembling as she came—hell, it was fucking hot. His cock, still in his jeans, was painfully hard.

"Are you ready for me, Trixie?" he cried out, voice hoarse.

"Yes."

"Can you stand? Or lean against a barstool?" He remembered how intense orgasms left her boneless.

"Barstool," she whispered.

He helped her slide off the bar. She bent over the stool, baring her ass to him. Trixie steadied herself, then spread her legs apart. She had opened herself to him. Offered him the gift of herself.

"Fuck me, Andre."

Heat flared through him. He reached over the bar and grabbed a condom. This time it would not go to waste. Andre hastily unbuttoned his jeans to free his cock. Pre-cum glistened in the semi-darkness of the room. Condom rolled on, he pressed his cock at her entrance.

"Andre," she cried. "Now!"

He pushed into her slick heat, her tight muscles drawing him in. Her body was so soft, so hot. He could stay inside her forever.

She wiggled her ass and arched her back. He took a deep breath and grabbed her hips with both hands.

"You need to stop that unless you want this to end quickly," he said through gritted teeth.

Her ass stilled, but her inner muscles continued to torture him. Unable to hold off any longer, he withdrew slowly until only his head was inside her. Trixie whimpered. He thrust back into her.

"Yes. Don't stop," she cried out.

His body took over as he thrust again, burying himself deep inside her. Her muscles fluttered around his cock. He'd forgotten how well they fit together. How she stretched to take in his full length. How fucking good it felt.

Now he had her back. He would pleasure her—no, fuck her until she came so hard, she couldn't think straight. To make up for all the orgasms he'd failed to give her the two years they'd been apart.

"So. Close," she panted.

He needed to see her eyes when she came. He'd missed it the first time. He wanted to look into her eyes as pleasure overtook her. She was so fucking beautiful when she came.

Bodies still connected, he walked them backward until a dining chair hit the back of his legs. He fell into it, pulling her down with him.

"Turn around so I can watch you come."

She disconnected from him only briefly, but the seconds felt like hours. Straddling him, she eased herself onto his cock, now slick with her juices. Trixie closed her eyes and sighed as they became united again.

"Open your eyes, babe. Let me see them when you come."

She gripped the back of the chair. Her mouth fell open as she began riding his cock. Her head fell back as, groaning, she slid up and down his length.

He slipped his hand between their bodies. She pressed her mound onto his fingers until he found her swollen clit. Her muscles squeezed tighter, pulsating around his cock. She was close. So was he.

"Trixie," he cried out. "Look at me."

She snapped her eyes open.

"Come, baby. Let me feel you come on my cock."

Trixie cried out and rode him harder. Grinding against him, her eyes never leaving his. Feeling her convulse around him as orgasm overtook her.

Eyes locked, he grabbed her hips and thrust into her one, two more times. She grinned through her euphoric haze and kissed him. Tongues intertwined, she ground her hips and twisted her body, drawing him in tighter. She screamed into his mouth and came a third time as he exploded inside her.

For the longest time, they sat with bodies tangled. Trixie nestled her head on his shoulder. Her sweet scent swirled around his nose, adding to his pleasure-soaked haze. For the first time since his mom got sick, stillness overtook him.

At this moment, he knew everything would be okay. The stress of running this restaurant, Keisha's college tuition, medical bills—everything would work out. He never thought he'd see her again. Tonight they'd just had the best make-up sex of his entire life.

"Trixie," he finally whispered after what felt like an eternity. "I hate to move you, but my leg is falling asleep."

"Mmmm," she replied, nuzzling harder into his neck.

"Want to go back to my place?"

Trixie stiffened. She sat up and extricated herself from him. The disappointment in his eyes was impossible to ignore. *Way to ruin the moment.* The air between them grew awkward faster than a blast chiller.

"Um, I better go. Zoe will worry." Trixie avoided his eyes and straightened the skirt of her dress. "She's my roommate."

"I'll help you with your bags." He stood up, walking to the bar to grab a napkin. After removing the condom, he buttoned his jeans. He didn't bother to tuck in his shirt.

"I need to freshen up a bit." Trixie grabbed her purse and ran into the bathroom, locking the door behind her.

Whatever stress relief she'd gotten was replaced by anxiety and panic. Without the haze of lust, her line about sex for research was weak. A flimsy excuse to be with Andre again. This was supposed to get him out of her system. The result was the opposite. Another bad decision. Another failure.

"Dammit, Trixie," she muttered to herself. "Control your hormones. You have a drawer full of vibrators."

How desperate had she been to jump on him the way she had? Yes, Andre knew exactly how to touch her, but she'd fallen into their old roles. He needed to call the shots—even during sex. Though she was the one who'd started it, she gave him control as soon as he wanted it.

Trixie hated herself for it. Ceding control to him with sex would be the beginning. If she didn't pay attention, she'd let him take over her life. The life she'd built without him. She didn't need him to be successful. Or sex.

Knock, knock.

She jumped and checked the lock on the door.

"You need anything?" Andre's muffled voice was worried.

"Be right out!" she called back.

Once his footsteps faded away, she turned on the faucet and splashed water on her face. She couldn't take back the sex, but now she had to set better boundaries. And not cross them.

When she walked back into the dining room, all evidence of their sex was gone. The bar and chair reset for the next day. On a different table were two glasses of water. His warm smile greeted her as he gestured to the water.

Suddenly Trixie was very thirsty. She drained the glass, then set it down with a large clang.

"No one can know about this," she declared. She could at least pretend he was out of her system. Enough to convince Andre she was truly over him.

His smile disappeared.

"Why?"

"Everything is moving too fast. Until two months ago, we hadn't spoken in two years. When we finally saw each other again, you told me to never come back. I'm back and now— this."

"Glad it was good for you, too." Sarcasm, his defense mechanism, kicked in.

Trixie cringed. "That's not what I meant. You were unbelievably amazing, Andre. It's just—"

"Just what? Yes, I fucked up before, but you won't give me a chance to explain."

"So you can feel better about yourself?" She didn't want to ease his guilt. He had to live with the choices he'd made the same way she'd dealt with the blowup with her parents. Her only mistake was trusting his advice about her life.

"I'm really sorry, Trixie. I kick myself every day for what I did to you." He hung his head.

"That makes two of us."

Andre opened his mouth and closed it. She felt a twinge of guilt for her harsh words.

"We can't do this again."

"I'm not in the habit of one-night stands." He gripped the back of the chair. "I thought we were starting over."

"I meant starting over as friends. Not—" She waved a hand between them.

"Fuck, Trixie, I'm not asking you to marry me. Let's give us another try."

"There can't be an 'us.' I thought we were just having fun. But this—us—any relationship would be a distraction from my goals. I have to focus on myself and my boutique."

She reached out for his hand, but he pulled it away.

"I can tell you still care about me, Trixie. Life is too short to throw away what we have. Had." He held her gaze until she looked away. "We owe it to ourselves to try."

"Since I left New Orleans, I've been working my ass off to be financially independent."

"You're very successful and good at your job." His eyes were sincere.

"But it's still a job, Andre. I'm working for someone else. Building another person's dream. I want to be an entrepreneur."

"It's not as easy as you think," he scoffed. "Overseeing Mama Hazel's may look glamorous on the outside, but I'm putting in sixteen-hour days. Don't forget about paperwork and bills after dealing with customers during the dinner rush. Working for the man might be less stressful."

"I want to find out for myself. I'm so close to winning this contest, I can taste it. For the first time in my life, I'm good at something. Something that I want for myself. Not something that my parents or someone else chose for me." Her voice trembled as passion filled it.

"So you're saying that I don't fit anywhere into your life plan?"

Trixie's mouth opened then closed. He really thought that sleeping together one time meant they would get back together.

ANDRE GRABBED HER hand and pulled her to him. He kissed her. Pressed upon her lips the words he couldn't say out loud. That having her back in his life gave him a glimmer of the happiness he'd had before his mother got sick. A kiss to apologize for leaving her alone and ghosting her. To show her they could make them work the second time.

She returned his kiss, arms wrapping around his neck. Their tongues danced together. She shuddered against his body.

Trixie pulled away, panting. Her eyes were glazed, and her mouth was swollen from their kiss.

"You want this as much as I do. You want us."

"Not fair." Her voice was thick with lust. "We've always been good in bed together."

"What if I don't want a relationship with you?" Andre didn't know what he was saying until it was too late. "What if we have some fun, no strings attached?"

"Are you sure that's enough for you?" Confusion covered her face.

"I'm sure." If that was the only way he could have her back in his life, so be it. "I've never forgotten you, Trixie Nguyen."

"Flattery will get you nowhere." But she half smiled as she said it.

"Doesn't mean I'll stop trying." He smiled back, glad that she was no longer trying to bolt out of the restaurant. Maybe even out of his life. Though he certainly deserved it if she wanted to.

"Okay," she said so quietly he almost missed it.

"Okay, I can keep complimenting you? Or we can keep seeing each other?" He knew she meant the latter, but he needed to hear her say it. They were starting over, and he wanted them to communicate clearly with each other.

"Both."

He pumped his fist in the air. Embarrassed, he shoved his hand into his pocket. She stopped him and held his hand.

"Let's set some ground rules."

"Of course." His thumb caressed the back of her hand. Such soft skin, though not as soft as the skin between her folds.

"We tell no one. Not even Keisha. I don't want to make things awkward when I'm here for the pop-ups."

"She'll figure it out the next time she sees us together." He'd kept so many secrets about the restaurant's financial state that he didn't want to pile on more lies. "I'll only tell her if she asks, but I don't think she needs to know we used to date. She's already trying to play matchmaker. I don't want to give her more fuel for that."

"Fine," she conceded.

"What about your friends, the Boss Babes?"

"If you get to tell Keisha, then I'm telling the Boss Babes. We don't keep secrets from each other." She bit her lip and continued. "This is just sex. No relationship. No commitment. Just sex."

"Just sex. Got it." He gave a thumbs-up. Sex had turned him into a dork. "Every man's fantasy: a hot friends-with-benefits situation."

She tossed a gentle slap at his arm.

"If this friends-with-benefits affects my winning this contest, then it's over. No hard feelings?"

He answered with another kiss. He had no plans to give her up so easily. When they came up for air, she pointed to her bags.

"Help me take them to the car?"

Andre had no idea what he'd gotten himself into. All he knew was that he had a chance of winning Trixie back. The more time they spent together—naked or clothed—the more opportunity for her to fall back in love with him.

CHAPTER 17

I have exciting news. After last night's pop-up, I'm in first place!"

"Congrats!" Reina exclaimed.

"I knew you could do it!" Josie cheered. "I told you those spreadsheets would keep you on track."

"I can't believe I have a chance at winning this thing. This month, I'll get bonus points for selling Whimsy, the new couples toy. I haven't used it with anyone, but it's gotten rave reviews online. This contest is in the bag!" Trixie almost pinched herself. After two years of coming in third place, she might actually take home the ten-grand prize!

"I'm so proud of you, Trixie." Zoe enveloped Trixie in a hug. "You took a big risk with your pop-ups and it's paying off."

"Speaking of risks, I had the worst heckler last night." Trixie told them about the woman in red and how Andre volunteered to help demonstrate the massage oil.

"I can't believe you poured half a bottle of Pants-on-Fire on his arm!" Reina exclaimed.

"You should have seen the look on his face when he realized how hot it got!" Trixie gasped, trying to keep her laughter contained so she could recount the story. "I have never sold so many sets of Blow Me warming massage oil in Pants-on-Fire and Candy Apple flavors!"

The Boss Babes' laughter echoed in the Vietnamese restaurant.

"I think it's romantic," said Zoe once the laughter had died down. "He came to your rescue. Your knight in shining armor."

"Speaking of armor, that sculpted bustier you're wearing is gorgeous. Is it part of your new cosplay line?" Trixie attempted to change the subject.

"Nice try," Zoe deflected. "We're talking about Andre and his armor."

"Too bad his armor wasn't heat proof," shot Josie. They all cracked up again.

"Nah, Trixie doesn't need rescuing," said Reina. "She takes care of herself, don't you, babe?"

"Actually, he did rescue me."

Her friends froze, drinks in midair. They all started talking at the same time. Trixie smiled and snuck a fried shrimp chip off the green papaya salad. Finally, their leader held her hands up for silence.

"Did you just admit to needing help?" asked Josie, who'd become the de facto leader of the Boss Babes because she formed the group. It probably helped that she was the oldest of five kids and was used to bossing people around.

"I didn't ask for help, but I needed it," she replied before grabbing another shrimp chip.

Everyone around the table mock gasped.

"Very funny." Trixie rolled her eyes but smiled at her girlfriends. "I was out of sorts that night because of the news about my dad."

"I'm glad Uncle Nguyen is doing better," said Zoe. "My mom

has some low-fat recipes she created for Phở-Ever 75. Want her to send them to your mom?"

"I might take you up on that—if my mom ever lets me get a word in during our phone calls."

"I'm glad your dad is out of the hospital, but I still want to know how Andre saved you," Reina demanded.

"The very drunk woman was so mean. She told me that I sucked at my job. Normally, I'd shut her down with a snappy joke, but I was out of sorts. That pop-up could have been a disaster, but he saved it." Trixie then recapped the woman's rude remarks.

"Oh, sweetie. What a tough week for you." Zoe grasped Trixie's hand.

"He talked me off the ledge. I was such a mess when I got there. And then he went above and beyond when he offered to help me demo the massage oil."

Trixie left out the rest. She was most definitely not going to tell them about the mind-blowing sex they had after everyone left.

"I still hate him," Reina announced. "Unless you don't hate him anymore. Do you?"

"I don't know if I truly hated him. *Angry* might be a better word." That anger had dissipated and turned into lust last night. What had she gotten herself into?

Why did she have to make her life more complicated? Part of Trixie still wanted to hold a grudge against him for walking out on her. But that one moment shouldn't define him for the rest of his life. Had it been fair to judge him only on that day? He was much more than that Dear Jane note. Yet that note had broken her in ways she didn't know were possible.

Last night he'd awoken a hunger inside her, reminding her that the past two years, she'd focused exclusively on her career and not her sex life. The irony of it all: owning a collection of sex toys to suit every mood, but in the end, they couldn't meet her desire for emotional connection paired with the sensual touch of a person.

Not just any person—Andre.

"Is there something you're not telling us?" Reina eyed Trixie. "Did something else happen between you two?"

"Well, there is one more thing." Trixie hesitated. "Please don't be mad at me!"

The Boss Babes had helped her refine her five-year life goals. Sleeping with Andre was nowhere on that spreadsheet Josie put together for her. She hated disappointing them.

"We could never be mad at you." Zoe touched Trixie's shoulder and nodded encouragingly. "Boss Babes are here to support you. Right, ladies?"

"Always," assured Josie.

Reina narrowed her eyes, studying Trixie's face. She gasped. "I know that look from college. You got laid!"

"About time," Josie cheered.

"Was it Andre?" Zoe asked. "I noticed you came home pretty late last night."

Trixie's face flushed, and she nodded.

"I didn't mean for it to happen. We could never keep our hands off each other. After the stressful day, he wrapped me in a hug and, well, one thing led to—"

"Sex? A hug led to sex?" Reina interrupted.

"I saw this side of him that he didn't show me often when we were in New Orleans. He talked me through my panic about my dad, then he opened up about worries about Mama Hazel's. Andre has changed."

"From a big asshole to a smaller one?" Reina broke in. "He was so rude to you at the bachelorette party. It's hard to believe he could change so much in just a few weeks."

"Reina's got a point," Josie said. "He walked out on you, remember? Guys like him don't deserve a second chance."

"I'm afraid I have to agree." Zoe pressed her lips together.

Of all the Babes, she expected disapproval from Reina, but Zoe and Josie, too?

"I hope you're not going to sleep with him again." Reina crossed her arms.

"Didn't you say I needed some work-life balance?"

For once Reina was speechless.

"We agreed that it's sex only—no strings attached." Trixie added as much conviction as she could. "Besides, now I have a research partner for my products!"

"If that's what you really want." Josie wasn't convinced. "But be careful. He's already hurt you once."

"Maybe we should stop by your next pop-up and meet Andre," Zoe said pointedly to Josie and Reina. They reluctantly nodded.

"Now that you're done discussing my sex life, tell me how your businesses are doing this week." Trixie was ready to talk about something besides Andre.

"Wait, I have one more thing to add," said Josie. "Let's go one step further to make your dream shop into a reality. I read about this in a self-help book."

"Oh no, here she goes," Reina groaned. "What woo-woo stuff are you reading now?"

"As I was saying"—Josie nudged Reina, who rolled her eyes—"You trick your brain into thinking that a dream is reality. Like a vision board. You put up pictures of what you really want. Your brain is so used to seeing your goals, it wants to make them a reality."

"How do I do that?" Trixie asked. "Like visit a sex toy boutique?"

"Almost. One of my photography clients has an opening in her co-op boutique. I told her you might be interested." Josie leaned back and crossed her arms, very pleased with herself.

"But I don't have enough money saved for a deposit. I'll need a loan and collateral. A store name—" Trixie's brain spun. "I need to make a list and plan it all out."

"Trixie, breathe." Josie tugged her arm. "I'm not saying you have to commit. Just look."

"I don't want to waste your client's time if I can't commit."

"I'll put you in contact with my broker, Kait Garcia, who helped me find my photography studio. Kait owns the co-op boutique. She invested early in District Market and got a great deal. The boutique is designed to be a stepping-stone for new women entrepreneurs. Get your start in a small space until you've saved up for one of your own."

Josie's photography studio was amazing. Big windows with plenty of natural light for her boudoir sessions. A great location out in Southwest by the Wharf, before real estate prices skyrocketed because of the new development. Gentrified, like Andre's neighborhood.

"I don't know." Even though opening a boutique was her ultimate goal, Trixie thought she had a few more years before it was even a real possibility.

"Look, it won't hurt to look. I'll tell Kait you're checking out your options."

"She'd do that? I won't be wasting her time?"

"Nope. This co-op is her passion project. She knows that some women don't have the funding to start a big business. Kait started with nothing, and this is her way to give back to the community. She's very dedicated to her work. In fact, she took me to over twenty locations before I fell in love with my studio."

"Are you sure she wasn't trying to get into your pants?" Reina tilted her head as she studied Josie's face. "Taking a sexy woman like you to twenty empty studios. Just you and her alone?"

"She's very professional." Josie blushed.

"Oh my God!" Reina practically bounced in her seat. "You like her. Your real estate broker!"

"We're supposed to be helping Trixie right now," Josie replied, shifting uncomfortably under their stares. "Besides, I'm seeing Taye."

"What if you had coffee with her, Trixie? Feel her out first?" Zoe suggested, letting Josie off the hook. Always the mediator.

"I guess it won't hurt," Trixie conceded.

"Great! I'll intro you two via email." Josie's eyes crinkled as she smiled. "You're gonna love Kait."

Trixie's heart raced at the thought of looking at storefronts. A co-op meant that her start-up costs would be manageable. Her prize money might cover the bulk of the lease and some inventory. Her first-place position meant she was one step closer to achieving her dream.

Everything was falling into place.

CHAPTER 18

A ndre padded down the stairs of his mom's row house. He yawned and followed his nose to the kitchen, where Keisha had brewed a pot of coffee. Working the busy bar during the busy pop-up followed by the late night pressed against Trixie's body had worn him out.

"I can't believe you slept in," Keisha said from the kitchen table. Textbooks and papers surrounded her. "What time did you get home last night?"

"Late." He fumbled with his I ♥ NOLA coffee mug and filled it to the top with coffee.

"Late, doing what?" Keisha raised an eyebrow. "Most of the cleaning was already done when I left."

"The bar was really messy last night." He squinted at his coffee before taking a sip. "I had lots of glasses to clean."

"Oh." Keisha's face fell.

"What did you think was gonna happen?" Andre avoided her eyes and put two slices of bread into the toaster. He wasn't surprised that she wanted to play matchmaker for him and Trixie. If he told her about Trixie right now, Keisha would declare her success and never let him forget it. Nope. Getting back with Trixie was his plan alone.

"Nothing." Disappointment flashed over Keisha's face, but she covered it with a small smile. "I forgot to tell you. Your etouffee and scorched rice was a hit last night!"

"Really?" With everything that happened last night, he'd forgotten about the new dish. "What did people say about it?"

"Once I explained what it was and how to eat it, they loved it. People liked the crispiness of the rice mixed with the rich etouffee."

"Well, damn." Andre couldn't believe it. "Did they think it was too hard to eat? Or wasn't authentic?"

"Andre, I said they loved it." She shook her head at him. "In fact, we ran out of it before anything else."

"Okay, cool." He rubbed the back of his head. The last twenty-four hours had been, well, a lot. He'd volunteered as a guinea pig for massage oil. He and Trixie were on their way to making up. And his new dish was a hit.

"I think we should add it to the menu." Keisha's eyes shone in the way they did when she had a new idea. "I mean, we already serve it with rice, but now we just burn it a little."

"Maybe. Let's not get too excited. It's just one pop-up. Let's see how it sells during regular meal service." Andre *was* thrilled, but Trixie's family had inspired the unconventional pairing. He couldn't add it to the menu without telling her.

"People will love it." She turned back to her notes. "I hate accounting. Why do I have to learn all this manual stuff when there are computers that do all the work for me?"

"I'm sure your professor has a reason." Andre didn't really know. He didn't go to college and all the accounting he knew he'd taught himself via internet searches and YouTube videos. "You're welcome to take over and automate our bookkeeping when you graduate."

Keisha rolled her eyes. "You just want to pawn off work you don't like onto me."

"Maybe." He held back a laugh. She wasn't wrong.

The toast popped up, and he slathered each piece with homemade peach jam. Mrs. Harris made a huge batch every year and gifted the entire neighborhood with jars of it. It was the best peach jam he'd ever tasted—outside of his mom's. Not that he'd ever tell Mrs. Harris.

"Can I talk to you about something?" Keisha pointed at the chair next to hers.

He sat down with his coffee and toast. "Look, I told you once you graduate, you can help—"

"That's what I wanted to talk to you about," Keisha interrupted. She drummed her fingers nervously on her notebook. "Promise me you won't get mad."

That didn't sound good. His brain raced. Did something terrible happen? Was she sick? He took a deep breath.

"I promise." No matter what happened, he'd take care of Keisha.

"I want to quit school and help out at the restaurant full time," his sister blurted.

"What!" He set his coffee mug down so hard that coffee splashed onto her notes. Andre grabbed a towel and dabbed furiously at her papers. "Sorry I ruined your accounting notes."

"See, if I didn't have to learn how to do this on paper, I could have pulled out my backup from the cloud." She pressed her lips together when he didn't respond to her joke.

"You're halfway through your bachelor's program. Why quit now?" He forced himself to take a bite of his toast. Chewed slowly so he could figure out how to convince Keisha to stay in school.

"You need help at the restaurant."

He opened his mouth, but she held up her hand.

"Let me finish. We can't afford to hire any more staff. I can work full time in the restaurant and be your apprentice during off hours. I know enough accounting to do books for Mama Hazel's." She chuckled nervously.

"I thought you liked school."

"I don't hate it. Mama was right that an education is important, but tuition is expensive. Next semester I'm supposed to take on more classes. We can't cover tuition and hiring someone to take my place while I'm in class during the day."

"I told you I would figure things out." His jaw clenched. Why didn't she believe him? As her big brother, he'd take care of her no matter what. "I'm considering closing the restaurants on Tuesdays and Wednesdays until things pick up. You can pick up your extra classes on those days."

"Andre," Keisha said softly and touched his hand. "I miss Mama, too. Working at the restaurant makes me feel closer to her, you know?"

He nodded as his chest tightened and his throat started to close. Andre took another bite of toast, trying to ignore the sadness that bloomed in his chest. Though it had been less than two years since she passed, grief snuck up on him when he least expected it.

"I've always wanted to put Mama's recipes into a cookbook. Quitting will give me time to work on it. Please, Tre. I really want to do this." Tears spilled out of her eyes.

Andre blinked quickly to rid the tears from his eyes. He'd do anything for Keisha, but this was her future. She wouldn't make it far without a college degree. She'd just be stuck working as a waitress or bartender—like him. Mama wouldn't want that for her.

"How about this? We've already paid for the fall semester. Finish it and register for the winter. If we can't make our finances work to cover winter tuition, you can defer." He took a deep breath. Maybe this would give Keisha more time to reconsider quitting. "You can pick up more shifts during winter break and help me out in the office. I promise it's not as exciting as you think it'll be."

"You're the best brother I've ever had!" Keisha kissed him on the cheek and hugged him.

"I'm your only brother." He returned her hug. "I'd better finish getting ready. Those receipts will multiply if I leave them alone for one day."

He left Keisha studying for her test and headed upstairs for a shower. Under the water, his brain tallied up all the things spiraling out of control. Mama's medical bills, the low cash flow at Mama Hazel's, the damned fryer on the fritz. Now Keisha wanted to quit school. While it seemed like a good idea right now, he knew it wasn't what his mom wanted for her. At least one Walker kid should have a college degree.

He'd figure it out. Somehow. Everything would work out, and Mama Hazel's would thrive with him at its helm. If the paperwork didn't bury him first.

By the time he'd come downstairs, Keisha was gone. Study group, she'd texted him. The mid-September humidity hit him as soon as he stepped outside his home. Beads of sweat formed on his brow.

"Morning, Mrs. Harris," he called across the street.

The heat and humidity didn't seem to bother her. She spent most mornings on her porch knitting. She also knew everything that went on in their neighborhood.

"Leaving late today, aren't you?" she replied, her knitting needles a blur of movement. "Noticed you didn't get home till after midnight last night."

Andre sighed. Mrs. Harris and his mom had been good friends, but it didn't mean he cared for her nosy if well-meaning questions.

"We had a private event last night." He crossed the street so he didn't have to yell. "Left a huge mess, so it took me a while to clean up since Keisha needed to study for an exam."

"Private parties, huh? Like our Monday dinners?"

"Something like that." If Mrs. Harris knew what was going on at the restaurant, he'd never hear the end of it. And the entire neighborhood would know, too, in minutes. "Turns out there are white folks who are willing to pay good money for Mama's food."

"They should. She was a good cook. And she taught Luis well." Her knitting needles paused.

"Thank you, ma'am." Andre checked his phone. He had two hours before lunch service started. If he stood here any longer, she'd start up about the collard greens again.

"Everything she cooked was good. Except for her greens. She never did take my advice on the smoked turkey necks."

Right on cue.

"I should get going, Mrs. Harris. I'm already running behind." He held up his phone to show her the time. "Keisha told me Mr. Harris is still fighting a cold. I'll send over some gumbo."

"Thank you, dear. Don't work too hard, Tre."

"I go by Andre now, Mrs. Harris." He was tired of asking her to call him that, but his childhood nickname grated even more. It reminded him too much of the immature kid who ran away from home.

"It's not good to work all the time." She ignored his request. The needles began moving again. "You need a woman in your life."

"No time for that right now, Mrs. Harris." Andre waved at her. "Have a good day."

Great. On top of everything else, he had Mrs. Harris's hawklike eyes to worry about.

After a brisk walk, he made it to the restaurant in time to prep for lunch service but not work in his office beforehand. Several people were standing by the front door. Maybe the pop-ups were bringing in customers already. Keisha was right about partnering with Trixie.

Once he came closer, he recognized Mr. Jackson, his landlord. He was chatting with two white folks in business suits. A brunette in a pantsuit and heels snapped photos of the building while a man in a dark gray suit and shiny black loafers took notes on his tablet. He seemed to be in charge.

"Afternoon, Mr. Jackson." Andre offered his hand. The gray-haired man's grip was surprisingly strong for someone in their early seventies. "What's going on here?"

"I thought y'all didn't open until lunch." He looked back at the corporate types behind him and walked Andre to the side. "We're almost done. I'll be right back."

Andre caught only a few words of the conversation, but there were plenty of smiles and nodding from everyone. Something about his landlord's lawyer calling. Then dark-gray-suit guy handed a large yellow envelope to Mr. Jackson before he and his partner got into an SUV and drove off.

"What was that about?" Andre asked.

"Andre." Mr. Jackson sighed and rubbed his bald head, which still held some patches of salt-and-pepper hair. "I didn't mean for you to find out this way. I know Hazel helped make this neighborhood better, but—"

"Who were they?" Andre interrupted. His landlord took frequent visits down memory lane that involved plenty of meandering. Normally, he'd humor Mr. Jackson, but he was already late.

"They want to buy the building. As is." He gestured to the cracked steps and worn bricks. "A generous offer. I can finally move to California and be near my son and grandkids."

"What?!" Andre shook his head. "But what about the restaurant and the bookstore? And the hair salon?"

Like Mama Hazel's, the bookstore had seen better days. There were probably more people browsing than actually buying books. He and Xavier spent many hot summer days enjoying the free air-conditioning there.

"I'm sorry, Andre. I can't keep up anymore. This building needs fixing up, and I don't have the money for it."

"What are they going to do with it?" He tried to keep the panic out of his voice. Mama Hazel's was just starting to do better. He needed more time.

"Either condos or office buildings." Mr. Jackson shrugged. "Something that'll bring more people to District Market."

"You can't do that! People depend on our family dinners. And the bookstore—where else can kids buy books for a dollar?"

"I'm seventy-four, Andre. I'm tired and I miss my son."

The man he'd known since he was a kid had gotten old. Deep wrinkles etched his warm brown skin, while his posture had become more stooped. Everyone and everything around him kept changing. Pretty soon no one around would remember Mama.

He had to do something.

"How much did they offer you?" Andre blurted. "What if we"—he gestured to the other tenants—"bought you out?"

"I suppose that would be all right. I'd rather keep it in the family, so to speak."

"Okay, let me talk to everyone. When do you need to tell the developers?"

"They're drawing up the papers for my lawyer. A couple of weeks max." Mr. Jackson put a hand on Andre's shoulder. "I know things are tough right now. Make me a good offer and I promise to talk to my son about it."

"Yes, sir."

Two weeks was not enough time, but he had to try.

CHAPTER 19

Friday's brisk lunch service kept Andre busy. He noticed several first-time customers. Maybe the pop-ups were helping. He meant to ask where they had learned about the restaurant. Running from table to table taking orders and keeping up with drink refills didn't leave much time for socializing with his customers. They were just busy enough to need another person but not making enough to hire one.

He stretched out on the futon in his office, exhausted. After his late night with Trixie and lunch service, he needed a nap before they reopened for dinner service in a few hours. Lying in his dark office only made his problems feel larger.

He couldn't fault Mr. Jackson for selling their building. The timing sucked. Like Mama Hazel's, the hair salon and used bookstore had also lost business due to District Market. He doubted the three of them could come up with a good counteroffer. Unless one of them had a fairy godmother tucked away somewhere.

Right now Xavier's joke about finding a sugar mama was very appealing.

"Andre? What are you doing in the dark?"

Keisha flipped the light switch.

"Ow!" Andre rubbed his eyes and blinked quickly to adjust to the light. "A warning could have been nice."

"Sorry. Lights!" She giggled.

"Very funny." He sat up on the futon. Sisters were so annoying, even as adults. "You're here early."

"My study group was tired, so we split." She sat down next to him, pushing him aside with her body. "How did lunch go?"

"Lunch was busy for once. We had some new customers. I could barely keep up."

"I knew it!" She clapped her hands. "The pop-ups are working."

"Don't get too excited. I think it's too soon to tell."

"Party pooper." She stuck out her lip in an exaggerated pout. "You need to think positive."

"How's this for positive? I think I figured out how to manage lunch service so you can keep taking classes."

"I told you I'm not sure I want to finish school, but I'm listening."

"What if we made the buffet a permanent thing? But only during lunch while you're in class. With a set menu, I don't have to take orders. I can focus on serving drinks and clearing tables."

"That's brilliant!" She smacked his arm with the back of her hand.

"Hey, that hurts."

"Since we have a buffet for Trixie's pop-ups, we know how efficient it is," she continued, ignoring his pain. "Do you think we can start next week? Luis and I can plan the menu over the weekend."

"I was thinking about trying out some of my new recipes for the buffet. A different one for each day, like a daily special." He stopped, unsure if it was too much risk.

"Finally, he sees the light." Keisha raised her hands up as if they were at a church service. "I've been saying this for months."

"You think Mama would have approved?"

"Not at first," she said quietly. "But once she realized how good your food is and how much people like it, she'd approve."

He thought about the arguments they'd had over his new ideas. How she never wanted to try anything new. If something wasn't broken, then why fix it? Mama Hazel's wasn't currently broken, but it wasn't thriving either.

"I think she'd understand that we're changing things up." Andre was relieved that Keisha was on board with his idea.

"Do you remember how to update our website?" Keisha had pulled out her notebook and scribbled furiously on it. "If you handle that, I'll work on social media."

"I almost forgot Mama Hazel's was on social media." While he was away in New Orleans, Keisha had convinced their mom to get the restaurant into the twenty-first century. "You said you knew some food bloggers, right?"

"Yes!" She smacked him on the arm again. "I already made a list on my phone. We should invite them over for lunch to try out the new buffet."

"I wish you'd stop hitting me when you get excited." He exaggerated rubbing his arm. "You're supposed to give me positive reinforcement when I have good ideas."

"Here's the plan if we're going to launch next Thursday," she continued, ignoring his pain. "I'll work on social media promotion, including the food bloggers. We should wait a week before we invite them."

"That will give us time to work out any kinks in the buffet service."

"Exactly." She added something to her list. "Luis and I will come up with a base menu that's cost-effective and can be served every day. You have the hardest job. Coming up with the daily special."

Andre nodded. The new lunch service was a solid plan but adding new dishes that he hadn't perfected yet was tricky. With a buffet, he could serve the new recipes without too much risk. If the customers didn't like it, they could eat one of their tried-and-true dishes.

"Can you give me a list of dishes and short descriptions in a couple of days? Luis and I will make sure there's a good variety for each lunch menu." She stood up and kissed him on the cheek. "Good job, big bro. This is your best idea yet."

"I hope so." He preferred to keep their expectations realistic, but his sister's excitement was rubbing off on him. This would hopefully give Keisha one more semester in school. They would figure things out one semester at a time.

With this problem solved, Mr. Jackson's talk with the developers didn't feel as daunting. After months of feeling lost and hopeless, Andre felt like they could win the battle against gentrification.

It didn't seem like a coincidence that it took Trixie coming back into his life for him to feel hopeful again.

CHAPTER 20

When Andre's sister immersed herself in a project, she jumped into the deep end. Over the weekend, Keisha hounded him with questions about fonts, graphic colors, and the actual text for their website and social media. Then there was her constant check-ins with menu questions and what recipes he wanted to add.

He was glad the restaurant was now closed on Tuesdays and Keisha was in class. She couldn't bounce into his office every ten minutes with another question. Andre officially had decision fatigue.

He was also procrastinating. All the recipes he'd jotted down in his leather notebook were terrible. The twists he'd put in them were too weird. Who would come to Mama Hazel's to eat collard greens cooked with kimchi?

He flipped to a blank page and tapped his pen. What if he took hush puppies and stuffed them with—no, that was terrible. The surprise texture of the almost-scorched rice made the etouffee fun to eat. Andre would have never used that crispy rice at the bottom of the pot until Trixie's mom served it to him. Before then, he considered it inedible and tossed it in the trash.

Trixie. Andre needed to see her again—before the next pop-up, when they weren't surrounded by people and had a million things to do. A place more conducive to talking. Not that he minded their explosive reunion after the last pop-up. She felt so fucking good in his arms. Her body wrapped around every inch of his—

Sex was no way to win her back. He pushed away from his desk. One of the chair wheels caught on a desk leg, dragging the desk a couple inches before escaping. The motion jarred his now cold cup of coffee. The dark brown liquid splashed onto a pile of past-due bills.

"Crap!"

He ran out of his office and into the supply room to grab napkins.

"Get your head straight, Andre," he muttered as he blotted the stained papers.

Xavier was right. He had to tell her what happened. Maybe their time apart would make it easier for her to forgive him. Or at the very least to understand what he'd been going through before he broke things off.

After cleaning the mess he'd made of his desk, he pulled out his phone. Should he call or text her? It'd been so long since he dated anyone, he had no idea what the rules were anymore. What would Xavier do? Good grief, did he just ask himself what his player best friend would do? Xay would text. Definitely text.

Andre's fingers tapped quickly.

Trixie, need your help with cocktail pairings for the next pop-up. Can you drop off samples of Blow Me flavors?

He hit send, then sent another:

Want to help taste test?

And maybe talk about why he'd left New Orleans so suddenly after a couple of cocktails? That was what he wanted to add but didn't. He tapped send before he lost his nerve.

Trixie's reply popped up almost immediately.

Great idea! I'll bring some stuff over—be there in 30 minutes.

His phone buzzed in his back pocket as he ran around the dining room turning on lights around the bar. Now that they were closed on Tuesdays and Wednesdays in addition to Mondays, Andre hadn't even walked into the front of the house yet. He'd told Trixie to just ring the bell at the back door, but a quick glance at his latest text confirmed she was waiting for him to let her in.

On my way, he texted as he raced to the back.

Sunlight flooded the dark hallway when he opened the door to let her in. He couldn't decide if it was the sudden sunshine that blinded him or Trixie's wide grin. A sweet citrus scent swirled around him. Andre inhaled as a huge weight lifted from his shoulders. How could one woman have so much power over his moods?

"Are you going to stand there looking like Lestat seeing the sun after a hundred years or help me with my bag?"

"Still an Anne Rice fan, I see." He forced his eyes open.

"It's hard to avoid her when you grow up in New Orleans." She shrugged. "How do you think Brad Pitt made it on my hall-pass list?"

Andre blinked and the rest of Trixie came into focus. She was fucking glowing. Her black hair was still wet. A purple T-shirt emblazoned with PLEASURE IS POWER hugged her chest. Now that his eyes adjusted to the sunlight, he took in the rest of her.

In her right hand was a tote bag overflowing with bottles and satin bags. The same satin bags she stored her demo toys in. Did she expect him to make cocktail pairings for the vibrators? How the hell was he going to do that?

"Sorry." What kind of gentleman was he? Staring at her body

while she carried a heavy bag. Andre eased the bag out of her grip. "Oof. Did you bring your entire kit?"

"Of course not." She walked past him into Mama Hazel's. "Only the most popular items."

"Are those vibrators I see?" He shut the door. The once sunlit hallway suddenly felt too dark. The lighting too fluorescent. The walls too narrow. Trixie's body so close to him was distracting. Her sweet fragrance invaded his nose again, but instead of relief washing over him, a rush of blood heated his cock.

"I thought we could create drink pairings for some luxury toys. Highlight them and increase my average order size." She was all business, not even acknowledging what happened between them after the last pop-up.

"Uh, sure." Andre cleared his throat. "How about we set up on the bar? I turned everything on over there."

Including himself apparently. Maybe working at the bar wasn't such a good idea. Not after what happened there the other night. He needed to keep his lust in check if he were to clear the air between them. Except it didn't make sense not to work at the bar, because that's where he kept the liquor. At the bar. Like most restaurants.

"I love the idea of drink pairings for our pop-ups." She walked past him down the hallway.

Even in the dimly lit hallway, he couldn't help but notice the way her hips sashayed as her low heels clacked on the tiles. Damn, her ass looked fine in those jeans. The denim must have been painted on because they hugged her curves. His fingers itched to peel them off her and suck her clit until she came in his mouth.

"Coming?" Trixie stopped and turned around.

That's exactly what he wanted. Buried deep inside her while she came around his—

"I don't mean to rush, but Zoe wants me to stop by her boutique later and look at her new cosplay designs."

Focus, Andre. She might not want anything to do with him after this conversation. He was tired of dancing around it. If she couldn't understand why he left her and New Orleans, then maybe they didn't have a future together after all.

TRIXIE TOOK A deep breath as she made her way into the front of the restaurant. The blinds were closed, but the bar glowed under the lights like a beacon, calling her to climb on top of it and let Andre have his way with her again. A familiar warmth flared through her body.

No, she wouldn't have sex with him today. They may have agreed to a friends-with-benefits arrangement, but she was here to work. Eyes on the ten-grand prize. She couldn't let her lust derail her plans. The boutique would finally prove to her family—and herself—that she could be successful without becoming a lawyer, doctor, or pharmacist. That she didn't fail miserably at everything she tried.

"Your Pants-on-Fire appletini was delicious. What other pairings did you have in mind?" Trixie pulled herself onto a barstool. She patted the stool next to her. "Hand me my bag, and I'll show you all the flavors."

He did as she asked and made his way to the other side of the bar.

"These are the top five flavors of Blow Me." Most of the products' names were loaded with innuendo. Or blatant sexual come-ons. Her cheeks grew warm as she thought about wrapping her lips around his—

"Want some water?" Andre interrupted her thoughts. "I'd give you a Diet Coke, but it'll mess up your taste buds as we test out cocktails."

She cleared her throat and sipped the water he'd placed in front of her.

"Let me guess"—he looked up and made a show of holding his chin thoughtfully—"Pants-on-Fire and Wicked Juicy Apple."

"I guess they made an impression on you during the demo." Trixie chuckled at the memory of him flailing as the massage oil overheated his skin. She pulled out those two flavors and three more: Va-Va-Voom Vanilla, Chocolate Explosion, and Berry Sexy.

"You could say that." He leaned closer to her and his voice deepened. "How could I forget the names after what we did with them?"

Trixie froze, her heart pounding. The way he'd lapped the cinnamon-flavored sweetness off her thighs. Even though she'd sold hundreds of bottles of Blow Me, that had been the first time she'd used it with someone else. The warming massage oil truly worked as promised. She resisted the urge to close her eyes and let the memory of his touch awaken her body.

"Andre," she whispered hoarsely. "We're supposed to be working."

His eyes bore into hers. Andre licked his lips, opened his mouth, and closed it again.

"Please. I'm not ready for whatever this is between us." She broke eye contact with him and rummaged through the tote bag. "Here are the deluxe vibes. Figured if you paired them with a cocktail, people would see past the price tag."

Andre nodded silently. He seemed—anxious? horny? Did he ask her to come for a booty call and she completely misread the signs? This was exactly why she hated flirting through texts. She had a life and a career. He needed to understand that this was serious for her and she didn't just drop everything for sex.

"What is going on?" She set the satin bags on the bar with a thump. "Did you really want to make cocktail pairings, or did you want sex?"

"Cocktail pairings." He rubbed the back of his head. "I'm not Xavier. I don't play games with women I'm in a relationship with."

"We are not in a relationship, Andre." Trixie pulled a notebook and pen out of her tote. "You asked me here to work on our businesses. To save your restaurant."

Andre's nostrils flared. His jaw tightened.

"I know what's at stake here." He hastily grabbed pint glasses and cocktail shakers. A shaker fell out of his grip and clattered onto the floor. Andre ignored it and reached for another one. "I see it every day when I walk into this nearly empty restaurant and see the bills piling up in my office. I'm doing everything I can to save this place. You don't have to remind me."

Having sex with him the other night had been a mistake. Andre might be more in touch with his feelings, but his outbursts made it hard for her to be professional. She had plenty to do on her own without tiptoeing around him.

"This is a bad idea."

Trixie grabbed her products off the bar and tossed them into her tote bag. She reached for Jack of All Trades, but Andre had grabbed the other end. There was no way she'd get into a tug-of-war with him with a rabbit-shaped vibrator.

"Let go," she growled. "Stop being childish."

"I'm not letting you run away." He pulled the toy toward him, but she refused to let go. "I'm sorry I snapped at you."

Did Andre Walker just apologize to her? Trixie let go of the toy suddenly. Andre's body flew backward, his hands still holding the satin bag. Panic crossed his face and he threw his hands out to catch himself on the bar. The vibrator sailed over his head and crashed into a row of liquor bottles behind him.

Trixie gasped. "Are you okay?"

Andre's wide eyes glanced behind him. A sigh of relief escaped him when he realized none of the bottles were broken. She wasn't sure she could say the same about Jack.

"Oh my God, did you just throw my bestselling vibrator at your liquor?" Trixie tried to sound horrified, but she giggled instead. Her shoulders shook and laughter bubbled out of her. "Andre Walker, it's a good thing you're a bartender and not a sex toy salesman."

"That wasn't funny," he replied, a bit miffed. "I could have died. Or broken my leg at the very least."

"Now that would have been a funny trip to the ER. Excuse me, nurse, my friend broke his leg because we were fighting over a rabbit vibrator." She couldn't help it. Trixie opened her mouth wide and laughed.

"Couldn't be any worse than when we took you to the ER because you caught that watermelon like a fucking quarterback," he shot back, ego obviously hurt.

Not this argument again. Another example of him trying to take care of everyone around him. Trying to be the big man when she didn't want help.

"That wasn't my fault. You threw it at me."

"Because we were in a watermelon-throwing contest at the parish fair! The one *you* signed us up for."

"We could have won if you hadn't made me go to the ER." Trixie put on an exaggerated pout. In hindsight, it had been pretty funny, especially as a parade of ER nurses asked them to retell the story.

Andre didn't look amused right now. He was in angry mode again.

"I told you I was fine!" she cried out.

"Your arm was going numb!" Andre shook his head, then breathed in and continued in a lower voice, "I was worried I'd hurt you."

His change in tone stopped her. Trixie took deep breaths to slow down her racing heart. Why in the hell were they arguing over something that happened over two years ago? Her shoulders sagged. She was tired of fighting.

"But then you did hurt me, Andre." Trixie looked across the bar at him, but he avoided her eyes. "Why did you do it?"

THEY WEREN'T TALKING about watermelons anymore. He didn't have a plan on how to approach the topic of their past, but this sure as hell wasn't it.

Andre bit his lip and kept his eyes on the row of highballs under the bar. He grabbed two and set them on the bar. With a practiced twist of his body, he grabbed the bottle of Patrón tequila from behind him. It didn't matter that it was barely lunchtime. He needed some liquid courage to have this conversation with her.

He added Diet Coke and lime to her glass. Orange juice and grenadine to his. He slid them across the bar.

"It's too early to drink." Trixie pushed the glass away. "If you don't want to talk about it, then I should go."

"Wait." He walked around the bar and pulled himself onto the stool next to her. This wasn't going to be an easy talk, but he wanted to have a clear view of her face. To be able to reach out and touch her without the bar between them.

"Five minutes." She ignored the drink he'd made for her. "I waited five months to hear from you because you'd never leave without an explanation. Eventually Reina convinced me to move on. Now all you get is five minutes."

"If that's all I get, I'll do my best."

"Clock is ticking." Trixie turned her phone to show the running timer on its screen.

"I—Trixie—" Andre gulped his tequila sunrise. "Walking out on you was the worst decision of my life. Back then, I thought I was doing the right thing. And now . . ."

"Now what? You want me to take you back because we're good in bed?"

Technically, it had been the bar. Making love to her in the restaurant had been hot as fuck, but it wasn't about the sex. It was the way she cared about others. How she was on a mission to help women love themselves more and become the confident woman he saw in her now. He'd seen that part of her when they had been together, but now everyone could see how beautiful and smart she was.

"No! I mean, I want us to be together again if that's what you want."

"Go on." Trixie picked up her Diet Coke and tequila and sipped.

"I hated that I was the reason you and your parents stopped talking. Family means so much to you. To me. I couldn't take that away from you." The words were finally out. Andre drained the rest of the highball.

"Are you kidding me?" Trixie's expression was a mix of incredulity and disgust. "You are so full of yourself. My falling out with my parents wasn't your fault. I know that now."

"But I'm the one who convinced you to switch to becoming a therapist. Without warming your parents up to the idea. Maybe if you'd given them more time to get used to the idea, they wouldn't have cut you off."

Trixie eyes shimmered. She looked upward and blinked away her tears.

"It wouldn't have mattered how much time I gave them. It's been over two years now and they still hate my decision."

"I never told you this, but I tried to talk to your dad."

"What?"

"I—I felt horrible that your parents cut you off. I mean, my mom wasn't happy about me leaving DC for New Orleans, but she gave me her blessing. I thought if I explained to him how great you were at helping others, the way you talked to people while you sat at the bar, waiting for me to get off work. I wanted him to understand that pharmacy school wasn't your passion."

Trixie laughed bitterly.

"Your dad told me that it was my fault for making you think that passion was more important than family. That I put crazy American ideas in your head. How being with me made you forget about your duty to your family."

"My father did what?!" Trixie set her drink down hard. Tequila and Diet Coke splashed all over the bar and onto her hands.

He grabbed a stack of cocktail napkins and handed her a few before soaking up the spill.

"I didn't agree with him that your ideas were too American, but I understood what he meant about duty to your family. I ran away from mine."

"What do you mean? I thought you came to New Orleans to learn its cocktail history."

"That's only half true. I came to New Orleans to learn more about my dad."

"I thought he died when you were little."

"He did." Andre took a deep breath. The only person he'd talked to about this had been Xavier. Back then his best friend hadn't understood why he'd left Mama and Keisha when they needed him the most.

"Mama didn't talk about him very much," he continued. "Everyone here expected me to be like Mama, but I had to know what he was like. What parts of him were in me. I didn't want to be just like my mom."

"You wanted to find who you were without your parents around." Trixie nodded. Of course she understood his desire. She was struggling with the same thing when they were dating. "Did you find what you were looking for?"

"Yes. And no. My dad was controlling and didn't support my mom's dream of opening a restaurant. He had old-fashioned ideas about his wife's responsibility." Relief flooded Andre. Telling Trixie this secret about his family was freeing.

He took a swig of his drink. Trixie turned off the timer on her phone and set it facedown on the bar.

"I ran away to New Orleans because I didn't want to take over Mama Hazel's. I ran away from my duty to my mother. I thought she'd always be here, and we had years left." He'd resisted changing his mom's recipes after she died because she'd fought against people who loved her in order to open the restaurant. "I needed to find myself, so I started going by Andre instead of Tre. And I didn't talk about my mom. Not even to you. I should have and I'm sorry."

Trixie remained silent, but her hands were clenched into tight fists. He couldn't tell if she was angry at him or what he'd revealed. She didn't accept his apology nor did she refuse it.

"I saw how important yours was to you when I came to your family dinners. At your celebrations. Like the big backyard crawfish boil where I only understood half of everyone's conversations."

Her family had welcomed him with open arms but didn't change who they were to make him feel more comfortable. When they were all together, a mixture of English and Vietnamese flew out of her family's mouths. He'd only caught every third word. Even then, he understood the feelings and tones of the conversations. Ribbing jokes followed by raucous laughter. It was hard to miss the love between everyone.

"Then later, when your parents were so mad, it seemed like the right opportunity to set you free from me. I wanted you to have your family back." With that, Andre's shoulders felt lighter. He'd finally told her the truth. "I thought by leaving you the way I did, you wouldn't try to find me. That without me, you'd have more space for your family."

She sighed, unclenching her fists. Trixie stirred her drink with the tiny plastic cocktail stick before knocking the rest of it back. When she finally spoke, her voice was low and resigned.

"My parents seem to forget that they raised me to be American," Trixie said. "So I could fit in and succeed." There was a faraway look in her eyes. "It's confusing to be the daughter of immigrants. Trying to figure out which part of me is more important. There's no guidebook on which situation requires me to be more Vietnamese and which one needs me to be American."

"I can't imagine what that's like," he said softly. He reached for her hand, and she didn't pull away. "It must have been hard."

"I called him after he was released from the hospital. I thought after what happened, he'd talk to me." Trixie shook her head.

"I'm sorry, babe."

"That part isn't your fault. He's mad because I rejected his dream for me and moved away. In his mind, when I gave up on pharmacy school, I gave up on them."

"What about your mom?"

"Oh, she still calls me almost weekly. Supposedly it's to tell me how she's getting old and will die at any moment." Trixie laughed. "But she's really checking up on me. You know my parents don't talk about their feelings."

"They still love you." Andre ran a finger around the rim of his empty glass. "I'd give anything to hear my mom's voice again."

"Fuck, I'm sorry, Andre." She grabbed his free hand.

"No, it's okay. I miss her every time I step into this place." He gestured at the dining room. "It's gotten easier over time, but . . ."

Trixie slid off her seat and wrapped her arms around him. He let himself relax into her hug as the clean, sweet scent of her damp hair filled his nose. After what felt like minutes, she let go and pulled herself back onto the barstool.

"As much as I've fought with my parents, I can't imagine them not being around."

"That's why I left you, Trixie. I couldn't bear to see you at odds with your parents. I thought if I left, you'd work things out with your dad. And Mama needed me. I'd shirked my duty long enough. It was time to come home and man up."

"But—"

He held up his hand. "Let me finish. Please?"

She closed her mouth and nodded.

"I thought if I could give you a few months to work things out—

after all, you'd sprung your career change on them suddenly—
then I'd come back once the air was clear."

"That's the dumbest thing I've ever heard."

He barked with laughter.

"I can see that now." Andre traced her knuckles with his fingers. "I wanted to text you, but the longer I waited, the harder it
was. I shouldn't have left you with a note. I deserve your hate."

"I hated you so much then. Reina probably hated you even
more."

"The very next day Keisha called to tell me about Mama." His
voice caught and he closed his eyes. "That she had cancer and the
doctors had found it too late. I couldn't avoid coming home any
longer. I took the next flight to DC. Once I got back, everything
was a blur of doctor visits, working at Mama Hazel's, and then she
just— I failed her, Trixie."

"Why would you say that?"

"I turned my back on my family. Wasn't there for them when
they needed me the most. Mama had wanted me to take over the
restaurant, but I wasn't ready. So I ran off to New Orleans. But if
I'd stayed or come home earlier, the doctors might have caught
her cancer sooner. Then maybe . . ."

"Andre, it's not your fault." She held his face with her hands.
"You came back when it mattered. You were there for her until she
passed. You're here for Mama Hazel's right now."

She kissed him. Her lips were warm and soft.

"I'm sorry for calling you names and badmouthing you to my
friends." She kissed him again.

"No, I'm sorry. I deserved it for ghosting you." He returned the
kiss. "Can we start over? For real this time?"

She nodded and caressed his lips with her thumb.

"I don't want to start over, though." She ran her hand down his neck. "That would mean pretending what we had before never happened."

He smiled, relieved to hear her say that. "Okay. Then we won't." Andre wrapped his arms around her waist, pulling her until their bodies were pressed together.

Trixie gasped at his hard heat pulsing against her body. "Let's keep this fun—no strings?"

He nodded.

"We have some lost time to make up for," he whispered, before crashing his lips onto hers.

CHAPTER 21

For the last two years, Trixie had held on to the anger and shame of his leaving. Mad at him for walking out when the shit had hit the fan with her parents.

Being forced to be on her own had taught her so much. She learned that she could take care of herself financially. That she was allowed to fumble around until she figured out what to do with her life. The Boss Babes had cheered her at every step.

In a way, his leaving her had been a gift. He broke her heart, but she came out stronger and more determined to succeed.

Now, with each searing kiss, the hate and anger she'd clutched so tightly dissipated. She'd gotten used to associating those feelings with Andre. No longer. It was time to let go of the past.

Trixie returned his kiss with all the power of two years of pent-up longing. She wanted her lips to ease the pain of his mother's death. To hold him up as he fought to keep his restaurant alive. To communicate that she'd help him. That he didn't have to do this alone.

"Andre," she moaned into his mouth.

He kissed the side of her neck, nipping his way down to her shoulder. She closed her eyes, letting each brush of skin against skin ignite her. He wrapped his arms around her waist, and proof of his desire pressed against her. Heat flared from her core.

"I want you. Need you," she gasped.

"Not here," he rasped. "In my office."

In the corner across from his desk was a worn IKEA futon, but they didn't make it that far. She grabbed the belt loop of his jeans and pulled him in for a kiss. Her hands made quick work undoing his belt and unbuttoning his fly. Trixie reached into his boxer briefs and wrapped her hands around his silky hardness.

She was rewarded with a groan from Andre. His hips pushed, rubbing his erection against her hand. She pulled down his shorts, freeing his cock. Her fingers brushed across the tip, eliciting another groan from him. Finding him already wet, she gasped.

"If you keep doing that, I'm going to throw you on this futon and fuck you until you cry for mercy."

"Promise?" She scraped her nails gently down the length of him.

He hissed in pleasure. Then pulled her hands behind her back. She arched as he grabbed both wrists with one hand. With his free hand, he untucked her T-shirt from her jeans.

"Andre, please." Her voice sounded not her own. Deeper, lustier. Her core ached for his touch.

"Please, what?" His fingers circled her nipple through the cotton of her shirt. Her nipple puckered, making a peak under the shirt. He gasped. "You're not wearing a bra."

"It's a special bra. Zoe's new design."

"You wore a special bra for a business meeting?" His deepbrown eyes bore into hers. "What happened to keeping things separate?"

"I thought maybe after we were done planning . . ." Trixie trailed off.

"You were mad because you thought I tricked you into a booty call, but"—he reached for the hem of her shirt—"you dressed up for me?"

"Yes. I'm a complicated person." She shrugged. She'd wanted him as much as he'd wanted her.

He let go of her wrists and stepped back. His jeans slid down his legs, revealing muscular thighs. Without looking away from her, he removed everything from the waist down. He looked magnificent. She wanted to run her hands down his dark brown thighs and all the way up to his cock. Before she could stop herself, she licked her lips.

"My eyes are up here."

Trixie looked up. "Sorry, I was distracted by the view."

Andre's heart leapt. Wearing a special bra meant that she still wanted him. Cared for him. He sat on the futon, leaving Trixie standing disheveled next to his desk.

"Show me." He wrapped his hand around his cock and stroked it slowly.

Trixie's eyes darted down. But she pulled her chin up and looked right into his eyes. "Why don't you unwrap me yourself? It's more fun this way," she said with a smirk on her face as she tucked her shirt back into her jeans.

Dammit, why did she insist on doing things her way?

"Come here." Fine, he'd strip her naked, but she had to come to him. To his surprise she walked over until she stood between his legs.

"Take off your shirt," he demanded.

"You take off yours first." Trixie's eyes dared him to make the first move. "It's my turn to be in charge."

"I like the sound of that." Andre meant it. He was tired of making all the decisions all the time. Demanding Trixie was so fucking hot.

He let go of his cock and grabbed the hem of his T-shirt.

Trixie's eyes widened as Andre began to pull up his shirt, revealing taut, sexy muscles. He actually heeded her demand. Would he let her call all the shots this time?

"Your turn." He tossed his shirt onto the floor.

"Not yet. I'm admiring the view." Trixie bit her lip. "Hot damn."

Enjoying the attention, Andre struck a model pose. With a thoughtful expression, he straightened his stance and set his hands on his hips, cock jutting out as he turned side to side.

Trixie giggled.

"A lesser guy would take offense at your laughter." He placed his hands on his heart in mock hurt. "But as you can see"—he swiveled his hips, swinging his erection side to side—"I'm not a lesser guy."

She couldn't keep it in any longer. Laughter bubbled out of her. Past Andre had never been this playful during foreplay.

Enjoying her laughter, he transitioned into a montage of poses including the Thinker, a muscleman, and more. With each pose, she couldn't help but follow the hard lines of his body and his bobbing erection.

"You missed your calling as a nude model."

"Hell, no. I'm only doing this for you. I don't show the goods to anybody."

His playful expression changed into one of lust—no, affection.

"In that case, let me express gratitude for the impromptu show." Trixie closed the distance between them. She pulled his head up to hers for a kiss.

Andre returned her kiss, deepening it. This kiss was different from their rough, lusty kisses from earlier. With only kisses, they apologized to each other. For all their misunderstandings. For the time they lost because they'd hidden the truth from each other.

Trixie broke their kiss to pull off her shirt. She slid her jeans down her legs. Commanding him to do her bidding turned her on even more. He'd done as she demanded, and knowing she held that power made her want to toss him on the futon and have her way with him.

"Holy. Fuck."

She stopped with one leg still in her jeans. Andre's mouth hung open.

"You're fucking beautiful."

Trixie slipped off her pants and spun around to give him the full view of the black lace bra and panty set. The underwire bra was designed to support, yet left her nipples free.

"Women buy beautiful lingerie only to toss it off during sex. Zoe wanted to design some that didn't need to be taken off during sex." Trixie felt beautiful in all her friend's designs, but seeing the look on Andre's face—she truly understood why Zoe created this line.

"If you don't take off those panties and come closer, I'm going to rip them off," he growled, and reached for her.

"Don't you dare!" She swatted his hand. "They're crotchless."

With those words, he pulled her onto the futon next to him and kissed her hard. His mouth seared kisses onto her chest, forcing her to lay back. He circled his tongue around her nipples. Suckled them until they were hard and aching. She gasped for breath between the bolts of pleasure zapping through her body.

"Nope, we're doing this my way." Trixie pushed him away from her until she could slip out from under him.

"Yes, ma'am." He stood up and put his hands out in surrender. "Your wish is my command."

With a playful push, he fell back onto the futon. She climbed onto his lap, grabbed his hand, and slid it between her legs. She guided him to the lace opening, which was soaked with her arousal.

"Fuck, Trixie." He groaned. "You're so wet. Hot and soft like velvet."

His fingers curved, finding the bundle of nerves inside her. She moaned. When his thumb pressed onto her clit, she lifted her hips up to meet him.

"Harder," she gasped.

"As you wish." He withdrew his fingers and thrust them back inside her.

She grabbed the back of the futon and rode his fingers curled up against her G-spot while his thumb pressed harder against her clit with every thrust.

"Take what you need, baby," he growled into her ear.

She grabbed his shoulders and undulated her hips faster. His tender yet sexy words coupled with the curling and uncurling of his fingers was almost too much to take.

"You're so beautiful when you're in charge." He nipped her neck. "I'll give you everything you need. Anything you want."

With that promise in her ear, her world exploded as waves of pleasure radiated throughout her body. This was a man who accepted—no—encouraged her to be her true self. He believed in her dream and wanted her to succeed.

"I need you, Trixie. Need to be closer to you." His voice was gravelly with desire.

"Andre, let me fuck you." She stared into his eyes, challenging him to cede control to her again.

He extricated his fingers from inside her. She gasped at the emptiness.

"I can't think of anything better," he replied, his eyes never leaving hers. "There's a condom on the desk, can you reach it?"

Her short arms couldn't reach, so she disentangled herself and swiped it off the table. Andre reached for the foil packet, but she pulled it out of his reach.

"Allow me."

He grunted. "Hurry, please."

Feeling heady with power, she opened the condom in slow motion, making a show of studying it before sliding it onto him. This was a feeling she could get used to.

Trixie straddled him again, this time hovering over him, teasing him. He bucked his hips to reach her, but she pulled away.

"Now, now, what's the rush?" She gently ran her nails down his chest.

"This will be over really soon if you don't sit on me," he said through clenched teeth.

"Poor baby," Trixie crooned. "What's the magic word?"

She lowered herself so his cock rubbed against the lace opening of her panties. Andre had become putty under her touch. She wasn't ready to give into his pleas, but the euphoria from her previous orgasm was waning.

"Please," he moaned.

She lowered herself onto him, his cock stretching her and filling her with his heat. Closing her eyes, she focused all attention on their bodies together. Riding him, taking from him all he offered to her.

When she came for the second time that day, Andre covered her mouth with a kiss, swallowing her cries as waves of pleasure rolled through her. She held on to his shoulders and rode her orgasm until he shuddered in pleasure, crying out her name as he came.

Trixie wrapped her arms around him as they caught their breath. She was glad they were finally able to put the past behind them. She wasn't sure what was next for them, but keeping her emotions out of it wouldn't be easy. Right now all she wanted to do was bask in the afterglow of their pleasure. She'd figure everything out later.

CHAPTER 22

Zoe!" Trixie called out as she walked into her roommate's plus-size lingerie shop, Something Cheeky.

The shop was empty except for her roommate, who sat on a stool by her cutting table. She loved visiting Zoe's zone of genius. The window display featured curvy mannequins dressed in a mixture of structured pieces like corsets and flowing chiffon robe-and-nightie sets.

Trixie knew firsthand how sexy the lingerie made her feel. Now so did Andre.

"Sorry I'm late, but I brought bún thịt nướng." She made her way past the racks of bras and negligees to the sewing area. Zoe's fingers flew across her laptop. Instead of silk or lace, sketches were strewn across the cutting table.

"Let me finish this blog post." Zoe didn't look up from her laptop. Using an alias, she ran a very popular fan site about her favorite graphic novel series, Trưng Rebellion, based on the famous Vietnamese sisters who fought off the Chinese army in their village. Only the Boss Babes knew about Zoe's secret online identity and would do anything to keep it safe.

"What are you writing about this time?" Trixie peered over her friend's shoulder. "Trưng Rebellion is being made into a TV show?"

"Ugh, don't get me started. They're whitewashing the show." Zoe shut her laptop. "I'm starving. Please tell me the noodles are from my parents' place."

"I wouldn't dare bring you Viet food from anywhere except Phở-Ever 75 less you expire from the guilt." Trixie rolled her eyes. Even though she teased Zoe about it, she knew the power of a Vietnamese mother's guilt. "I even brought you cà phê sữa đá. Actually, your mom practically pushed the coffee into my hand."

"That was very thoughtful of you to grab lunch." Zoe checked her phone. "A very late lunch, I should add."

Trixie ignored the dig about her lack of punctuality.

"Make sure you thank Auntie Trinh so she won't guilt you for being ungrateful. Or me for not reminding you." Trixie shuddered. "I can only handle guilt from one Vietnamese mom at a time."

"Very funny. But true. I'll text her after we eat. Let's eat here so I can show you my latest cosplay designs for the next Capital Comic Con." Zoe tore off a long sheet of brown craft paper that she used for making patterns and set it on the table. "There, easy cleanup, and I won't have to worry about grease staining the next fabric I cut."

They dug into their bowls of rice noodles topped with grilled lemongrass pork and fresh cucumbers and carrots tossed with nước chấm, a sweet-salty-tangy fish sauce. As they ate, Zoe scrolled through sketches on her laptop while explaining her interpretation of each character. Trixie didn't understand all the sewing terms or know all the characters, but she immersed herself in her friend's creative energy.

Way too soon, they reached the end of Zoe's sketches and the bottom of their takeout bowls.

"Oh, the bún hits the spot." Trixie rubbed her stomach. "I had worked up an appetite after—"

She stopped, but it was too late.

"Wait, is that why you were an hour late?" Zoe set down her chopsticks and studied Trixie. "You slept with him again!"

Zoe's mouth hung open.

Suddenly, Trixie found the swirls of condensed milk at the bottom of her coffee fascinating. She stirred it with her straw to mix the remaining thick sweetener into the strong espresso.

"You're practically glowing," Zoe said after recovering from shock. "Does he make you happy?"

"Right now, yes." Trixie let out a sigh. "Today was just, just . . ."

"That good, huh?"

"It was better than good. Dare I say it was the best sex we've ever had?" Trixie couldn't stop smiling. "I saw a different side of him. He was playful and vulnerable. Willing to let me take charge."

"Wait, did you do something kinky?" Zoe's eyes grew bigger. "I mean, if that's what you like, but I didn't know that about you."

"No, not like that. When we were dating, he always had to be in charge of how we had sex. Even if I'd initiated it." Trixie chewed her lip, trying to find the right words. "I guess it never bothered me before."

"How was it different today?"

"We had a moment where he tried to take control again, but I wasn't feeling it. So I challenged him to do what I wanted."

"That's my Trixie! Don't you say at your shows, we should tell our partner what we want in bed?"

"I'm surprised at myself. Giving the advice and actually doing it was different." Trixie realized that she hadn't challenged for control consciously. She knew what she wanted at that moment and demanded it. "I liked being in charge during sex."

"You've really come into your own since we've met. I'm so proud of you."

"I'm proud of me, too." A few months ago, Trixie would've brushed off the compliment. Yes, she was happy about her job and her vision for a boutique. She'd thrived in DC with a "fake it till you make it" attitude and the support of the Boss Babes. By standing up to Andre and later confronting him about how he'd dumped her, she'd proven to herself that she didn't have to feign confidence and success. She'd already succeeded simply by going after her heart's desires.

"What was his reaction when you took charge?" Zoe set her elbows on the table and leaned in closer. "I'm guessing by that giant grin on your face that he didn't mind."

"Not only did he go with it, he became playful. As if the weight of the world disappeared and he was—happy." She wondered if Andre realized how he'd changed in that moment. It was as if he was relieved *not* to be in charge. That he trusted her to take care of him. After all, he'd spent the past two years or so taking care of everyone else. The idea both thrilled and scared her.

"Wow." Zoe was wide-eyed, her smile filling up her face. "Sounds like you two really connected."

"Yeah." Trixie sighed.

"There's a *but*?"

"After today, I could see myself with him again. DMV Andre is sensitive, if broody. He loves his sister and his neighbors. And he still cares about me. But I can't take it if he breaks my heart again."

"Oh, sweetie." Zoe rubbed Trixie's shoulder. "Those are normal feelings. But since I've known you, I haven't seen you this happy outside of work and the Boss Babes. You've been working so hard. It's okay to have fun. Enjoy the moment."

"You're saying I'm overthinking this."

"No, I'm telling you to take it one day at a time," said Zoe. "You two agreed to have fun with no strings attached. There's nothing wrong with that. No expectations for it to become more."

"You're right."

For the past two years, everything Trixie did served a purpose: to find her true life's calling and prove to her parents she could be successful without their guidance. It felt strange to do something that was just for fun. Just for herself.

Yes, she'd have fun and break things off before her heart got involved. Trixie had everything under control.

CHAPTER 23

Trixie was in total control when she found herself in Mama Hazel's kitchen the next day. Today's visit was purely professional. Andre invited her over to taste some new dishes that he'd been working on. How could she say no to free and delicious food?

"Close your eyes and open your mouth." His voice was low and sensual. He held a bowl behind his back.

"Why are you being so mysterious?" Trixie tried to see what was in the bowl without any success. Being spoon-fed was too sensual, too intimate. Not keeping things professional. She crossed her arms. "I'm a grown woman. I can feed myself."

"You think I'm trying to seduce you with food?"

"What am I supposed to think when you talk to me in that voice?" she shot back.

He blinked innocently as if he didn't realize the effect he had on her.

"I promise not to seduce you right now. Scout's honor." He held up three fingers.

"You were a Boy Scout?" Instead of feeling annoyed that this was yet one more thing he'd never shared about himself, she was excited. Yesterday had unlocked a gate, and now he spoke freely about himself and his past.

"Nope." He snorted. "But I wanted to be one."

"Stop clowning around," she scoffed. "Hand me the bowl already! I'm starving."

"Oh, hangry Trixie is feisty," he teased.

"I am not even close to hangry. You don't want to see that." She gave a half smile. He was kind of cute, this playful Andre. Everything between them had changed yesterday. Instead of butting heads or avoiding each other, they were talking instead of tossing barbs. Hanging out was comfortable and safe.

"Okay, I'm nervous about you tasting this, because you inspired this dish."

"How did I do that?" That tidbit made her even more curious. She leaned to the side, hoping to see around his back, but he'd covered the bowl with a kitchen towel. On cue, her stomach growled.

"Fine." He slid the bowl onto the stainless-steel table and sat across from her. "I want your honest opinion."

"Even if I hate it?" She picked up the spoon and met his gaze.

"Yes, especially if you hate it. I don't want to serve a terrible dish and ruin the restaurant's reputation."

"You're being dramatic," she teased. When she saw vulnerability in his eyes, she gave him an encouraging smile. She was relieved that his openness wasn't a one-time thing. That he was able to share the full range of his emotions with her.

With the flair of a celebrity chef, he pulled off the towel. The bowl was wide and shallow, not deep like the one they served gumbo in.

"It's shrimp etouffee." The way he acted, she expected something else. Like something from a cooking show they used to watch together. Instead it was a very familiar New Orleans comfort food.

"Don't look so disappointed." His face fell. "I know it doesn't look like much—"

Trixie set the spoon on his lips and shushed him. "Let me taste it before you jump to conclusions."

Andre didn't realize how nervous he was until it was time to share with Trixie what he'd made. Would she hate it or accuse him of appropriating her family's food? If she did either, he'd fix the dish. Make it into something Mama would be proud of.

He trusted Trixie's opinion. Ever since the moment she declared her hatred for him, he knew she would always tell him the truth. This new version of Trixie stood up for what she believed and what she wanted. Like the way she'd demanded control yesterday.

If he hesitated any longer, the food would be cold. He took the spoon out of her hand.

"Before you dig in, make sure you get a little bit of everything in one bite." He handed the spoon back to her.

"You're telling a native New Orleanian how to eat etouffee?" With the same playfulness that was in her voice, she took the spoon and carefully scooped up a small amount of each element of the dish.

Andre held his breath. As her luscious lips wrapped around the spoon and the food hit her tongue, he watched her face for a reaction. She closed her eyes and set the spoon back in the bowl as she chewed. How was one woman this incredibly sensual when eating a bite of food?

He was glad that she'd refused to let him feed her. This afternoon's taste testing would have been derailed. He didn't plan to see her again so soon, but Keisha was on him about finalizing the daily specials. Trixie loved his idea for a lunch buffet, and Andre wanted an impartial taste tester.

He was nervous. Serving her a dish inspired by her family was ballsy. Keisha and the initial taste testers liked it, but he didn't want to serve it if Trixie hated it.

"Oh!" Trixie mouthed in surprise. She swallowed. "It's crunchy. Is that—"

He exhaled and nodded. Recognition blossomed on her face, and she gasped. She dug in for another bite. Relief flooded his body.

"This tastes like"—she spoke with her mouth full—"both parts of me. Vietnamese and New Orleans."

"I meant to have you try it at the last pop-up, but things didn't go as planned." He was glad for that night, because it'd brought her back into his arms. "I wanted your approval before officially putting it on the menu."

"Andre, it's delicious! You have to add it to the menu. I can't believe you remember eating cơm cháy at my parents' place."

"I wasn't sold when you translated it to 'burnt rice.' I only tried it so I could make a good impression on your parents."

"You've never told me that! You realized that the rice at the bottom of the pot is the most coveted section?" She laughed. "It meant a lot that my mom offered it to you."

"Really?" Maybe she did tell him that, but he'd been so nervous about meeting her parents that he ate everything they put in front of him. "It made an impression on me."

"Is this the first time you've been back in the kitchen, since—um." Trixie paused awkwardly.

"Since Mama died?" He rubbed the back of his head. "Yeah, it is."

He shouldn't have left everything to Luis, but it had been too hard to work in the kitchen, tracing the steps his mom took every day as she cooked from her heart. Sticking to the bar was easier. Since they added it after she passed, there were no memories sneaking up on him there.

Andre had let his guilt and grief keep him away, but preparing all the dishes today was therapeutic. He only hoped the rest of the dishes honored his mom even though he added his own twist to them.

"How does it feel to be cooking at Mama Hazel's again?" she asked before shoveling another spoonful into her mouth.

WHEN TRIXIE WAS a kid, her classmates laughed at the burnt rice and caramel stewed pork belly she brought for lunch. Burnt rice was what she called it because that was the literal translation. They made fun of her stinky and burnt food. She still loved her mom's cooking but had insisted that she eat school lunch after that.

Now Andre had taken this humble food and combined it with his family's food. He'd remembered it all these years, even through their time apart. Her chest swelled with tenderness and—no, not that word. This food reminded her of home and made her emotional. That was it. Nothing more.

"It feels weird because Luis has been in charge since Mama got sick. I feel like I'm stepping into his domain."

"I bet he's glad to have you in here." Time to steer the conversation back to something more work-related. "What else do you have planned?"

"We only need four different daily specials for the buffet now that we're closed Monday through Wednesday. I made small batches of the two if you want to try them. I'm still working out what the last dish will be."

"If they're half as good as this etouffee with scorched rice, I'm in." Discussing details of the menu made it easier to ignore all the warm feelings rising up inside Trixie.

"I'll dish them up, but they still need work." He walked over to the stove. "They'll probably need some tweaks. Which is why you're here."

He came back with two plates piled with food. The smell made her mouth water. She forced herself to wait until he was ready for her to try them.

"This one is collard greens cooked with kimchi."

Trixie raised an eyebrow. When did he get into kimchi?

"I know it sounds like they won't go together, but Mrs. Kim used to give mom jars of her homemade kimchi. I went through a phase where I ate kimchi with everything. It gives the greens a punch and extra umami."

She grinned. He was so adorable, talking like a contestant on a cooking show.

"I love that it's inspired by your neighbors." She pointed at two sliders. "What's this?"

"Fried catfish nugget sliders on corn cakes with homemade tartar sauce."

"They're so cute!" Trixie grabbed one and took a large bite.

The cornmeal crust was seasoned perfectly, while the catfish was moist and tender. The bun was comprised of two small corn pancakes and added a hint of sweetness to contrast with the fish and tartar sauce. "These would go great with beer."

"My thoughts exactly." Andre was beaming. "I talked to my beer guy. Starting next week, we'll have Abita on tap."

"No way!" Trixie clapped her hands. Abita was their favorite New Orleans beer. She was happy to find bottles of it at the liquor megastores in the Maryland suburbs, but it was ten times better on tap. "Please say you'll serve Purple Haze, my favorite."

"Did you forget it's my favorite, too?" His wide smile transformed his face. He was so happy.

"You did good, Andre. Mama Hazel's is going to take off faster than you think," Trixie said before finishing the slider.

She was so proud of him. He'd come such a long way. From hiding his creativity from his mom to finding a way to honor both her food and his ideas. Andre had found his calling and asked her to be a part of it. She wanted to celebrate this moment by hugging and kissing him. But she resisted.

If Trixie wasn't careful, she could find herself falling in love with him again.

CHAPTER 24

Andre's phone buzzed. The clock on the wall surprised him. Was it almost noon? He'd been so engrossed in receipts and paperwork that he didn't realize how late it had gotten.

Another buzz helped him dig out his phone from under a stack of unopened mail. He grinned. It was a text from Trixie. He hadn't seen her since last week when she'd tried his new dishes. Between the restaurant's evening hours and Trixie's schedule, there hadn't been much overlap for them to see each other. He was more than happy to push aside work to chat with her. Which often led to sexting. He had zero complaints about that.

Trixie: Are you busy today? I need a favor.

Andre: Catching up on paperwork until we prep for community dinner tonight.

Trixie: Can you tear yourself away from such fun work for an hour or so?

Andre glanced at the stacks of paper on his desk and the red numbers in his spreadsheet. Thanks to Trixie's pop-ups, the red numbers were going down, but not as fast as he'd like. The fryer was still acting up, and their supplier had raised chicken prices after a recent bird-flu outbreak. Things he couldn't control but nevertheless hurt their bottom line.

Worst of all, Mr. Jackson was still selling the building. The emergency meeting Andre had called confirmed his worries; they didn't have the money to buy the building. Like Mama Hazel's, his neighbors were barely making ends meet.

Rubbing his eyes, he closed the spreadsheet. He needed a break from numbers and computers. Spending time with Trixie was a hundred times better than paperwork.

Andre: As long as I'm back by 3.

Trixie: You got it! I'll swing by in 30 minutes.

Maybe he'd convince her to get cozy on the futon in his office again. If that was the case, he needed to wash his face. The bleary, staring-at-the-computer-all-morning look was not sexy.

When the bell to the back door rang, he looked at his watch. Thirty minutes had not passed. Was she here early to surprise him? He got up to let her in.

"I hope this favor includes an encore from last week, Trixie!" Andre swung the door open and met Xavier's confused expression. Andre wiped the grin off his face.

"Whoa, bro!" Xavier stepped through the door and walked through the kitchen.

"Go ahead. Make yourself at home," Andre muttered sarcastically.

Andre tried to keep the disappointment from his face, but

Xavier didn't notice. Andre shut the door and walked briskly past Xavier into his office.

"Back up, Tre. An encore of what?" Xavier ran after Andre. "Did you two hook up?"

"It wasn't a hookup." Andre scowled. "Don't talk about Trixie like she's one of your one-night stands."

"Those one-night stands were one-hundred-percent consensual. With a little sixty-nine." His friend winked.

"Save your fuckboy act. I know you care deep down. I've read your poems."

"Hey, I let you read those in confidence." Xavier leaned closer and whispered, "If word gets out that I write about feelings, I'll lose my street cred."

Andre almost laughed but realized Xavier was serious. He hoped Xavier would share his talent with others someday. Those poems were tight.

"I'm not going to tell the world you actually have feelings that don't involve your dick."

Relief flooded Xavier's face.

Andre closed the door to his office. He might as well tell Xavier, since he practically let it slip at the back door. "We're back together. But you can't tell anyone."

For once, Xavier was speechless. His mouth gaped open and closed, like a Muppet.

"I want Keisha to hear it from me. If you breathe a word of this to her, I'm going to tell her that you're the one who cut off her Barbie dolls' hair when we were kids."

"You helped, too, if I recall." Xavier chuckled. "Man, we were some troublemakers back then."

"Who will she believe ruined her dolls, me or you?"

"That's low, man." Xavier plopped down on the armchair in Andre's office. "You better tell her soon. We all see how you look at Trixie during the pop-ups. Now tell me everything."

"We called a truce after her last pop-up. After everyone was gone. One thing led to another and things got hot between us."

"I knew you still had it in you!" Xavier reached out for a fist bump.

Andre glared at his friend until he dropped his hand. Xavier shrugged, unfazed by the rejection.

"We're not dating. It's just, um, friends with benefits."

"Wait, you're friends now? Are you cool with that arrangement? I know you dig relationships." Xavier shuddered at the word. "But if it's what you really want from her, I got your back."

"There's more." Andre sat on the side of his desk, ignoring the papers he displaced. "I want her as my girlfriend. The more time we spend together, the more she'll warm up to me. I told her why I never called after I left New Orleans."

"You did? I'm proud of you, man."

"I told her everything—about Mama getting sick. Finding out about my dad."

"No shit! Look at you, Mr. Communication." Xavier grabbed a handful of mints off Andre's desk. He threw them in the air and tried to catch them in his mouth, failing spectacularly.

"I wasn't going to, but after we talked about my mom, it came out. Then she kissed me. And well." Andre shrugged. "We didn't talk much after that."

"You dog!" Xavier punched him in the shoulder. "Dry spell for two years and now you're getting more action than me!"

"Watch it," Andre growled. "You're talking about my girlfriend. And clean those up." He pointed to the mints littering the rug.

"She ain't your girlfriend yet. Y'all are still friends with benefits." Xavier ignored the discarded ones and reached for the bowl.

Andre snagged it first and pushed it out of reach. "Why are you here so early?"

"I took today off. Luis is teaching me how to make Miss Hazel's roux. Maybe we could grab some lunch before my lesson."

"Nope, you need to leave." Andre pointed at his office door. "Trixie will be here soon."

"Easy there, stud. I won't stand in the way of beneficial rewards. At least not my best friend's."

"I'm going to win her back," Andre said too emphatically. Was he trying to convince his best friend or himself?

"You never do things halfway. Look, don't set yourself up for disappointment. Or make promises you can't keep. You did her wrong and she has every right to keep things casual. Take it slow and give her time to trust you again. Just don't get your heart broken, bro." Xavier stood up and mock saluted Andre. "I'll wait for Luis in the kitchen."

Xavier was right. Of course, Andre cared about Trixie and their relationship. What was the point if he didn't put his whole heart into the important people and things in his life? The only reason Mama Hazel's was still here was because he cared. Cared about his mother's legacy. Cared about Keisha. Not to mention Mr. and Mrs. Harris, Luis, and everyone else who came to their Monday-night dinners.

He still cared about Trixie. The more time they spent together, the sooner she'd realize how much she meant to him.

He'd invite her to family dinner and truly let her into his life this time.

CHAPTER 25

The back door to Mama Hazel's flew open.

"I'm meeting with a—" Trixie's words were cut short when Andre pulled her into the doorway for a deep kiss. Her toes curled and heat flooded her body.

"Hello," she whispered when they finally came up for air.

"I've missed you." Andre leaned against the doorframe, looking sexy as hell in another pair of ass-hugging jeans and a forest green Henley. If this were a movie, his teeth would sparkle. "Five days is five days too many without kissing you."

His kiss had awakened all the other parts that ached for his lips.

"I've missed you, too. But we don't have time for a quickie." She grabbed his hand. "Lock up, and I'll explain on the way."

"Not even a super-quick quickie?" He raised their linked hands and kissed the soft skin below her knuckles, sending tingles up her arm.

"As tempting as that sounds, I can't." She laughed at his puppy dog eyes. "I have an appointment in fifteen minutes, and it's a ten-minute walk. So, no."

His face fell. Did she give him the impression this was a visit for sex? She felt a little guilty. Her texts had been vague.

"Maybe later?"

"I'll hold you to that promise, but it's not going to be a quickie. I want to kiss you all over until you beg me to fuck you," he whispered into her ear.

She shuddered, and her heartbeat fluttered. Now, that was a very tempting promise.

"You said we had to be somewhere in ten minutes?" Andre stepped out of the doorway and locked the door. He tapped on his phone. "Told Keisha I'd be back in a couple of hours. Didn't want her to worry."

"I wish my siblings and I were as close as the two of you. They're so much older than me." Not to mention they were stereotypical Asian overachievers while she was just average. Obviously, mediocre Asians existed, but no one liked to talk about it.

"Keisha's the only family I have left." He shrugged. "I have to take care of my little sister."

"You've been so strong through everything. Keisha worries about you." Trixie fought the urge to grab his hand as they walked down the street. She wasn't ready to announce their relationship to the public.

"I had to do what needed to be done." Andre's jaw tightened. "Tell her I'm fine and stop worrying about me."

"I didn't mean to upset you. We don't have to talk about it." Trixie sighed. He seemed more closed off today than the last time they were together.

"Sorry." Andre stuck his hands in his pants pockets. "Mama's cancer grew too fast for me to think about how hard things were. She didn't want to close Mama Hazel's so I ran it as best I could in between her doctor appointments and treatment sessions."

"I know you prefer to take action instead of talking, but it's okay to talk about your feelings. I'm a good listener." Trixie avoided his eyes and checked the directions on her phone. She hadn't told him where they were going, and he didn't ask. If she told him, he might not agree to come along.

Trixie stole a glance at Andre. His eyes crinkled as he smiled.

"Our entire neighborhood—we're like family. Mrs. Harris watched me and Keisha while my mom worked several jobs in order to make ends meet," he continued. He pointed at some of the shuttered stores. "As you can see, things are lean in our neighborhood. Many people depend on our weekly hot meals. I refuse to let them down."

"Monday-night dinners mean a lot to you." Trixie recalled how Keisha's eyes lit up every time she talked about the free dinners at Mama Hazel's.

"Even when Mama was sick, she thought of others. She started Monday-night dinners to pay back our neighbors, who helped a single mother of two get on her feet in a new town. No matter how tough things get for the restaurant, I will do everything in my power to make sure Mama Hazel's survives. It's part of my mother's legacy."

"I wish I could have met her."

"I think you two would have gotten along." He grabbed her hand.

"You think so?" She squeezed his hand.

"She would have liked your drive and passion for helping others." Andre sounded far off, distracted. His eyes darted between the closed stores as if remembering them when they were thriving.

Out of the corner of her eye, she noticed how his other hand had clenched into a fist. He was determined. New Orleans Andre had been quiet and serious—like he was searching for something. Now she knew he'd been searching for his dad's family and, by extension, himself. He returned to DC and had to take on responsibilities no one his age should've.

He was still serious at times, but now he had more playful moments—at least with Trixie. In the last couple of weeks, he'd rediscovered joy in cooking and was breathing new life into Mama Hazel's.

"Keisha told me word is spreading about your lunch buffet," she replied softy. "You'll keep Mama Hazel's going."

"I still don't like that we're closed three days of the week instead of one," he said, shaking his head. His fist unclenched, and he ran his hand over his head. "It's going to take a lot more customers before we can reopen on Tuesdays and Wednesdays."

"I'm so sorry, Andre."

She turned to him so she could—what, hug him? It was getting harder to separate how much she cared about him and her desire to keep things business only between them. He looked straight ahead, avoiding her eyes.

"How's your dad doing?" he asked, changing the subject.

"Fine, I guess." She shrugged. "He's driving Mom crazy about his new doctor-recommended diet. She says he hates brown rice. Prefers the white jasmine rice he grew up eating."

"If I served brown rice at family dinner, everyone would throw their cornbread at me." He chuckled. "So he's still not talking to you?"

"Is it sad to say that I've gotten used to it? I mean, I can't ignore the Viet-parent guilt, but at least it's predictable." She laughed, but the sound was hollow to her ears. Every time she called home, she hoped he would answer, but only her mom picked up the phone.

"Don't give up on them. They might surprise you."

"I hope so." Trixie sighed.

She wanted him to be right, but she couldn't wait for her parents to come around. Even in his weird mood, Andre was so easy to talk to. The Boss Babes were also convinced that Trixie's parents would accept her career. But hearing Andre say it made reconciliation seem tangible. He'd met her parents. He knew what they were like.

"I'm glad you're here. The DMV agrees with you." Andre smiled at her and bumped her shoulder with his. "You're doing so much to help people. Teaching and volunteering at the clinic. Helping women all over the metro area find their happy endings."

He remembered the name she'd picked out for her boutique! Trixie resisted the urge to hug him. She squeezed his hand again instead and glanced at the walking directions on her phone. They passed in comfortable silence through the next block, though people waved and greeted Andre by name, volunteering to help with the weekly family dinners. He'd done so much for his neighbors and they all wanted to pitch in.

Everyone here adored him. This was where he'd grown up, but she understood why he'd had to leave. She knew how stifling it was trying to find herself when everyone around her had different expectations for her.

Late September was usually hot and humid, but today's weather was a fluke. It was still warm, but not enough to make you break into a sweat as soon as you stepped outdoors. Maybe this meant fall would arrive in DC on time this year.

When they were a couple of blocks away, her stomach twisted. Maybe she wasn't ready for this. It was a horrible idea. She grabbed his hand and squeezed it hard.

"Trixie, are you okay?" He caressed the back of her hand with his thumb.

"No, I'm not okay. Maybe this is a mistake." She slowed her pace and he matched it. "Josie had this crazy idea to introduce me to her real estate broker friend, Kait Garcia, who runs a co-op boutique on the side and has an open space I could rent. Josie is super bossy and said I needed to see it so my brain could believe my dream could come true."

"Sounds like something my mom would say. Except less eloquent. Fake it till you make it."

Trixie laughed. Her nervousness began to fade.

"That's who we're meeting. In approximately one block."

"Why do you need me? You've got this."

"I've only done sales presentations in people's homes and pop-up shops at your restaurant. I don't know anything about running a brick-and-mortar shop, but you do."

"You want my opinion on the place?" His face brightened.

"Exactly. Walk through with me and give me your honest opinion about it."

"Running a restaurant isn't anything like an adult boutique, but I'll do my best."

"Great! Let's go. We're two minutes late." She hated being late for anything.

Trixie resumed their earlier pace, and Andre kept up easily since his stride was longer than hers. They reached the end of the block and turned the corner to District Market. She looked at the map on her phone.

"It's the next building. Suite C." She looked closely at the shiny new numbers and stopped in front of a glass door. "Here it is!"

The shop was closed, but a handwritten note told Trixie to come in, so she pushed the door open. Andre followed her.

"Wow, look at this place!" Trixie turned in a slow circle to take in the large room.

The store had soft, warm lighting and modern hardwood floors. In one corner was a display of handmade soaps, tubs of bath salts with scoopers, and a shelf of body products. The scent of lavender permeated the air. Next to that was a stationery store that had spinning racks of greeting cards, stacks of letter-pressed notebooks, and an array of pens.

Toward the back was an empty section the size of her kitchen. Big enough for a starter shop, though Trixie wasn't sure how her products would fit in with the other vendors. Their products seemed so normal compared to vibrators. Then again, everything probably looked strange next to a Jack of All Trades.

A tall Filipino woman walked out of a back room. She had a short haircut and wore a stylish dark gray pantsuit accentuated by a dark orange scarf. No wonder Josie had blushed at the mention of her name. The real estate broker oozed elegance and beauty.

"You must be Trixie! I'm Kait Garcia." She smiled as she shook Trixie's hand. "And you brought a friend."

"This is Andre." Trixie turned to him. Was it her imagination or was he scowling just now?

"Nice to meet you, Andre." Kait stretched her hand out.

"Likewise." He shook Kait's hand quickly. Then stuffed his hands in his pockets. Serious Andre had returned.

Trixie didn't know why she'd expected him to use his bartender charm here. He usually turned it on for new people. The real estate broker didn't seem fazed by Andre's curtness. She focused on Trixie, making sure to ask about Josie. It was obvious Kait and

Josie had a connection. Trixie didn't know what was going on be-tween them, but she couldn't wait to tease Josie about it.

"I'm not sure this is a good fit," Trixie said. "Josie told you what I want to sell, right?"

"Of course she did. You're empowering women, just like the other shop owners here." Kait chuckled at Trixie's confused ex-pression. "Let me give you a quick tour."

Kait guided her and Andre to the body products. "Over here is CBDare. Kelly here makes a line of cannabis-infused body prod-ucts to help women relax. I highly recommend this crème for cramps. It comes in handy every month."

"I had no idea that even existed." Trixie studied a box with bright yellow packaging. "Does this tea say it increases your libido?"

"I'm a satisfied customer," Kait mock whispered.

No wonder Josie and Kait got along so well. This woman was full of surprises.

"Then we have Fresh Out, a line of irreverent, hand-lettered sta-tionery. This one is my favorite."

Kait handed her a greeting card.

"'Save a horse, ride a cowboy'?" Trixie read.

Behind her Andre snorted.

Trixie read the other cards on the rack. "No Fucks Left" and "Sorry I was late, I was masturbating" were written in colorful swirly letters and embellished with glitter.

"Oh my God, I love these." Trixie couldn't wait to tell Reina about these cards.

"As you can see, a mini sex toy boutique would fit in perfectly." Kait walked over to the empty area. "This would be your space. I have some extra shelving you can borrow, but you'll have to bring in your own fixtures."

Trixie envisioned her store in the tiny space. Small displays with demo toys and tasting stations over there. A rack featuring some of Zoe's crotchless panties here. She'd put everything on casters so she could set out chairs for small workshops.

"Each person also has access to storage space in the back room. If you need more room, talk to your fellow tenants. You'll find them easygoing and flexible. We want everyone here to succeed."

Kait gestured at a set of curtains hung over a doorway. Trixie peered in. The back room was spacious. She didn't think she needed a lot of room. Boxes of toys and lube didn't take up much space. It was the perfect starter boutique.

"This space is so warm and elegant. I can already see how I'd set up my displays," Trixie raved as she took pictures on her phone.

Josie was right. Standing in this store made everything more real. Opening her own boutique was truly within her grasp. Now she wouldn't have to worry about meeting Bedroom Frenzy's goals or try to push a product she didn't love. She could promote women-owned brands. Even teach workshops without the pressure of selling products. Trixie could make money *and* help other women without compromising her values.

"As you see, District Market has plenty of foot traffic." Kait gestured at the people walking past the store windows. "Even though it's only been open for a year, businesses have seen a consistent uptick in clientele. I think a body-positive, empowering boutique such as yours would be an asset to the co-op. What do you think?"

While Trixie gushed, Andre merely walked behind them. A grunt or murmur could be heard, but nothing else. When she did look at him, she couldn't read his face.

"Can you explain how the co-op aspect works?" Until today,

she hadn't considered co-ops as an option for her business. Kait's open mind and forward thinking meant Trixie could put vibrators in the hands of people who'd never attend one of her Bedroom Frenzy pop-ups.

"The lease is based off square footage. Electricity, water, and internet access are included. If you want or need a landline, you're responsible for that. Plus a commission of your sales. I try to keep the entry costs low so you can get up and running quickly."

"Wow, that sounds amazing. When do you need an answer?"

"There's a waitlist for this space, but Josie spoke very highly of you." Kait looked at her phone. "I can hold it for two weeks. Any longer and you'll need to submit a nonrefundable deposit."

"Suppose I was ready to move forward. What would you need from me?" Were those words really coming out of her mouth? This would push her plan ahead by months. No thanks to her car problems, her savings account was almost depleted. But what did Mama Hazel say? Fake it till you make it.

"You'll need to fill out an application. Provided your credit check goes through, it's a minimum six-month lease, plus deposit." Kait pulled out a note card. "You can apply at this website. Make sure you have all your documentation before you start."

"How much per square foot?" Andre's deep voice echoed in her empty future shop space. She'd asked him to help pose the right questions and he waited until now? All he wanted to know was the rent? Trixie shot him a look, then smiled broadly at Kait.

"I'm personally funding the shop, so my budget is very tight," said Trixie. "I don't want to waste your time if it's not a good fit."

"There're three other shops here, so you all split the rent based on your square footage. Rent for your space would be approximately eight hundred dollars a month plus a five percent commission from all your sales." Kait looked at Andre. "Yes, I'm trying to help other businesswomen, but I want to make money, too."

"That sounds too good to be true!" Trixie couldn't believe it.

"I handpicked all the businesses in here and yours would complement them. Their customers will love your toys." Kait smiled encouragingly. "It's a lot of info, so think about, and I'll call you in a few days."

"Yeah, it's a lot." Trixie realized how not ready she was to start her business. Winning the contest would cover her rent and some setup costs, but not enough to make her comfortable. In her mind it seemed so easy. Take the prize money, open the shop, and boom! Customers would come. That part of her goal had been a dream for so long, but she'd enjoyed the dreaming part more than actual research. Because she thought she had plenty of time to figure it out. She needed a crash course from the Boss Babes, who all had their own spaces.

Trixie was scared. What if the store—what if *she* failed? She had no backup plan. No way would she go crawling back to her parents again. Maybe she should stick with Bedroom Frenzy. Or find a more stable, practical job like her parents had suggested too many times.

"Are you okay, Trixie?" Kait asked. "If you're feeling overwhelmed, I suggest you talk to the Small Business Administration. They have lots of resources for women business owners."

"Sure, I'll do that." This had been a mistake. She didn't need to set herself up to fail. Not when she was at the top of her game at Bedroom Frenzy. Her chest tightened. She needed fresh air.

"We have to go. I have another appointment." Trixie grabbed Andre and pushed him out of the store.

CHAPTER 26

Andre let Trixie push him out the door. Once outside, he stuck his hands in his pockets and walked back to Mama Hazel's. He looked straight ahead, because it hurt to look at the shiny new chain stores and boutiques.

Instead of designer clothing stores, he saw the fried fish takeout place that used to live on that corner. The one where he and Xavier would share the five-dollar plate as kids. Or the hole-in-the-wall Chinese restaurant next to it that gave him fortune cookies for sweeping their stoop. Mr. Chen passed away while he was in New Orleans. Their kids convinced Mrs. Chen to close the restaurant and move in with them in California.

All that history had been demolished to build District Market. The fucking town center changed everything good in his life. Ruined it. Took away small businesses. Brought in so much competition it forced his mom to work herself so hard that she neglected to see her doctor for regular checkups.

He hated it and everything it stood for. Now Trixie wanted to open her boutique here of all places.

"Andre, you've been very quiet." Trixie huffed, trying to keep up with him. "What did you think of the store?"

He increased his pace. Behind him, her breathing became labored as she tried to catch up. He shouldn't take out his anger at the town center on Trixie. Andre stopped so she could catch up.

"You're upset about something," Trixie sputtered between catching her breath.

"Not here." He searched the people around them to make sure there was no one who knew him. He couldn't be sure and didn't want anyone in public to overhear him.

"What aren't you telling me, Andre?"

"I have to get back and help set up for dinner tonight. The community depends on us," he said, still looking ahead. He couldn't look at her. Andre was relieved he hadn't invited her to dinner that night.

He didn't give her a chance to respond. Instead, he resumed his brisk pace back to the restaurant. She huffed behind him, breathing too hard to speak. Soon the sign to Mama Hazel's appeared before them.

Trixie sped up and stepped in front of him. He had to stop, or he'd knock her over.

"Are you mad at me?" she demanded.

Andre wanted to be happy for her, but he couldn't. Not right now. She deserved to know what was happening with Mr. Jackson and the building. Seeing her gush over the co-op in District Market—it hurt. To see her moving forward with her dreams while Mama Hazel's death was imminent. It wasn't fair. He hated that he felt that way. He walked around her to the back of the restaurant.

"Seriously?! You're mad at me about something and you won't tell me why?" She threw her hands in the air but followed him through the back door, all the way into his office.

"This is so typical," she gasped. Sweat was dripping down the sides of her face. Her breasts heaved as she tried to catch her breath.

He grabbed a bottle of water from his desk drawer and handed it to her. Trixie collapsed onto the futon in his office. The cap clicked as she twisted it off and downed half the bottle.

Even through his anger, Andre couldn't help but notice how beautiful Trixie looked with a sheen of sweat on her face. The same way she glowed after their lovemaking during New Orleans' humid nights.

"Why can't you just tell me how you feel?" she demanded once the bottle of water was empty.

"You want to know what's bothering me? Fine!" Andre twisted the cap off a new bottle so hard, water splashed all over the papers on his desk. Ignoring the spill, he squeezed the water into his mouth and swallowed. "Our landlord is selling the building." He wiped his mouth on his shirtsleeve.

"Oh, Andre." She got up, walked over, and wrapped her arms around him. "I'm so sorry."

"No, I'm sorry," he replied into her neck. The scent of sweet, citrus shampoo calmed him. He pulled back to look at her face. Worry and sadness were all he saw. None of this was her fault.

"I was a jerk." He rubbed a thumb over her soft cheek then pulled her in for a kiss.

She returned the kiss but cut it short. "Now talk. How long have you known about the building being sold?"

"Two weeks, maybe three?" He rubbed the back of his head. Andre recounted his conversation with Mr. Jackson outside the building. "We held an emergency tenant meeting to consider his buyout offer, but . . ."

He trailed off. She grabbed his hand, encouraging him to continue.

"He came by again this morning before you came over. Mr. Jackson received another offer, better than the first one. They're signing the paperwork this week."

"Oh, no." Trixie squeezed his hand. "How long do you have?"

"I don't know. The new landlord will send details soon, I guess." He shrugged.

"What did Keisha say about all this?"

"I didn't want her to worry. She's got school to focus on." He'd gone out of his way to keep the news from his sister. He'd scheduled the meeting when she had class and made everyone promise not to share the news until they had a solution.

"Andre, you need to tell her."

"That town center is taking away everything good about this neighborhood and our community," he continued, pushing aside her chastising. "So when you fell in love with that co-op, it felt like you sided with the enemy. The gentrification that's slowly erasing us."

"Why didn't you tell me about Mr. Jackson sooner? Maybe there are loans or—"

"It was my problem. Not yours." He shook his head. "I let everyone down."

"You're not a superhero, Andre. You can't save everyone."

He wasn't trying to save everyone. He only wanted to save his mother's memory and provide for his sister. And continue meals for— Yeah, so maybe he was.

"Do you know how much rent has gone up since that place was built?" he continued. It was as if she unlocked the box where he'd hidden his hurt and anger. "They started rising a month after construction broke ground. My neighbors were barely making ends meet before that. Which is why our community dinner is more important than ever. It's all we have left."

Torn, Trixie's heart sank at his words. She felt terrible for Andre, but if she turned Kait down, someone else would just take the space. It wouldn't solve the neighborhood's issues.

"There's gotta be a way to save Mama Hazel's." Trixie brainstormed out loud. "Have you looked into grants or historical societies? There's so much history here—we can't let it disappear like that."

"There's nothing." His shoulders slumped.

"Have you looked? Don't give up yet, Andre. I can help."

"You can help by not renting that space for your boutique. Go out in the suburbs where it'll be cheaper. Like Wheaton or Silver Spring."

"Even in the suburbs it would take me years to save up. I don't want to be part of the gentrification problem, but I can't give up on my dream, Andre. Kait's offer is once-in-a-lifetime."

"It's another nail in Mama Hazel's coffin," he tossed back. "If this is your decision, I can't be with you while you help District Market grow."

That's it? He was breaking things off again?

"You're an ass, you know that! Reina was right," Trixie fumed. She had tried to be understanding, but he was stuck in this pit and refused to ask for or accept help. "I thought you were so strong to take over after your mom passed away. But you're not. You're a coward."

It was too late to take the words back. Even if she meant them. He stood up, looming over her. Trixie took a step back.

"Putting the best interests of my sister and this neighborhood first is not cowardly."

"No, but refusing to change is." She wanted to smack some sense into him. Instead she kept her clenched fists by her side.

"I'll fix it. I'll find a solution." He took a step closer.

This time Trixie stood her ground. She was tired of giving in to others without putting herself first. This co-op was the first step to owning her very own shop. If he couldn't support her dreams, she didn't need him.

"You can't do this by yourself." She looked into his dark, sad eyes. "There are people who want to help you. Your sister. All your neighbors who stopped you during our walk. It's obvious that they adore you. They'd want to help."

"They're just being nice."

"Ugghhhh!" Trixie screamed. "You are so hardheaded!"

She couldn't help someone who didn't want to be helped. And she wasn't going to give up on a store that practically landed in her lap.

"I thought you were going to be excited for me. At least help me make the right choice for me. Not for you." She reached over to the futon for her purse. "I have to tell the Boss Babes the good news. At least they'll support me."

"Trixie." He placed a hand on her shoulder. "I'm sorry. I panicked."

She swung the purse strap over her neck and shoulder. *Count to three and walk out,* she told herself.

"I'm not good at asking for help, but I—I don't want us to fight." He ran his thumb across her cheek. "It's hard enough to keep Mama Hazel's running, much less figure out how to stop developers from turning my restaurant into a condo."

Trixie leaned into his touch and sighed. He brushed a kiss on her lips. She pulled back.

"Maybe us being together in any capacity is a bad idea," she said. "We want different things." Things had gotten complicated between them fast. So many feelings for a friends-with-benefits relationship.

Andre reached for her hand.

"Stop. I'm still mad at you." If she let his touch distract her, they'd only postpone the argument.

He pulled his hands away from her and stepped back. His eyes fell.

"Can't we talk about it later? Your skin is so soft, I can't help touching you." He shrugged. "Besides, it's not like we can solve gentrification right this second."

"Sure, stick your head in the sand until it's too late to do anything," she huffed.

"I'm not—"

"I learned my lesson in New Orleans," she said, cutting him off. "I waited too long to tell my parents what I really wanted to do with my life. I've lost too much time with them already."

"Oh, babe, it's not your fault they didn't—"

"Let me finish." Trixie's words were sharper than she intended, but they had the effect she wanted.

Andre sat on the edge of his desk. He nodded, ceding the floor to her.

"I was so scared of how they'd react, I made bad decisions because of my fear. I should have eased them into my decision sooner. I should have talked to them about what I was feeling and what I wanted. I didn't trust them to love me unconditionally." Trixie blinked rapidly.

Until now she hadn't thought of the blowup with her parents that way. She'd chalked it up to how her immigrant parents didn't understand what she wanted. But she'd blindsided them with her decision to change her career path. Which is what Andre would be doing to Keisha if he didn't loop her in right away.

"I am a little scared," Andre whispered. His shoulders slumped as he avoided her eyes. "I already let down Mama when I stayed in New Orleans longer than I should have. Now I'm losing the restaurant."

"Andre, you don't have to do this alone." Trixie would tell him again and again until she got it into his thick head. "You have Keisha and a community who adore you. Believe me, they don't want to lose Mama Hazel's either."

Trixie closed the distance and grabbed his hands. Andre looked up, his brow furrowed. He pressed light feathery kisses onto her hands. Her skin tingled as his kisses traveled up her arms. Andre pulled her closer and continued until his lips reached the soft spot on her neck.

"Promise me you'll talk to Keisha right away? She's smart and knows this neighborhood as well as you do. I wouldn't be surprised if she came up with five solutions."

"I'm not good at asking for help," he said, and sighed.

Trixie reached for his cheek and rubbed her thumb over his prickly stubble.

"Promise me."

He nodded.

"Say it out loud." She ran her thumb over his lips.

He blew out a breath and nodded.

"I promise I'll talk to Keisha—on my terms." He turned and kissed her thumb. "Soon."

Trixie sighed. Getting him to admit he was scared and needed help was already a big step. She'd pushed him enough for one day. Once he told his sister, the three of them would come up with a solution to save the restaurant and open her boutique.

"You know I'll keep asking you until you tell her." Trixie closed her eyes and let the familiar heat flush her body.

He sighed loudly. "It's hard to get into your pants when you're talking about my sister."

"You know we can't fix everything with sex," she replied half-heartedly, her body already giving in to his touch.

"At least let me apologize for yelling at you." His hand cupped her ass. "If you'll let me," he whispered into her ear.

Trixie's willpower slipped away with each kiss and caress. Dimly, she knew she wouldn't be so mad if she didn't care for him so much. Mixing business and pleasure was too complicated. She wanted him, even if he could be a hardheaded jerk sometimes.

"Okay, but only if I'm on top." Trixie pushed him against his desk. He grinned and pulled off his shirt. She reached for his jeans and resolutely pushed everything else out of her brain.

CHAPTER 27

"Since our massage oil comes in so many flavors, I've asked our resident bartender, Andre, to help us demonstrate them." Everyone turned as Trixie gestured to the bar. Today he wore a burgundy long-sleeved shirt that accentuated his hard chest. "Let's give him a warm welcome!"

The women cheered and hooted. Trixie grinned as Andre played to the crowd. He flexed his biceps and pumped his fists in the air as he strutted to her demo table. Like he was accepting an award for Best Bartender in the Universe. She didn't know enough bartenders to be certain of that title, but he absolutely won Sexiest Man Alive.

Using Andre as a guinea pig for the warming massage oil had been so successful, Trixie asked him to volunteer for all her pop-ups. The women—and some men—in the crowd swooned over his muscular forearms and his charm. Not only did her sales double, but she liked having him as a demo partner. They planned out the flavor pairings beforehand. During the pop-up, she made sure to add only a few drops of the flavor combo on his arm. After the tasting, he announced that evening's specialty cocktail.

Including Andre as part of her pop-ups was fun. She'd been so focused on the contest this year that she had forgotten how fun her job was. She could be stuck in a stuffy law office shuffling paper! Instead she talked about sex toys and helped others discover how fun sex could be. With Andre next to her during these pop-ups, she experienced the products through his uninitiated eyes and felt rejuvenated after each one.

Andre was good in front of a crowd. His charm and easygoing manner put people at ease. Demoing the massage oil together also meant she had an excuse to touch him.

At first, things had been awkward after their meeting with Kait. Following her personal decision to keep things uncomplicated, she didn't bring up the co-op again. Asking him to go with her to the co-op had been a moment of weakness. She didn't need his advice or support when she had the Boss Babes. What she needed, however, was to continue their very successful pop-ups. Every dollar she could put toward the co-op would help her succeed.

Once the pop-up was done, they could continue touching each other in the privacy of his office. Sometimes she even grabbed a bottle of massage oil for "research and development." So they could plan the next pop-up's signature cocktail.

"Whew!" Andre mocked fanning himself as Trixie blew on his arm. "Is it getting warm in here?"

"Maybe a taste will cool you down?" Trixie replied, winking at the crowd. Tonight, they had chosen Pep-in-Your-Step Peppermint, with a peppermint chocolate martini to pair with it.

The diners chuckled at Andre's exaggerated happily surprised reaction as he licked the sweet peppermint oil from his well-massaged arm. Trixie repeated the flavor options while everyone wrote them down. The crowd clamored to order that evening's signature cocktail. Trixie took the brief break to straighten the items on her demo table.

"You two are hilarious together!" a familiar voice spoke behind her.

"Zoe! What are you doing here?"

"The food, of course." Zoe rubbed her stomach. "After all the rave reviews from you and Reina at our Boss Babes meetings, I had to see for myself. And the studio was dead, so I closed early and came here."

Zoe handed her a chocolate martini. She nodded at the bar. "You've been talking about Andre nonstop, so I wanted to meet him. I finally understand what all the fuss is about."

"Well, he knows how to work a crowd." Trixie sipped the drink. "Wow, this is really good. Did you get one for yourself? Put it on my tab."

"Of course. I can't resist chocolate alcohol." She pointed at an empty barstool where a martini glass waited for her.

"What bad things is he saying about me?" Trixie joked.

"He sung your praises—that was before he found out I was your roommate."

"I'm glad you approve. Let's hope Reina doesn't show up and threaten him again."

They both chuckled.

"That man is head over heels in love with you," Zoe said.

Trixie coughed and set down her martini.

"Why do you say that? We're keeping things uncomplicated." There was that word again.

"I'm not so sure about that. Every time he said your name, his eyes did this sparkle thing." Zoe flashed jazz hands next to her eyes to imitate an anime character.

"Stop it!" She had to squash the thought before it took hold. "It's only sex between me and Andre."

The room went suddenly still. Crap, that came out louder than she'd intended.

"I knew it!" Keisha screamed from somewhere near the kitchen door. She pumped her fist in the air and ran to hug her brother.

When Trixie finally caught Andre's attention, he bowed. The crowd cheered. Trixie opened her mouth, but closed it when no words came.

"I'm so sorry," Zoe whispered, and escaped to the bar.

Leaving Trixie alone in front of twenty-five pairs of eyes. She did her best to keep her personal sex life out of her work. Until today. Her cheeks grew hot and she avoided looking at the bar. Maybe there was still time to save the moment.

"A gal's gotta do some R&D, right?" She forced a laugh. "How else will I be able to tell you what works?"

Everyone chuckled and nodded. She blew out a breath. Keisha hadn't returned to the dining room. Trixie hoped they could talk after everyone had left.

"Now, let's move on to the more, ahem, buzzy part of the evening." Trixie picked up a small silver egg-shaped vibrator and a small remote control. "Don't let its small size fool you. The Rock My World Bullet has eight different settings starting with 'Hellooo, baby" all the way to 'OMG.'"

"I want two of those!" yelled a dark-skinned woman with braids.

Her friends chuckled, murmuring, "Of course she does."

Trixie breathed a sigh of relief as everyone turned their attention back to the products instead of her sex life.

"This is a good toy for first-timers and more advanced users alike. It's perfect if you prefer clitoral stimulation, but you can also insert it vaginally. You can even use it during intercourse."

"Because not everyone can have an orgasm with just penetration, right?" someone interjected.

"Exactly!" She loved it when they remembered what she'd said earlier in her demo.

"How does it work for intercourse?"

"Great question. It all depends on what position you're in and how flexible you are. You'll need one hand to hold it in place and the other to adjust the settings. Those hands don't have to be yours. Try holding the toy against your clit and handing the remote to your partner."

The crowd reacted with "No way!" and "That's amazing!"

Trixie smiled. It was so fun to see people expand their preconceived ideas of how to use the toys. More chimed in as they visualized how to use the toy.

"How loud is it?"

"Can I wear it to the club?"

"How far can you keep the remote?"

"I'm glad you asked," Trixie said in response to the rapid-fire questions. She pointed to the woman with braids. When the woman stepped up front, Trixie handed her the bullet. "Take this in your hand and walk slowly toward the bar."

The woman giggled and did as she was told. Trixie pressed a button, and the woman jumped.

"It's vibrating!" the woman squealed. "From all the way over here!"

"Wow, I didn't even hear it until she called out!" They were suitably impressed. Wait until she showed them the rest of the toys.

"Now remember, just because a toy is phallically shaped doesn't mean it's just for people with vulvas. You can also use it on other parts of the body, such as nipples, the sensitive underside of a penis, or even your perineum," Trixie said as she set down Jack of All Trades.

"Many toys were designed for all body types and genders. Take this O-Bunny." She held up a vibrator slightly bigger than her hand. It was shaped like the outline of a rabbit's head but was flat and thick like a jelly-filled donut. It was even embossed with a nose and whiskers like a bunny's.

"Looks innocent, right? Wrong." She pressed a button on the bottom. "There're so many fun ways to play with this. You can sit on it and ride it—gives new meaning to 'sit on my face.'"

"Yes!"

Trixie went on to explain how the rabbit "ears" could be used on other erogenous zones for different types of bodies. Sharing these kinds of toys was her favorite, because gender and body type shouldn't exclude anyone from pleasure. She noticed several people added O-Bunny to their wish lists as the vibe was passed around.

"Our company is releasing a brand-new toy next month, but I got my hands on an early sample." Trixie pulled out a medium-size lavender satin bag and held it up. "Who wants to see it?"

Cheers and hollers mixed with "Yeah!" echoed throughout the restaurant. Trixie smiled. She loved talking about new, innovative toys. This one was her favorite yet.

"Meet Whimsy." Trixie pulled out a flat, dark purple toy about ten inches long. The flat side of one end had three raised bumps. On the other end were short silicone bristles.

"Looks like a giant toothbrush," said a blond woman wearing purple cat-eye glasses. "They know we don't have teeth down there, right?"

Even Trixie roared with laughter. Now that the toothbrush reference had been made, she couldn't unsee it. She would, however, keep that joke for her next show.

"Whimsy is designed for everyone, no matter your body type. It might look like a toothbrush now, but not for long," Trixie continued once the laughter died down. "What makes this baby special isn't the medical-grade silicone or travel-lock function."

Trixie grabbed both ends of the toy and folded them toward each other. Then she pulled the ends in opposite directions. The crowd gasped.

"With Whimsy, you get endless possibilities because it bends in various positions. That's right, you become your very own sex toy designer." Trixie held up the toy, now curved into a relaxed *S* shape.

"There're five different motors embedded along Whimsy. They all vibrate independently. You can bend it into an *S* curve like this and use it on your G-spot. Or—" She manipulated the toy again. "Or make an ergonomic handle and tickle your fancy with the soft, silicone bristles. Make it curve for your body and ride it hands-free. You can even use it with your partner during intercourse or oral sex!"

"Won't that be awkward?" Heads turned toward the woman in braids. "Does it really fit during sex? With his penis, I mean."

The heads swiveled back to Trixie. They were relieved the woman had asked the question out loud.

"Since I only received them yesterday, I have not had a chance for any R&D." She laughed at her joke. It was a perk of her job, after all.

"Maybe you should try it out and get back to us!" someone near the buffet suggested. "What do you say, Andre?"

Trixie threw a quick glance at Andre. He grinned and gave her a thumbs-up. Trixie blushed and looked away. She'd intended to ask him to help her test it, but life had kept them busy. He'd been deep in his backlog of paperwork. She hadn't seen him since her samples arrived. She always ordered one for her demo kit and one for herself.

"As you know, vaginas are very adaptable. Bend it into a U for intercourse so the soft bristles stimulate your clit while these three nubs"—she pointed to the raised dots on the other end—"do their magic on your G-spot. Turn on Whimsy and both of you will vibrate your way to orgasms."

"I'm getting one! Me and Samantha are going to try it." A Latina woman on the left pointed to a very embarrassed woman who had to be Samantha.

"If you'll give me my first testimonial on the product, you can have it at cost!"

"Sold!" The woman pulled Samantha close and gave her a deep kiss. Their friends hooted and whistled.

The rest of the evening flew by as she turned on various toys and suggested ways to use them. For most pop-ups, this was the quiet part as everyone took notes, asked questions. Some laughed in surprise as they discovered the different settings of each toy.

Thirty minutes later, the last guests walked out, leaving with full stomachs and small bags of lubes and lotions to tide them over until their orders arrived. Even with the disruption from her accidental announcement, tonight's pop-up had gone very well. She even sold a few Whimsy toys.

"Want some help?" Without waiting for an answer, Zoe began removing batteries from the vibrators.

"Um, thanks." Trixie opened her suitcase and pulled out the small takeout container she used to store her batteries.

"I am so sorry," Zoe whispered, not very quietly. "I didn't mean to announce your personal life to your customers. I know you hate that."

"Nothing we can do about it now." She glanced at the bar. Andre was meticulously cleaning the bar. As usual. "It might have even helped with sales."

"Glad I could be of service." Zoe curtsied, looking very elegant in her purple maxi skirt. "You haven't dated anyone since you moved here. Or slept with anyone."

"We're not dating." Trixie shrugged. "We're just sleeping together. Having some fun. That's it."

"Sure. You also have a giant plastic bin of vibrators you could have fun with," Zoe scoffed.

"They're not the same and you know it."

Zoe raised her eyebrows.

"We're two consenting adults. We can keep our emotions apart from the physical stuff."

"That means you're still not talking to him about the co-op? You have to give Kait an answer in a week."

"I know time is running out," Trixie whispered. "But talking about it would involve emotions, wouldn't it? And no. It's better that way."

Trixie was trying to convince herself as much as Zoe. Since they stopped talking about her co-op and losing his building, sex had been fantastic. Because they didn't fight about it. You can't have fights about topics you didn't discuss. In fact, she looked forward to going back to his house tonight.

"I only remember the state you were in when you moved into

our apartment. I don't want you to get hurt again." Zoe handed Trixie the last of the papers and pens. "You can't hide your emotions forever. I see how you look at each other."

"Thank you for being such a good friend. I have it under control. It's only sex. Nothing more. He knows it, and I know it."

"I'm not an expert, but he's got it bad for you. Even if you can keep your feelings separate from the sex, he might not be able to."

Trixie could see the worry on her face.

"Don't lead him on if that's the case."

"I'll try not to," whispered Trixie.

"And tonight is totally a story for our next Boss Babes lunch!" Zoe clapped her hands and giggled.

"Don't tell Reina and Josie about my accidental confession," Trixie pleaded. "It's so embarrassing. I'm supposed to be a professional."

"You know I have to tell them." Zoe laughed, then hugged Trixie. "All we want is for you to be happy. Now let's finish putting away all your things."

The two quickly broke down her demo table. Zoe had gone to shows with Trixie in her early days, when Trixie needed emotional support, and knew exactly what to do and where everything went.

"How about I pick up some wine on the way home? We can watch *Crazy Rich Asians* again and pause on all the sexy man chests." Zoe placed the back of her hand on her forehead in an exaggerated swoon.

"So that's why that movie is so popular," Andre spoke from behind them.

"Andre!" How much of her conversation with Zoe had he heard? Trixie looked past him and glanced around the room.

"Keisha left. She has to study for her midterms."

"Already? I wanted to chat with her about what happened," said Trixie. "Is she okay with me and you—us?"

"She was thrilled. Keisha has been trying to play matchmaker since you walked into this restaurant."

"Thank goodness," she said with relief, then punched Andre in the arm.

"What was that for?" He rubbed his arm. "That really hurt."

"That's for not telling Keisha about us as we said you should."

"Trixie, relax. We talked about it, and she's very happy for us. Don't be surprised if she starts hinting about a ring."

"You told her we weren't serious, right?"

"I tried, but once she gets an idea in her head, I can't stop her."

"You two have already met, but let's make it official. This is my roommate and one of the Boss Babes, Zoe Tran." Trixie quickly introduced them.

"I thought she was your sister." Andre turned to Zoe.

Trixie gasped at his horrible joke. Zoe glared at him.

"You have so much in common. You're both beautiful and will kick my ass if I hurt Trixie." He flashed her a toothy smile.

Trixie shook her head, embarrassed for him.

"You got that right." Zoe grabbed the hand Andre offered and pulled him to her. Andre's smile turned into confusion. He cringed when Zoe squeezed his hand.

"You hurt Trixie and I will double knot you into a corset so tight, you won't be able to breathe. Then I'll kick your ass."

"Zoe!" Trixie held back a laugh. Most people assumed Zoe was sweet because of her quiet, thoughtful demeanor. Trixie knew better.

"Yes, ma'am." Andre looked Zoe square in the eyes. "I only have good intentions toward Trixie."

"Not too good, I hope. That would be a waste." Zoe released his hand. "How about a rain check on girls' night? I think you two have some things to talk about."

"I'll text you on my way home." Trixie hugged her friend and whispered, "Thank you for being you."

"Remember what I said about earlier. Cut him loose before he falls too hard."

Trixie nodded, worried it might be too late.

CHAPTER 28

I'm scared of her," Andre mock whispered as he locked the door behind Zoe.

"You should be." Trixie laughed. "Zoe may be quiet, but she'll throw down for us if need be. We Boss Babes stick together."

"Want a drink?"

"But you just cleaned the bar."

"Why do we have to go through this every night you're here? I don't mind making you a drink."

"How about a pinot grigio? Then you won't have to dirty up anything but a wineglass."

"I'm always happy to dirty things up for you." He smirked and poured a very generous glass of wine. Then grabbed a beer for himself.

"What a night. I'm exhausted." She pressed the cold wineglass against her face. "That feels so good."

"You're supposed to drink it."

"Don't worry, I will." She took a large swallow. "So Keisha's been trying to set us up the entire time? How come you never told me?"

"I thought she was trying to push my buttons. I didn't know she really meant it." He shrugged. "She wants you to come to family dinner next week."

"Are you sure that's a good idea? Won't I scandalize your neighbors?"

Right. He did imply that before they officially partnered for the pop-ups.

"I don't care who knows we're together. You're talented, kind, and wicked smart. If they can't handle what you do for a living, then they'll have to fight me." He hopped like a boxer and put two fists up.

"You look so dorky right now. Sexy but dorky." She laughed, but then her laughter faded as she traced her fingers on the bar. "If I show up to your family dinner, then everyone will assume I'm your girlfriend."

"What's wrong with that?" He wanted to tell everyone she was his girlfriend, not just his "friend."

"We agreed to keep things chill between us. No strings," she reminded him.

"If it makes you feel better, I'll introduce you as my 'good friend.' If they pry, I'll change the subject and tell them that you tempted me with your flavored lube."

"You wouldn't!" She dipped her fingers in her wine and flicked it at him. "If I was going to tempt you, I'd pick something more exciting than lube."

"Like Whimsy?" Andre had been thinking about the toy ever since she demo'd it. "It sounds like a lot of fun."

"Yes, I've been dying to test it out." She pointed at her purple suitcase with her products in it. "I convinced my manager to send me two testers. One for my demo kit and one for me."

"What are we waiting for? Let's go to my place!" He dumped out her wineglass and washed it.

"Hey! I wasn't finished with that."

"I promise to make it up to you." He pressed his lips on her cheek. "Multiple times."

"I'll hold you to that." Trixie turned her head until their lips met. She pulled him in for a deep kiss.

"Let's wrap everything up and head home," he said when they finally broke apart. "You grab that toy and put it in your purse."

It was almost midnight when they finally locked the door to Mama Hazel's. They'd decided it was better to leave her car parked there and walk to his home. After some back and forth, Trixie relented and let him carry her demo kit as they walked the few short blocks.

The early October night was crisp and a little chilly. He'd forgotten to grab his jacket from his office. Trixie wore a sweater dress that clung to her body in all the right places. It must have been thin, because she shivered in the light breeze.

"Cold?"

When she nodded, he wrapped his free arm around her waist and pulled her close. They walked in sync down the street, stepping over sidewalks split by oak tree roots. Everything about this moment was perfect. He tried to memorize the way her black hair tickled his cheek when the wind picked up. How the curve of her hip bumped against his as they walked under the yellow glow of streetlamps.

"Ready?" he asked when they arrived at his stoop.

She nodded. Andre picked up her suitcase and carried it up the six short steps onto his small porch. He motioned for her to walk softly as they made their way upstairs.

"I feel like a teenager sneaking back into my room after staying out past curfew," he whispered as he locked his bedroom door behind them. "I don't want to wake up Keisha since she has her exam in the morning."

"What were you like as a teenager?" she asked, untucking his shirt. "I can't imagine you as an awkward teen."

"I was the worst teenager." He lifted his arms as she pulled the shirt over his head. "Awkward and horny."

Trixie giggled. Her warm breath sent shivers across his chest. "I don't believe it."

Her hot tongue circled his nipple. He inhaled sharply.

"There's no awkward bone in your body. Horny, on the other hand . . ." She dropped kisses on his chest. One after the other, traveling down until she reached the waistband of his jeans.

"I can think of at least one," he groaned.

She unbuttoned the fly and slid both jeans and his boxer shorts down to his ankles.

"Found it," she whispered as his erection was freed. She kissed the head of his cock.

Andre inhaled sharply and braced himself against the door. Trixie went down on her knees and cupped his balls. She licked the underside of his cock, sending electric shocks down his legs. He was about to lose his mind, and her hand had barely touched him.

"Aren't we supposed to test Whimsy?" he gasped as she swirled her tongue around his swollen head.

She paused and pulled away. Cold air hit his cock as she released it from her grasp.

"Oh, yeah. Let me grab it out of my purse. Don't move."

Trixie smiled to herself as she dug through her bag. She'd forgotten how much fun it was to tease Andre. Put him on edge this way. He preferred to be in control in the bedroom, but not tonight. Sometimes he needed to lean back and enjoy her attention. He preferred focusing on her pleasure but turnaround was fair play.

If he could tease her to the edge of orgasm and pull back, then he deserved a taste of his own medicine.

"Found it!" She pulled a small bottle of lube and the toy out of a satin bag. Waving it at him, she said, "I even charged it this morning before I came to the restaurant."

"Always prepared, my Trixie." He smiled in the moonlight.

"Since Whimsy arrived, I've thought of several different ways to try it out."

She grabbed his hand and pulled him to the bed. He sat down, cock jutting up between his thighs. What a sight he was to look at. The moonlight accentuated his jawline, the taut muscles of his arms, and his very hard cock. It took all her willpower not to mount him right then and ride herself into oblivion.

"I want to try all of them." His voice was husky. "But you're a bit overdressed for the occasion."

Trixie looked at her sweater dress and laughed. Setting the vibrator on the bed, she grabbed the bottom of her sweater and pulled it smoothly over her head.

"Better?"

"You're not wearing a bra. Or panties." His eyes widened. "When did you take them off?"

"I took them off while you were cleaning up the bar."

"Dammit, woman," he said hoarsely. "Come here."

Instead of sitting on the bed next to him, she knelt between his thighs. She squeezed a thin line of lube down the toy's length. Trixie rolled the ends of the bendable toy until it formed a circle. She slid it down his length.

"Sorry the lube is cold. It will warm up soon."

The room was dark, so it took her a few tries to find the controls.

After a few false pushes, the vibrator sprang to life. The buzzing sounded like a concert in the silence of the night.

"What the—!" Andre's hips bucked off the bed as the vibrations traveled across his cock.

"Shhh," she whispered, and rubbed circles on his inner thigh. "Relax and just feel."

He leaned back onto the bed, legs still hanging off the edge. His cock stood to attention, almost perpendicular to his supine body. Vibrations from Whimsy made his hard-on twitch. The tip of it glistened with his arousal under the pale yellowish streetlamp light that managed to bypass his window curtains.

Andre looked absolutely delectable.

She braced her hands on his knees and pulled herself up until her lips were a few inches from the tip of his dark brown cock. Wrapping one hand around the vibrator she'd rolled into a cock ring, she squeezed gently.

Trixie was rewarded with a sharp inhale from Andre. Opening her lips, she breathed on his cock. Goose bumps broke out on his thighs as they trembled. With a flick of her tongue, she tasted his offering.

A deep moan filled her ears. Taking that as encouragement, she wrapped her lips around his hardness and slid down until she could take no more of his length. Whimsy would help her with the rest. The lube allowed the vibe to glide smoothly across his skin, turning the bendable toy into a stroker.

"Oh, fuck," Andre muttered.

Feeling Trixie's warm mouth around his cock shot tingles across his abdomen and down his legs. Then she started moving the vibrator up and down his shaft.

The sensations overwhelmed his body. It was almost too much, yet he didn't want her to stop doing whatever the hell she was doing down there. When he'd suggested Whimsy, he'd imagined using it on her. Andre fought the urge to pull her up and flip her onto the bed. He wanted to be the one making her feel good. Be responsible for her pleasure.

But everything felt so damned good. It was all he could do not to roll his hips and pump himself into her hot, tight mouth. The vibrations skating up and down and up again on his cock didn't make it easier. He was losing his mind. Losing control of his body. If she kept going, he would explode in her mouth. And the evening would end much sooner than he wanted.

"Trixie," he moaned. "I'm going to come if you keep doing that."

"Mmmm," she replied as her head bobbed. She didn't stop.

"Want you to come first," he gasped, and reached for her. "At least twice."

"Not yet. I'm having too much fun."

Trixie relished taking control. Making him powerless to the sensations she gave him. She wanted to make him beg her for mercy. Beg her to finish him off.

She slid her mouth down again, this time taking him so deep that her lips touched the vibrator around his shaft. In slow motion she released him, her tongue swirling, drawing a code on his sensitive skin.

"You, my darling, are fucking tasty."

"Trixie, please," he begged.

Andre was right where she wanted him. His muscles were taut and his legs shook as he tried to hold back his release. But he didn't reach out for her or try to pull her on top of him.

Finally, he surrendered to her. Trixie's pussy throbbed at this realization. His willingness to let her be herself. Let her lead without hesitation.

"What a good boy," she crooned. "Good boys always get rewarded."

She pulled herself up and onto the bed. A quick reach into his nightstand and she pulled out a condom. Straddling his legs, she slid it onto him. Instead of taking him inside of her, she sat so his cock was nestled between her thighs.

"Feel how wet you made me?" She undulated her hips so he could feel her slickness over his still tingling and vibrating cock.

"Babe, I need you," he panted. "I want to feel you wrapped around my cock."

"What's the magic word?" She laughed at his demands and rolled her hips until his cock slid between her outer lips. Andre inhaled as wet heat surrounded him. His eyes rolled as the scent of her arousal reached his nose.

"Ask nicely, my human vibrator." She giggled.

Andre blinked his eyes open. Did she just call him a—

"Don't worry," she said as she reached between her thighs to grab his erection. "You belong only to me. I own the patent on the Andre-powered vibrator."

Before he could respond, she slipped him into her. Andre groaned as her tight muscles stretched to fit him. She straddled him, taking him as deep as she could with the toy wrapped around the base of his cock.

Trixie closed her eyes as her body began to hum. With the vibrator pressed between them, the buzzing spread over their bodies. They were vibrating together. The same frequency.

Never in his life had he felt so connected to anyone. Finally, she had claimed him as hers. She wanted him. No, *needed* him.

Andre grabbed her hips and began to slide her up and down his length.

"Yes, Andre." She flattened her palms on his chest and rode him. "Fuck, that feels amazing."

She felt amazing. He wasn't sure he could hold back his orgasm any longer. As their rhythm increased, neither of them could form words. Grunts, moans, hisses flew from her lips as she tilted her hips until his cock rubbed on her G-spot. Her inner muscles grabbed him with each pull. Tightened as he pushed his way back inside her. Their bodies vibrated together.

"Almost. There," she gasped. She sat up and reached between them to find her clit.

His hands dug into her hips as she moved faster. Her hand a blur as she rubbed herself. Muscles clenched his cock so tightly, he had to pull her down harder to slide back in. Trixie's head lolled back, but her hand continued moving.

"Come," he gasped as he felt a heat rush over his body. "Come on my cock."

Trixie arched her back and cried out. Her orgasm shot through her body. Hands still on her hips, he continued pumping into her. He felt every shudder as pleasure exploded through her body.

"Andre, come with me!" she moaned. Trixie leaned over and sealed her lips over his mouth. Their tongues clashed as she rode him hard.

That was all he needed to take him over the edge. With one deep thrust, he exploded inside her tight heat. His body quaked as his orgasm overtook him. When his hands dropped to his side, she continued to roll her hips, letting him ride out his waves of pleasure.

"Damn, babe," he whispered.

She slid off him and removed the toy. He'd almost forgotten about it, but its vibrations were too intense for their now very sensitive bodies. Trixie turned it off and set the toy on his nightstand.

"You were amazing, Andre," she said. Her body was still humming, as if she'd drunk a cà phê sữa đá. Taking charge energized her. She needed to do it more often.

"Let me take care of this." He disposed of the condom and slid back into bed. Trixie turned to face him.

"I think Whimsy is a winner," she declared. "Thanks for helping me with R&D."

She knew it would be good, but tonight had been mind-blowing. Maybe it wasn't just the toy, but the power it gave her. No, the power was hers. She earned it.

"Anytime. I'd do anything for you, Trixie. Not that it was a great sacrifice."

"Andre, thank you."

"For what?" He pulled her tighter against him.

"For inviting me to help at community dinner. You've talked so much about your neighbors. I want to meet them." Trixie wanted to meet the people who shaped Andre as a kid. The ones for whom he'd taken responsibility without being asked. Now that he was older, his love for his community was what gave him purpose.

ANDRE'S HEART LEAPT. She wanted to be part of his life that didn't involve his bed. And meet his neighbors, no, his extended family.

"I'm glad you agreed, babe." He kept his voice steady, as if this wasn't a big deal. "We can always use extra hands."

"Good. I'll come by early and you can put me to work." Yawning, she pulled his arm tighter around her waist. Andre buried his face in her hair and breathed in the lingering citrus shampoo.

Giving himself over to her tonight had been hard, but she'd given him no choice. He actually enjoyed it.

He felt safe around Trixie. That no matter how bad things got, she'd keep him moving forward. She had big dreams and wanted to lift others up with her.

"I should have never left you the way I did."

He stroked her hair. "Because I never stopped loving you, Trixie."

Crap. The words had slipped out. Things had been so good between them the past few weeks. Now he had to ruin it with the L-word. She wasn't ready, but hearing her talk about bussing tables for their community dinner—she wanted to be part of his life, too. Not just his bed or his business.

He waited for her to panic. For her to run out the door. She remained still.

"Trixie?" He brushed her hair aside and looked at her face. Trixie was asleep.

Andre closed his eyes, glad that she hadn't heard his declaration of love. Things had been so good between them, the last thing he wanted to do was scare her away. He'd tell her after family dinner, after she'd met all the important people in his life. They'd love her as much as he loved her.

CHAPTER 29

Trixie eased the front door to her apartment open as quietly as she could. She'd snuck away before Andre woke up. Sitting in Friday-morning rush hour gave her plenty of time to relive the previous night over and over. It wasn't the passionate sex that she replayed but what he'd confessed to her after.

Andre said he loved her. He still loved her and had never stopped. She'd been in such shock that she faked being asleep. Not the most mature way to respond, but he'd caught her off guard.

Zoe was right. Trixie had let things go too far. She cared about him, but she wanted to join the co-op, too. He'd made it clear that she had to pick a side. But what if things weren't so cut and dry? She didn't want to hurt him, but—

"Morning!"

Trixie shrieked. Zoe was making coffee in the kitchen.

"Sorry," her roommate apologized. "Why are you sneaking into your own apartment?"

"I didn't want to wake you."

"Actually, I've been up most of the night working on my blog. I'm chugging some coffee before I lay down for a nap. Want some?"

Trixie shook her head even though she was exhausted. She dropped her bags by the front door and threw herself on the couch. If she fell asleep, she didn't have to deal with her feelings about Andre. Or even what those feelings were.

"Oh, sweetie, what's wrong?" Zoe rushed over and pressed her coffee mug into Trixie's hands. "Drink."

"Last night Andre said he loved me." Trixie took a sip of coffee and handed it back.

"I see." Zoe had the grace not to say *I told you so*. Her roommate had warned her, and Trixie had brushed her off.

"I'm freaking out," Trixie confessed. She told her how they'd tried out Whimsy together. "Everything was fine until we cuddled up for pillow talk. I was sleepy from my after-sex glow. That's when he dropped the L-bomb."

"What did you say?"

"Nothing. I pretended I was asleep." Trixie covered her face and groaned. "I can't do this."

Zoe rubbed Trixie's arm, encouraging her to continue.

"He's not supposed to fall in love with me. We were keeping it strictly casual. And Keisha has joked about us getting married." Marriage was not in her five-year plan. Though Trixie was relieved that Keisha finally knew about her and Andre. They'd become close, and she didn't want to sabotage her friendship with Keisha. Though now it might be too late.

"That escalated fast. His sister only learned about you two yesterday."

"He said he'd never stopped loving me. He has no right to say that after everything he put me through. Like it's supposed to make everything all right?" Trixie was angry. At herself for letting him back into her bed. Angry at him for—what? For loving her?

All this time, she'd reminded herself over and over that Andre was only a fun detour. She thought she could handle keeping things physical only. Then he shared his feelings with her. He let himself be vulnerable around her. All things he didn't do back in New Orleans. He *had* changed.

"I think I love him, too," Trixie whispered. Saying it out loud scared her, but she repeated it. "Oh my God, I love Andre."

"That's not bad, is it?"

"When I'm in love, I make bad decisions," said Trixie. Like in New Orleans when she second-guessed her decision to tell her parents. "Not this time. I have to tell him I want to be a part of this co-op."

"Wait, what did I miss?" Zoe's eyebrows furrowed. "You just admitted to loving him and now you're talking about the shop?"

"I want to lease this co-op so bad, Zoe. It's one step closer to my dream."

"But?"

"By choosing the co-op, I'm choosing his enemy. How could I do that to the man I love?"

"Trixie, you are not his enemy," Zoe scoffed. "He should never have put you in that position."

"Why do I feel like I should turn down the co-op for him? I can't put my dreams on hold." Her boutique was just beyond her grasp. She only had to step forward. Once the co-op was open and flourishing, her parents would be proud of her again. Her dad would talk to her once more.

"I'm going to tell him after community dinner," Trixie resolved. "If he loves me like he said, he'll understand why this is so important for me."

"Wait!" Zoe held up a finger. "What if you don't have to choose between him and District Market?"

"What do you mean?"

"I have lots of space in my shop. Why don't you open Happy Endings at Something Cheeky?" Zoe's eyes sparkled as she clapped her hands.

"Wait, you're serious?" Trixie studied Zoe, whose body was visibly buzzing with excitement.

"It's a great pairing and we'd have so much fun together!"

Trixie could tell her roommate was mentally rearranging her shop to make room for Happy Endings. Zoe's spacious lingerie boutique had plenty of room, one of the luxuries of leasing a spot in a suburban Falls Church strip mall.

"Can I think about it?"

Zoe's face fell.

"Oh, no, I mean we would have fun together. My toys complement your custom lingerie so well." Trixie hugged her friend. "You're always so generous and I love you for it. I've had my heart set on my own shop for so long. It's hard to change your dreams overnight."

"I get it. I felt the same way about Something Cheeky and didn't want to settle." Zoe squeezed Trixie's arm. "You should never settle when it comes to your dreams."

"Thanks for understanding." Once again, Trixie thanked the universe for putting Zoe and the rest of the Boss Babes into her life.

"You have to do what's right for you." Zoe pointed at Trixie. "Not me. And definitely not Andre."

Trixie nodded. She had plenty of time to think about all of it before next week's community dinner. Then she'd talk it over with Andre. He loved her. She'd heard him. He would support her no matter what. He had to.

MAMA HAZEL'S WAS packed the following Monday for community dinner. Andre sent Xavier to the coffee shop two blocks down to borrow chairs. Columbus Day—or Indigenous Peoples' Day, as Keisha called it—was a federal holiday. In DC you couldn't throw a rock without hitting someone who had the day off. He hoped Luis and Keisha had prepared enough food.

The last time their dining room had been this full was his mother's celebration of life two years ago. Neighbors had packed into the restaurant to pay their respects and recall their favorite memories about his mother.

Andre was nervous. Tonight he was more or less introducing Trixie as his girlfriend to his elders. They'd all given him dating advice or remarked how he hadn't dated anyone since he came back home. He was pretty sure Mrs. Harris and the others wouldn't hesitate to share their opinions about his love life.

It didn't matter what his elders thought. He loved Trixie and wanted her in his life. After dinner was over, he planned to make it official and ask her to be his girlfriend. Their friends-with-benefits arrangement had evolved into more, just as he'd hoped. The two of them had connected on a deeper level than before. When he shared his fears and the pressure of saving the restaurant, she consoled him and offered to help. She understood his need to preserve this neighborhood.

Andre tried to ignore the jittery feeling in his stomach and looked for his Trixie. She never brought up his declaration of love from Friday night, which confirmed that she was asleep. He was relieved that she missed it. Telling her he loved her right after sex felt so cliché. Tonight was his chance for a do-over.

He spotted Trixie running from table to table with pitchers of soda and sweet tea. She wore a black T-shirt emblazoned with IT'S AN HONOR TO BE ASIAN and a pair of tight jeans that hugged her curves. Her eyes sparkled and a smile lit her face as she stopped to greet each person. His neighbors were enamored of her, too.

Seeing her in this part of her life filled him with happiness. It was a strange feeling. One he hadn't allowed himself to feel since his mother died.

"You got it bad, bro," said Xavier, sweat dripping down his face from dragging a dozen chairs into the restaurant. "Can I get a glass of water?"

"Yeah, I guess I do." Andre smiled and slid a glass over to Xavier.

"Did you just agree with me?"

"I'm going to ask her to officially be my girlfriend tonight. After everyone's gone." Andre turned his attention back to the dirty glasses under the bar. He knew Xavier would have a field day with his announcement.

"Ooooh, Andre has a girlfriend," Xavier sang. Right on cue.

"Shhh! Everyone will hear you." But Andre couldn't stop the wide smile creeping onto his face.

"I'm happy for you, man." Xavier clapped him on the shoulder. "Does she know how you feel?"

"I think so." Andre thought about last Friday. Their intense connection during—no, it was more than sex. They had made love. "She might even be the one."

Xavier and Andre watched as Trixie charmed every table she stopped at. Everyone beamed when she stopped at their table to refill drinks and take away their dirty plates. Even grumpy Mrs. Harris smiled at her, then turned to wink at Andre in approval. Trixie caught the two of them looking her way and waved. Andre waved back.

"Whoa. My man Tre is ready to settle down. Another one bites the dust." Xavier exaggerated a sad face.

"Don't make fun of me. You'll fall in love someday."

"Nope, love ain't for me. That's all you." Xavier emptied his glass and passed it to Andre. "I better get back in the kitchen and help Keisha."

"Thanks for grabbing the chairs, bro."

"I had to promise to read my poetry at their open-mic night. You owe me big time." Xavier gave a mock salute and walked back into the kitchen.

Andre's only regret about leaving New Orleans was leaving Trixie. He didn't regret coming back to take care of his family. Not just his mom and Keisha, but his neighbors. Even nosy Mrs. Harris. Now that his mom was gone, it was his job to keep his extended family together. Take care of them the same way she had.

Trixie had taught him that he didn't have to do it alone. As long as she was by his side, he could handle whatever life threw at him.

Andre's phone rang. A number he didn't recognize had been calling all weekend. Worried that it was a creditor or something worse, he declined the call. Someone from California had been calling the last few days but didn't leave any messages. Whoever it was, they could wait until tomorrow. Tonight he was going to focus on his friends and family.

The damned phone rang again. He had a feeling it would keep ringing if he didn't answer. He swiped the green button.

"Hello?"

"Hi, Mr. Walker? I'm calling on behalf of your new landlord. Do you have a few minutes?"

"Wow, I CAN see why you love these Monday-night dinners." Trixie wiped down the last table. "Do people usually stay this late?"

"Not usually," replied Andre, who was wiping down the bar. "I think we had such a great turnout because of the holiday."

It was almost midnight. He didn't look at all tired. She caught him humming after Keisha and Xavier had left an hour ago. Trixie had hoped to talk to Andre about the co-op sooner. The restaurant had been packed, and the mood festive. Now she was exhausted and didn't want to dampen his happy mood.

"Thanks again for letting me help out tonight," Trixie said after putting away the cleaning supplies. She didn't know where to start the conversation, but she didn't want the awkwardness between them whenever District Market came up in conversation.

Trixie had thought long and hard about Zoe's offer. Starting Happy Endings at her best friend's boutique was a good stepping-stone to having a stand-alone shop. But that wasn't her dream. She wanted to do everything on her own so she could show her parents what she was capable of. To prove to herself what she was capable of when she followed her heart.

"You were amazing." Andre came up behind her and wrapped his arms around her waist.

She let herself relax in his embrace for a few seconds. If this conversation didn't go well, this may be the last time he'd hold her.

"There's something I have to ask you." Andre gave her a light kiss on the cheek.

"Andre, we need to talk about the co-op."

She unlatched his arms and turned around to face him. She grabbed his hands. He bit his lip and his eyebrows furrowed, but he didn't speak.

"I want to do it." There. She said it.

"Do what?" His confused eyes searched her face. "You mean open your store at the co-op?"

Trixie released a breath she didn't know she was holding. "Yes. It's the opportunity I've been waiting for. It's a perfect starter space until Happy Endings can have its own store."

"I thought we talked about this already." He released her hands and stepped back. "Can't you see my side of this?"

"I understand you hate what District Market represents, but Kait's co-op isn't the enemy. Me turning down this lease won't stop what's happening in your neighborhood."

"If you cared about me and Mama Hazel's, you'd find a different way to open your store."

"You said you loved me. How does giving me an ultimatum show me that?" Trixie was livid. How dare he suggest she didn't care about him or this restaurant? After all the time she'd spent with him, to taste his new dishes and their pop-ups.

Andre was stunned. She'd heard him that night. Heard him profess his love to her and ignored it. Now she wanted to open her shop at District Market. Of all the places in the DMV, she had to choose that town center. He wanted her to be happy and succeed, but there had to be another way.

"I—I do love you," he whispered. "You heard me and didn't say anything."

"I'm sorry, Andre. I needed time to think."

"Do you love me?"

She opened her mouth and closed it.

There was his answer right there. She didn't love him. Or if she did, not enough. Now she was doing the one thing he didn't want her to do. And to think he was going to ask her to officially be his girlfriend tonight.

"We can save Mama Hazel's together," Trixie pleaded. "Once

I'm up and running, I'll send customers to Mama Hazel's for lunch. We can still do pop-ups here."

"It's too late." He shook his head. "I have a meeting with the new landlord next week. He probably wants to deliver the bad news in person."

"Do you want me to join you? What if Keisha and I get a petition started? We can call the news and see if—"

"Trixie, I need time to think." Andre's head began to pound. He'd finally felt a little happiness and now it was gone. Everything was tumbling down again. "I'll call you in a few days."

"I'm sorry you think I'm choosing between you or District Market. I'm not."

She leaned in to kiss him, but he turned away. Andre was all out of ideas. Maybe it was time to admit defeat.

Trixie opened her mouth and closed it. This time, it was she who walked out on him.

CHAPTER 30

I miss my Babes." Reina raised her drink for a toast. "I get out of sorts when we go too long between meetings."

"No kidding," Zoe said. "I'm up to my neck in custom orders. For which I have Josie to thank."

"My boudoir clients are looking for unique lingerie for their shoots, so I have to refer them to the very best," explained Josie.

"A toast to the Bitchin' Boss Babes!" Trixie raised her glass to meet her friends'.

"Bitchin'!" Reina declared. Trixie echoed her friends' cheers.

While her friends gave updates on their businesses and asked for advice, Trixie checked her phone again. Two days. The number of days since she'd heard from Andre. Their last conversation had gone horribly. She was giving him the space he asked for, but this was the longest they'd gone without any contact. It felt strange not to receive a meme or emoji from him every day.

"You all right, Trixie?" Josie waved a hand in front of Trixie's face.

Trixie blinked, remembering she was still with the Boss Babes.

"Tell them," Zoe prodded. "Unless you want me to."

Trixie shook her head. Though based on the number of times she'd recalled the conversation and overanalyzed it with Zoe, her roommate could retell it verbatim. Trixie quickly filled in Josie and Reina on what had happened between her and Andre. From when he said *I love you* to when he accused her of not caring about him or the restaurant.

"What are you going to do now?" Josie asked.

"I'm going to sign the lease. If you can loan me the deposit." Trixie looked at each of her best friends. They nodded. "Thank you. I'll pay you back as soon as I win this contest."

"And Andre?" Reina asked. Zoe tried to shush her. "Come on, we were all wondering."

"If I don't hear from him today or tomorrow, I'm going to assume things are over between us." She couldn't believe that she'd let him do this to her again. Ghosting her.

"If he can't support your dreams, then he doesn't deserve to be part of your life," said Josie. "We believe in you."

"You three are the best friends I could ever have." Trixie smiled through her sadness. "Thank you for believing in me."

"We've always believed in you," said Reina. "Let's go to Lucky Stiff tonight and celebrate. Drinks on the house!"

"I'm in. It's been too long since we went out together." Zoe grinned. "What's tonight's theme, Reina?"

"My dancers are very into superheroes right now."

"My two worlds colliding! Hot men dancing and cosplay." Zoe turned to Trixie. "Please say you'll go out."

"That does sound fun, but I have so much to do to get ready for my store."

"You have to celebrate your wins," Josie reminded her.

"Fine, twist my arm." Trixie didn't need much convincing to watch Reina's dancers perform. The shows were as much art as they were entertainment. "It'll be nice to hang out and not talk shop."

Tonight she'd go out with her friends and try to forget about Andre.

"Trixie, I heard you were here today." Keisha waved from the doorway of a meeting room. She had a backpack slung over her shoulder.

"I had some free time so I dropped by. I'm sending out donor letters." Trixie motioned to a stack of letters, envelopes, and stamps on the table. "Want to join me?"

"I was on my way to study group, then to prep for dinner service." Keisha pulled up a chair next to Trixie and set her bag on the floor. "Got a minute?"

"Sure." Trixie searched Keisha's face. Did Andre send his sister to check on her? She was now going on day three with no contact from him. There was nothing on Keisha's face that hinted at him or their fight.

"Thank you for helping out with dinner on Monday. With all the pop-ups and this week's community dinner, you must be tired of Mama Hazel's!"

"Not really." At least not until her fight with Andre. "Helping out at community dinner reminded me of home."

There was a sense of family among the regulars at their community dinners that made Trixie miss her large extended family. Though they weren't related by blood, they cared for each other. People like Mrs. Harris looked out for her neighbors, even if she came off as nosy.

"I'm glad you and Andre are together," blurted Keisha. "I was hoping from that very first bachelorette party that you two would hit it off."

So Andre hadn't told his sister about their disagreements. How much was he keeping from her? Trixie didn't have the heart to tell Keisha what happened after Monday's dinner.

"Did he tell you that we knew each other in New Orleans?" Trixie tested to see how much Keisha knew about their past.

"No, he didn't." Keisha gasped. "That makes so much sense now! That's why you two get along so well. You already knew each other."

"I guess you can say that," Trixie sputtered. Why did he keep so many things from his sister? Trixie debated telling Keisha the truth about their past.

"Maybe you'll be my sister-in-law someday," Keisha said hopefully.

"What? Andre and I—we're just casual." Trixie wasn't ready to tell Keisha that she hadn't talked to Andre since Monday night.

"Could have fooled me!" Keisha laughed. "I hear you doing the walk of shame in the mornings."

"Sorry for waking you." Trixie's cheeks burned.

"It's not just that. Andre hasn't dated anyone since he came back. Not even a fling. The fact that he's bringing you to the house means he's really into you. You make him happy."

"Oh." Trixie began folding the letters, carefully lining up the edges to create a trifold. She didn't know how to respond.

Andre might have been into her but not anymore. She'd given him space like he asked. The last three days of radio silence felt too much like he was ghosting her again. Trixie refused to feel that lost and helpless ever again.

"Look at me rambling on. I'll be late for study group." Keisha checked the time on her phone. "I'll be so glad when this semester is over, and I can work in the restaurant full time."

"Wait, you're quitting school? Aren't you halfway done?"

"Halfway done for a major I hate." Keisha sighed. "I thought a business major would give me a leg up on running Mama Hazel's, but so far it's just boring theory and lame accounting spreadsheets."

"Based on Andre's complaints, there're a lot of spreadsheets." Trixie nodded. "Running a business requires a lot of planning and work. I'm glad I have the Boss Babes to help me."

"I'd rather have real-life experience than textbooks written by folks who sit at a computer all day."

"Have you thought about changing majors?"

"Sort of. I've considered changing to hospitality management." Keisha pursed her lips and paused. "I have some big ideas to revitalize Mama Hazel's, but I'm worried Andre won't give them a chance. We have to make some drastic changes if the restaurant is going to survive. He thinks I don't know how bad things are, but I took accounting. I know how to read our books."

He'd promised Trixie that he would tell Keisha about the building being sold. It was obvious that Keisha knew nothing about it. There might not be a restaurant for her to manage soon. Once she quit school, it would be harder to go back. Trixie knew that firsthand. She silently cursed Andre for keeping so many secrets from his sister.

"Anyway, that's not why I wanted to talk to you," Keisha continued, oblivious to Trixie's discomfort talking about Andre. "The older ladies had a blast chatting with you at dinner. They wanted all the dirt on you. They could tell you and Andre are dating. He kept making heart eyes at you all night."

Trixie's heart softened. He had tossed her many sexy glances that evening. But she remembered how angry and uncompromising he'd been afterward, when she told him about leasing the co-op.

"They'd heard rumors about your pop-ups. After I explained what they were and your classes at the clinic—they want in on the fun." Keisha leaned in. "They want you to do a private pop-up for them."

"Really?" Trixie's mouth hung open.

"Andre is gonna kill me if he finds out. Mrs. Harris, Mrs. Kim, all of them helped raise us. They're like family. Which is why he does not want to think about our elders having sex." Keisha covered her face with her hands. "I'm not sure I do either, but they are sexual beings, too."

Trixie's heart beat faster. This was exactly why she loved her job. No one had taught her about sex. She learned it all from magazines and romance books. Most of the older women who attended her classes at the clinic never talked about sex with anyone. Not even their husbands.

"I'll do it!" She may not have a boutique of her own in which to hold classes, but the least she could do was continue teaching. Especially to eager students.

"Hurray!" Keisha clapped her hands. She pulled out her phone. "Let's pick a date. I'll make Xavier take Andre out for the night, so he'll be too busy to know what's going on."

Trixie consulted her calendar app and compared it to Keisha's.

"Since we're now closed on Tuesday and Wednesday nights, let's do one of those. It needs to be early in the evening. Mrs. Harris will give me an earful if we keep her up past her bedtime."

"How about next Tuesday? Is four days enough time to set everything up?"

"That should work. We'll have some decent leftovers from family dinner to serve beforehand. I can also fry up some chicken if needed."

Trixie added the date to her calendar app.

"Are you sure Xavier can drag Andre away from the restaurant?" she asked.

"Xavier is very creative," replied Keisha. "He got me out of a lot of trouble when we were kids. Of course, he was the one that got us into trouble in the first place!"

"Next Tuesday then. You'll get the word out?"

"It won't be hard. News travels fast around here."

"Great, I'll start planning." She'd take this opportunity to test out a new workshop idea for her co-op space. Trixie's mind raced as she created a mental list of her top products for postmenopausal women. She couldn't wait to tell the Boss Babes.

TUESDAY MORNING, SHE opened the Boss Babe's group chat on her phone. Over the past few days, Trixie had stewed over her conversation with Keisha. She was angry at Andre for keeping his sister in the dark about their new landlord. Keisha had a right to know, but Trixie wasn't sure if it was her place.

Her fingers flew across the on-screen keyboard as she explained her dilemma. In no time at all, her phone started blowing up with her friends' responses.

Reina: Tell Keisha. She deserves to know.

Trixie: Ugh, he told me not to tell her. He's so hardheaded!

Reina: Isn't that why you're sleeping with him?

Zoe: REINA!

Josie: 😵

Zoe: He put you in a bad spot. Not cool.

Trixie tapped her fingers on the arm of her couch. She and Keisha were friends. Trixie owed it to her. She'd given Andre plenty of time to tell his sister. But she didn't want to put herself in the middle of their family problems. She and Andre were already at odds about the co-op. Telling Keisha would only pile on to their fight.

Reina: Let's invite her to girls' night. Then I'll drop the info casual-like.

Josie: Don't ambush that poor woman.

Trixie: No time for girls' night. Am seeing Keisha at class tonight.

Reina: ☹ Fine. Make Andre tell her.

Trixie: He's not returning my texts. Plus he doesn't know about tonight.

Zoe: Kick butt tonight! Make sure they all buy vibrators.

Trixie grinned. She was looking forward to the pop-up. After talking to the doctor at the clinic about menopausal and postmenopausal women's bodies, she'd prepared goody bags filled

with samples of lube designed for postmenopausal women, en-
hancing creams, and edible lotions.

Trixie: Keep your fingers crossed Andre stays away from the
restaurant.

Reina: Tell him a bunch of old ladies are talking about vibrators.
He'll run! 😬

Trixie: Keisha says he'll flip out.

Zoe: Xavier will keep him away. Don't worry.

Trixie: He will because he's scared of Keisha. LOL.

Josie: Whatever happens, we're here for you.

Trixie: I have to get ready. Thanks, Babes!

She set her phone down and picked up her cold tea. Trixie had
no idea what she should do, but right now she needed to focus on
the pop-up.

CHAPTER 31

"Why did you drag me to open-mic night?" Andre was not in the mood to deal with Xavier's antics. He didn't know how to answer Trixie's texts, but now they'd stopped. Then there was tomorrow's tenant meeting with their new landlord.

"Because you owe me." Xavier handed him a pint of DC Brau pilsner. "Remember when I borrowed the chairs for last week's dinner?"

"Sorry, man." He'd forgotten. At least the coffee shop served beer. "I have a lot on my mind right now."

"I noticed. You want to talk about it or nah?" Xavier took a swig of his beer. "Hold that. Crap, I'm next."

Xavier set his beer down and dried his hands on his jeans. His best friend's swagger was replaced with nervousness.

"Xay, you've got this. Your poems are good." His friend didn't show him a lot of his work, but the ones Andre had seen were decent.

Xavier nodded and pulled out his phone. "We're finishing this conversation when I'm done."

His friend sauntered up to the small platform that served as a stage. Xavier pushed the stool aside and claimed the mic. He cleared his throat and tapped on his phone.

"Hi, I'm Xavier, and I'm reading one of my poems tonight."

The crowd clapped politely, except for Andre, who cheered for his friend.

> I deliver packages for a living.
> That's not a euphemism,
> But if anyone's looking for a sugar baby, hit me up.

Someone whistled. Xavier winked at the crowd.

> I deliver packages for a living.
> Boxes of all shapes and sizes.
> Every time I walk up to the door,
> I wonder,
> Is this the box that will change their life forever?

> Will they open the door with a smile?
> Or tap their toes impatiently because
> I stopped too long
> To pet Pumpkin, the chihuahua
> Who greets me when I drop boxes off
> At the brownstone off H Street?

> I deliver packages for a living.
> They're not just pieces of cardboard
> Filled with stuff.
> They're some folks' link to the outside world,
> The folks who are too sick to leave their home,
> The mom stuck at home with kids who drive her crazy
> But she loves them.
> Am I right?

Xavier looked out at the crowd.

You know she loves them hellions. Moms need breaks, too.
Or the dude who's new in town,
And I'm the one they wave at every week.
Their only friend until they're
Brave enough to go out alone.

The next time you see your delivery guy,
Think of me,
Your boy, Xavier,
The one who keeps dog treats in my pocket
for Pumpkin.
I deliver more than packages for a living.

Xavier bowed as the small crowd in the coffee shop cheered for him.

"Woooo!" Andre shouted. Xavier had killed it.

"Holy fuck, that was nerve-racking," said Xavier when he returned to their table. Sweat glistened on his forehead. He grabbed his beer and chugged the rest of the glass. "I want to do it again."

Andre laughed. It felt good to laugh and not think about his troubles for a while. He was glad Xavier dragged him out.

"What? It was thrilling. You should try it sometime."

"No," Andre refused. "I'm not a poet and I don't like public speaking."

"I beg to differ." Xavier tapped the table. "You get in front of strangers and demonstrate warming massage oil. If you can do that, you can take open-mic night."

Andre's face fell. He doubted that would be happening anytime soon. Trixie was probably planning demos in her fancy new co-op by now. He hid behind his drink.

"You all right, bro? You've been moody lately." Xavier elbowed Andre. "When was the last time you and Ms. Trixie hooked up?"

"None of your business."

"Oh, that long, huh?"

"I don't want to talk about it." Andre picked up the tiny menu card on their table. "I'm ordering nachos. You want some?"

"You're not getting away that easy." Xavier caught the waiter's attention and ordered loaded nachos. "Another round?"

Xavier didn't wait for Andre to answer and ordered another pint for both of them.

"We had a fight." Andre sighed.

"What, she didn't say 'I love you' back?"

"Will you stop joking for a second? This is serious." Andre tipped his head and knocked back the rest of his beer.

"I'm just messing with you, man." Xavier's cool-dude vibe disappeared. "Talk to me."

"After dinner last week, right before I was going to tell her, she dropped a bomb on me. She's opening a shop at District Market. A co-op."

The waiter dropped off their beers. Andre swallowed the cold amber liquid.

"That's great news!" Xavier held his glass out for a toast, but Andre didn't return the gesture. "What did you do?"

"I told her she had to choose between Mama Hazel's or District Market." Andre shook his head, angry at himself. He'd handled it all wrong.

"Aw, man." Xavier shot him a disappointed look. "You messed up big time."

"Trixie's not even my biggest problem right now." Andre sighed. He told Xavier about Mr. Jackson and the upcoming meeting with their new landlord.

"Why didn't you tell me?" Xavier whistled. "That's fucked up."

"There's nothing we could've done. I talked to everyone in the building about buying him out. None of us had the funds."

Andre rubbed his face. It wasn't until the stubble scratched his palm that he realized he'd forgotten to shave that morning. How did everything go sideways? When things had looked bad, at least he'd had Trixie by his side.

"What does Keisha have to say about it?"

"I didn't tell her."

Xavier's jaw dropped. "She will kill you when she finds out."

"She won't. You're not going to tell her." Andre gave his best friend a hard look.

"She's going to find out when you have to vacate the premises. You are a brave man."

"I thought I could handle everything on my own. Keisha is going to kill me." Andre slapped his forehead.

"Keisha may be shorter and smaller than me, but I'm scared of her the same way I was of your mama." His best friend shuddered.

Andre laughed, remembering their childhood games that his sister always won. She knew how to get what she wanted. Their nachos arrived, and the two men dug in. Andre was glad to have something to soak up the two beers that he'd guzzled.

"Are your finances getting any better?" Xavier asked after

they'd polished off the nachos. "Maybe you can move to a different location."

Andre shook his head.

"The sexy pop-ups aren't working? From what I can tell, you've had a full house for every one this month."

"We're basically breaking even. With the Monday family dinners, I'm still in the red."

"Shit, man. I'm sorry."

The two men drank their beers and half listened to the performers on the makeshift stage. Andre wasn't sure how much longer he could keep Mama Hazel's open. After Andre downed his third—or was it fourth?—beer, Xavier broke their silence.

"Mama Hazel would want you to be happy. What would make you happy right now?" Xavier asked.

"I'm not sure." Andre truly didn't know the answer to that. He thought leaving DC, away from nosy neighbors and expectations, would free him. Make him happier. New Orleans did, for a little while. He didn't realize how much he missed his family and everyone until his mom became sick. Right now, he didn't have time to worry if he was happy or not. Too many people depended on him.

"Does Trixie make you happy?"

"Yeah, I think so."

"You think?"

"When we're together, I feel free. Don't have the weight of bills and responsibility on my shoulders. I forget about them for a while."

"Must be some good sex."

Andre threw a light punch into Xavier's shoulder.

"She's doing big things," Andre spoke into his half-empty pint glass. "I don't want to hold her back."

"Do you love her?" Xavier asked.

"Yes, I love her." Andre bit his lip. "But she didn't choose me. She chose District Market."

"She didn't choose District Market, you idiot. She chose herself and her dream. If you want to save Mama Hazel's *and* win the girl, you have to fight." Xavier grabbed his shoulder. "You can't run away when things get too hard."

Like how he ran away to New Orleans. Xavier didn't have to say it out loud. They both knew why he left. He couldn't handle the pressure of being Mama Hazel's boy and heir to the restaurant. Xavier had been kind enough not to call him out on it back then.

"Yeah, yeah. Thanks for the pep talk." Andre rolled his eyes.

"Now if you'll excuse me, that lovely lady over there has been making eyes at me all night." Xavier tipped his head at a woman lounging on an armchair on the other side of the room. "You mind if I say hello?"

"Go. Have fun." Andre waved him off. He could trust Xavier to always be Xavier.

Andre was glad to drop the conversation. All those beers made it too easy to get sucked into his feelings. He tried to concentrate on the amateur guitarist, but he wasn't feeling it. Maybe Xavier was right. He'd spent most of his life trying to make the people around him happy. It was time he did something for himself. Screw responsibilities.

Except he'd promised Mama he'd keep her legacy alive. A deathbed promise.

His chest tightened. His throat closed, making it hard to breathe. The empty space his mom left felt gigantic. Andre would not let his mother's memory disappear.

The walls started to close in on him. Andre needed to get out.

His legs wobbled as he stood up. How many beers did he drink? He'd lost count. He tried to wave at Xavier to say he was leaving, but Xay was completely focused on his new lady friend. Xavier didn't need a wingman.

Whenever he missed his mother, he baked a peach cobbler. Not just any cobbler, but her recipe that was passed down from her mother. That's what his mom did whenever he needed cheering up. He needed the comfort of sweet peaches topped with a fluffy, sweet dough.

Andre pulled a couple of twenties out of his wallet and set it on the bar. He waved good night to the coffee-shop owner. The handwritten recipe card was in the safe in his office. They'd just received a delivery of late-season peaches on Monday.

He'd have the entire restaurant to himself to bake the cobbler. Maybe even eat the entire thing without being forced to share it with Keisha. Mama Hazel's was only a couple of blocks away.

CHAPTER 32

"Any questions about what we've discussed so far?" Trixie asked after she passed around the final toy. The women were one of the liveliest bunches she'd ever taught. Though they'd asked for a pop-up, she kept the structure closer to one of her clinic classes. More education and less selling.

"So, tell me more about this Whimsy toy." Mrs. Moore winked. "I got a gentleman I want to try it with."

"Mrs. Moore! I didn't know you were seeing anyone," Keisha gasped.

"I might be seventy-two, but I still have needs!" Mrs. Moore laughed. "I'm courting a seventy-year-old, and I need to keep up before he finds himself a younger floozy."

"My man needs one of them cock-ring things," Mrs. Allen added. "That old thing is so wrinkled and floppy you'd think it was already dead."

The women cackled. Trixie grinned and glanced over at Keisha. The horrified look on Keisha's face was priceless. Keisha covered her ears.

"I'm never going to be able to look at Mr. Allen again." Keisha shook her head.

Trixie's chest bubbled with laughter. The last hour and a half with these women had been a laugh riot. They were sassy and didn't care what anyone thought of them. Watching them tease each other reminded Trixie of her aunties. How they sat in a circle at family gatherings to gossip and rib each other. Though if her aunties talked about sex around her, she'd be as embarrassed as Keisha was right now.

An ache grew in her chest. Andre and Keisha were so lucky to have an extended family who loved them for who they were. This was the first time since she'd moved to DC that she truly missed her family.

She'd call her mom soon. As frustrating as their conversations were, Trixie missed her mom's voice. There was so much to do to get her co-op store ready. Once it was set up, Trixie would send pictures to her family. Then they could see that she figured out what she wanted and actually succeeded.

"Trixie, which one of these toys is the quietest? I want to use it after my Roy goes to sleep." Mrs. Harris's eyes were twinkling. "If it wakes him up, he'll expect something from me."

"Ruthie," Mrs. Allen chided. "Give him some whiskey and Roy will sleep through the whole thing."

"Or turn off his hearing aids," Mrs. Moore quipped.

The women howled with laughter.

"I don't remember the last time I had so much fun," Mrs. Kim said. "I never talked to my friends about this kind of stuff. We've been missing out."

Everyone murmured in agreement. Trixie beamed. She didn't care if they bought any of her products. Helping them open up about their sexual needs was exactly why she loved doing this.

"If there are no more questions, I have a surprise for you!"

Their wrinkled, eager faces looked around the room. Mrs. Harris threw her hands up in the air.

"My prayers have come true," Mrs. Harris called out. "Tell me you hired a stripper, Keisha!"

"I didn't bring any dollar bills," Mrs. Moore called out.

"There is no stripper." Keisha's voice cracked as she tried to speak over the women. Their laughter turned into murmurs of disappointment.

"This has been the best night ever. I had no idea you were such dirty old ladies." Trixie winked at Keisha, who was hiding in the back.

Andre will kill me, Keisha mouthed to Trixie. Her face was flushed.

"Damn skippy!" said Mrs. Allen. "Just because we're old doesn't mean we're dead!"

"I'm sorry, but there are no dancers scheduled for tonight. If you really want dancers, we should take a field trip to my friend Reina's male burlesque club another night."

Cheers rang out. From the back, Keisha tapped her watch. Xavier could only keep Andre away for so long. They still needed to clean the kitchen and dining room.

"Where was I?" Trixie said, laughing. "Oh, yes. I made you all goody bags! You'll find some samples and a mini bullet. If there's anything you want to purchase, you'll get the friends-and-family discount."

While Keisha passed out the bags, Trixie quickly packed her sales kit. A few women approached her to place their orders. What she saw in these women was the future of the Boss Babes. Funny, confident, and still rocking their sex lives.

There were two knocks at the front door. Keisha peeked out between the blinds before letting Reina inside.

"Sorry to show up unannounced, but I have a surprise." Reina turned on her southern charm. "When Trixie told me about you young ladies, I didn't want to miss out on the fun."

"This is one of my best friends, Reina."

"Trixie told us about you. You own that nightclub," Mrs. Harris said.

"Yes, ma'am. Lucky Stiff. In fact, that's why I'm here. I thought y'all could use someone to escort you home." Reina swung open the door and six of her very handsome, very buff dancers walked in.

"Hallelujah! There is a God," cried Mrs. Harris. "This has been the best night of my life."

Trixie's mouth gaped. She was used to seeing Reina's burlesque dancers in a lot less clothing. However, their formfitting black tees and dark blue jeans were a beauty to behold. The dancers worked their magic as they introduced themselves to the older women. Reina ran over to Trixie.

"Sorry to burst in, but I knew you had to get out of here before Andre got back. Since Xavier isn't around to walk them home, I brought reinforcements."

"It's genius." Trixie hugged her friend. "When the Boss Babes grow up, I want us to be just like them."

"I can see it now. Raunchy Boss Babes!"

"What the hell is going on?!" A voice boomed through the room. Andre stumbled through the door, looking like he'd had one too many drinks.

The restaurant grew quiet, except for a familiar buzzing sound. Everyone turned to look at Trixie. She shook her head. It wasn't one of her demo products. All the batteries had already been re-moved and put away.

"Whoops, that's mine." Mrs. Kim clutched her bag to her chest, grinning impishly. She fumbled around in her bag until she found the vibrator's off switch.

The eerie silence sucked the happiness out of the room.

"We better go. Ready, boys?" Mrs. Harris slipped her arm through one of the dancer's. The other hand had a tight grip on her cane and her goody bag.

The subdued ladies made their way to the door.

"Thanks, guys!" Reina called after them. "See you tomorrow night."

"Andre, I can explain." Keisha ran up to her brother. He ig-nored her.

"You're selling sex toys to—to my mother's friends?" He stumbled toward Trixie. "To the women who treat me like I'm their own son?"

"Whoa, you need to calm down." Reina stepped between them. "They wanted to learn more about toys. So I offered to teach a class about postmenopausal female pleasure."

"It's one thing to hold pop-ups for your clients, but how dare you intrude upon these women? They just want to live a quiet life. Enjoy what they can of this neighborhood before all the hipsters take over." Andre's eyes narrowed.

"Obviously, you don't know them as well as you think," Trixie countered. She tapped Reina, who stepped aside. "Just because they're older doesn't mean they don't enjoy sex."

"I don't need confirmation that they have sex." Andre shook his head. "I know how babies are made. These are my mother's friends. They're my family."

"Don't write off their desires and needs because you think they're too old."

"Why do you have to go and change things around here? Not all change is good. Look at what's happening to this neighborhood." He waved wildly. "Everything was fine before you showed up. Mama Hazel's is fine the way it is. I'm fine."

"No, Andre, you're drunk," Trixie said softly, and reached out for him. "How about we talk about it in the morning?"

He pulled back from her. She froze. Trixie had never seen him this angry.

"Everything changed the day you stepped into our restaurant. Keisha is quitting school. Mrs. Chen closed her Chinese takeout place. The developers are turning this building into condos." The veins in his neck bulged as the words and spittle flew out of his mouth.

"Did you say condos?" asked Keisha, who had been quietly watching the exchange from the back.

Andre cringed. Trixie glared at him. Reina looked at the floor.

"Andre, what the hell is going on?" When he didn't respond, she turned to Trixie.

"I'm sorry, Keisha. He promised me that he'd tell you," Trixie apologized.

Keisha stomped up to the rest of the group until she was face-to-face with Andre. He tried to look away, his intoxicated bluster suddenly gone.

"Mr. Jackson sold our building," Andre mumbled.

The older women, who had stopped at the entrance, murmured in surprise. Keisha pursed her lips, fingers drumming on her thighs.

"Mama left me half of this restaurant. I know that you're run-

ning most of the day-to-day so I can study, but this is ridiculous."
Her voice cracked. "You promised to include me in big decisions."

"Mr. Jackson said he'd consider any offer the tenants had for
the building, but no one had the money. I talked to everyone. He
sold the building, and there's a tenant meeting with our new landlord tomorrow."

"You didn't talk to me, your sister. Why do you have to do
everything yourself? We're all family here. People would have
chipped in to help. We could have held fundraisers. Now it's too
late. All because you couldn't let go of your ego enough to ask for
help." Keisha took a deep breath. "I—I can't stay here. I might say
something I'll regret."

Keisha turned to Trixie and grabbed her hand. Trixie pulled
her in for a hug.

"I'm sorry. I should have told you," she whispered into Keisha's ear.

"Since you're here, Andre, you're on kitchen duty." Keisha's
voice was ice-cold. "Turn off the fryer and put the leftovers away.
I'll wash the dishes in the morning."

"Keisha, I'm sorry," Andre said weakly.

"Just because you're my big brother doesn't mean you're wiser
than I am." Keisha grabbed her backpack from behind the bar.
"I like change. It means we're living in the present and not the
past. I'm not coming home tonight. Don't try to call me until
tomorrow."

Keisha threw open the door. Xavier stood in the doorway.

"You were supposed to keep him away!" she yelled.

"I left him alone for only ten minutes! What happened?" Xavier
looked at Andre, who didn't acknowledge his presence.

Furious, Keisha ran out the door. Andre fell into a chair and dropped his head onto the table. Trixie wanted to run after Keisha, but her feet were glued to the floor. Everything was happening so fast.

"Come on, Trixie." Reina pulled her elbow. "Let's go. You don't need him. You have a store to open."

"You signed the lease for the store in District Market?"

"Yes." Trixie stood as tall as she could, daring him to belittle her decision.

"I should have asked for help," Andre said to no one in particular. "Everything is ruined and it's my fault."

Trixie blinked away tears. She didn't want to leave this way, but he wasn't in the right frame of mind to talk.

"I'll make sure he gets to bed," said Xavier softly. "Go on home."

"Come on. There's no point in talking to him until he sobers up." Reina grabbed Trixie's bags and dragged her out the door.

CHAPTER 33

"The emergency Bitchin' Boss Babes meeting is called to order," Reina declared as she topped off everyone's wineglasses. "Now also known as the Andre Is an Asshole meeting."

Trixie and Reina took turns recounting the evening's events.

"That boy needs some sense knocked into him." Josie was completely serious. "Say the word and I'll do it. I can kick his ass and not even mess up my 'fro."

"No, he feels bad enough already," Trixie replied. "I shouldn't have told him about the co-op the way I did."

She should have talked to him about it sooner to warm him up to the idea. Instead she chose the worst way possible to tell him, so that he had a reason to let her go. If they couldn't even communicate their feelings to each other, then they didn't deserve to be together.

"What will you do now?" Zoe asked.

"First I'm going to drink more wine." Trixie finished her glass and held it out for a refill. She had to try to forget about Andre. They'd given things another try, and it didn't work out. "Then I'm going to become the best sex shop in all of DC—with your help."

"Hell, yes!" Reina held out her glass for a toast.

"If you don't mind staying up late, I could use your help writing out my business plan for my new store." Time to move on. Trixie didn't need him to be successful. He was holding her back.

"I'll grab my laptop," said Zoe.

"We'll need more wine," declared Reina. "Write drunk, edit sober."

"Together, we Boss Babes can do anything."

Josie was right. All she needed in life were people who supported her and cheered her on when things got tough. The Boss Babes would never let her down.

TRIXIE BLINKED. THE sunlight was too bright for late October. She'd fallen asleep on the couch. How much wine had they drunk while working on her new business plan? She squinted and counted at least six empty bottles.

"I made some coffee," Zoe called from their kitchen.

"Thank God." Trixie wrapped the throw around her and joined her friend.

"When did Reina and Josie leave?"

"An hour before you woke up," Zoe replied. "I think you have a solid business plan. Might need some editing since we wrote it drunk."

"How are you not hungover?" Trixie's head pounded.

"I think you and Reina drank most of the wine. Hungry?" Zoe pointed at the breakfast bar.

On it were two plates with eggs, sausage, and toast. Next to them were mugs of Vietnamese-style coffee. The phin—single serving tin filters—on top of the mugs were still dripping the dark roast into the sweetened condensed milk at the bottom. She preferred the hot version this early in the morning. No đá—ice.

"Cà phê sữa!" Trixie hugged Zoe. "This reminds me of home. Thank you."

"After the late night, I think both of us need the extra caffeine."

Trixie grabbed the Sriracha hot sauce from the fridge before sitting down. Her stomach growled, reminding her that she hadn't eaten last night. She scarfed down her breakfast.

"Wow, that hit the spot." Trixie leaned back and rubbed her stomach. She removed the phin from the mug, setting it onto the upturned lid. The deep chocolate fragrance hit her nose as she stirred her coffee. "I can't remember the last time I had a cà phê sữa at home."

"Me neither. I had to google how to use the filters!" Zoe laughed. "My mom always said that no Vietnamese person in the States brews coffee this way anymore. They only do it in restaurants for the white people."

Zoe's parents would know. Phở-Ever 75 in Falls Church had made *Washingtonian* magazine's best cheap eats three years running. The restaurant was very popular with both Vietnamese and non-Vietnamese diners alike.

"I don't care how it's made. It's delicious." Trixie chuckled. "Do you hear that sound?"

"I think it's your phone. Let me find it."

"If it's Andre, let it go to voicemail. I'm not talking to him ever again."

"It's your mom." Zoe handed Trixie the phone.

"Má, sorry I haven't called," she said after putting her on speaker.

"Your dad had another heart attack. A big one this time."

Zoe gasped.

"Ba! When?"

"This morning. I called an ambulance, and they took him to the hospital. Lucy is driving me there to meet him now."

The panic in her mom's voice scared Trixie.

"Má, I'm coming. I'm coming home." She didn't care if her dad wanted her there. Trixie was going to New Orleans. "Oh my God, Ba."

"Don't pay for parking at the airport. It's too expensive." How could she think about frugality at a time like this?

"Zoe will take me to the airport, and I'll book the next flight." Zoe nodded.

"I'll have Lucy text you when we get to the hospital. We're almost there. I'll talk to you when you get here." Her mom hung up without their customary good-byes.

"I—I should go pack." Trixie shook as she picked up her phone.

"No, you sit. I'll pack for you." Zoe hugged her. "Go sit on the couch."

Trixie zombie-walked back to the couch she'd woken up on not long ago. When she'd left New Orleans, he was strong and healthy. Now he was in an ambulance, and she had no idea of his condition.

Her embarrassment and pride had kept her away from her parents for too long. Her mom always insisted that Trixie not spend money on a flight. But her mom would never ask her outright to come home. Deep down Trixie knew this. If she knocked on their door, her parents wouldn't have turned her away. Not even her dad. They loved her. Trixie didn't want to lose any more time with them. It was time to go home and mend their relationship.

CHAPTER 34

The room felt much too bright, even with his eyes closed. Andre's head pounded. He sat up, groaning. The pounding didn't stop.

"Xavier, open up! Is Andre in there?" The pounding continued.

He watched through a haze as Xavier slipped on boxers—wait, he slept naked?—and opened the door.

"Xavier, is Andre—" Keisha stopped when she spotted him on Xavier's couch. "You look like shit."

He deserved that. "I feel like it, too."

"I got a call from Mrs. Harris. There's smoke coming from Mama Hazel's."

"What?" he said loudly, and immediately regretted it.

"I told her to call 911, and that I was on my way."

"Wait, 911?"

"I had to find you first. Left my keys in the restaurant last night. I need your keys." She held out her hand. "Right now."

"I'm coming with you." Andre found his jacket and threw it on. He tried to ignore the pounding inside his head.

"Me too," said Xavier as he tossed on jeans and a shirt.

Mama Hazel's was only a few blocks away, but they could hear the commotion. There were sirens and a crowd gathered near the restaurant.

Andre broke into a run.

There was smoke billowing out of his mother's restaurant. Out of the door and windows. The air shimmered from heat emanating from the building. Andre stopped when he ran into a wall of heat. This couldn't be happening. Not Mama's place.

Flames shot out of the windows, cracking the glass. The fire easily spread to the bookstore next door.

"Sir, you need to move back!" A firefighter tried to escort him farther away. "It's not safe."

"But that's my restaurant," he said weakly.

"I'm sorry, sir, but you'll still need to move farther back." He pointed to a cordoned-off area.

"Andre." Keisha had caught up with him. "Come on. Let the firefighters do their jobs."

He overheard the firefighters as she and Xavier dragged him away.

"Chief thinks it started in the kitchen. Fryer or stove," a different firefighter called out. "We're going to need foam to control it."

The fryer! He'd forgotten to turn it off. Keisha told him before she rightfully stormed out of the restaurant. This fire was all his fault. Andre put his head in his hands. He'd fucked everything up.

He heard a sob before realizing it was his. Keisha wrapped her arms around him. He sobbed into her shoulder. They held each other as firefighters worked hard to douse the flames.

After what felt like hours, Xavier jogged over to them. "I heard the firefighters say they've got everything under control. The building will be saved."

Andre stared at the building, but all he could see was smoke and flames. Xavier sounded hopeful, so maybe he was right.

"Let's find somewhere for you Walkers to rest," suggested Xavier.

"I can't leave until the fire's out." Keisha shook her head, eyes glued to the building. She pulled Andre and Xavier closer to her.

"Excuse me, are you Andre Walker?"

The three of them turned around, the heat of the fire now on their backs.

Andre wiped his eyes, watery from the smoke. A tall Asian man stood in front of them. He looked familiar.

"Mike Chen? Is that you?" Andre studied Mike's expensive suit, which probably smelled like smoke. They weren't very close as kids, but had sometimes played pickup basketball together. Then Mike got into MIT and never came home. "Didn't you move to California?"

"I'm back in town for business. I was on my way down here—" Mike looked at the fire. "I'm sorry, man."

Andre sighed.

"I know my timing sucks, but we were supposed to have a meeting this morning," Mike said.

"We were?" Andre was confused. "The only meeting I had was with our new landlord."

"That's me. I bought the building."

"You're our new landlord?" Andre laughed bitterly. "I'm sorry about your investment. I guess it'll be easier to bulldoze for your condos."

"Who said I was building condos?" Mike made a disgusted face. "No way. I grew up here, just like you. This isn't the right time to go into details, but I have an idea for how to revitalize the neighborhood. But I need your help."

The three of them stared at Mike in disbelief. It was too much to take in.

"How about we talk later. You have more important things to deal with. And I promised my mom I'd drive her to see some old friends while we're in DC." Mike handed his card to both Andre and Keisha. "I know things seem bad right now. Hell, I didn't expect to find the building I'd just purchased on fire. But we can figure things out. Call me, please."

THE PAST SIX hours had been the longest in his life. Andre stood at the entryway of Mama Hazel's, now blocked by yellow caution tape. The fire chief deemed the entire building unstable but not a total loss. The charred remains of his mother's legacy were soggy and smoky. It was unlikely that anything could be salvaged.

Luckily, they were able to contain the fire before it spread to the buildings next to it, but everything in their building was gone. The hair salon, the bookstore, and worst of all, his restaurant. Everything that reminded him of his mom had disappeared under smoke and flames.

He dropped down onto the front stoop. Andre didn't know if he was supposed to laugh or cry. What the hell was he going to do now?

"It's going to be all right, Andre." Keisha sat down next to him. She held up a plastic shopping bag. "Hungry? Mrs. Kim made us some SPAM kimbap."

His stomach growled at the mention of their neighbor's Korean rice-and-seaweed rolls. He hadn't eaten anything since the nachos and beers from the night before. Oh God, his drunken rant. He'd been an ass.

"I'm so sorry, Keisha." He wrapped his arms around his sister. His only sister. "I was such an asshole."

"What's new?" She handed him a bottle of water and set a black plastic takeout container on her lap. "Mrs. Kim was worried about us, so she cooked."

"Food is love no matter where you're from." He tossed a roll into his mouth. "Wow. I'll never get tired of these. Remember when she bribed us with kimbap?"

"You mean she bribed me to tutor her son. I just shared them with you."

"Thanks for sharing these with me," Andre said softly. "Thank you for sharing Mama Hazel's with me, even if I was terrible at it."

"I'll accept your apology if you promise no more secrets."

"I promise. I'm sorry I didn't tell you about Mr. Jackson selling our building," he apologized.

"Or Mike Chen buying it," Keisha added.

"That I didn't know about. I'd only talked to his admin, and she was super secretive about everything."

"Can you believe Mike Chen is a tech millionaire now?" Keisha laughed. "He was so awkward and nerdy in high school. I guess it paid off."

"I bet you regret not going to prom with him now," Andre teased.

"Very funny." Keisha squeezed his hand. "I'm just glad you were at Xavier's and not sleeping in your office."

"You can't get rid of your annoying big brother that easily." His joke fell flat. Things could have gone very badly today.

"Ha. Ha. Not funny." Keisha punched him in the arm, the way she always did when he annoyed her.

"I've let down Mama." Andre rubbed his hand over his head. "Everything she worked for is—just gone. And it's my fault."

"You're not God. Why do you think you can control everything, and when it doesn't go your way, that it's your fault?"

"The fire chief did a walkthrough after you went home to search for Mama's recipes. She said the fire started in the kitchen." He swallowed hard. "It was the fryer. I was so upset and drunk last night that I forgot to turn everything off."

"No, Andre." Keisha shook her head. "Xavier turned everything off last night. I texted him to be sure. It's not your fault."

"I failed Mama. She had only one wish before she died." His voice cracked. "And now it's in ashes."

"It's okay. We can start over."

"With what? We have nothing. No savings. Piles of bills. Insurance will barely cover replacing the equipment." This was the first time he'd said it out loud to Keisha. Why had it taken him so long to tell her that they were in over their heads?

"Don't forget about Mike Chen. He said he had a plan. Even if he doesn't want to rebuild, we'll make it happen. I don't know what the new Mama Hazel's will look like, but I have faith in us Walkers. We're tough."

"Maybe you are. Being tough was what got me in trouble." Andre could finally admit that he didn't need to be tough all the time.

"Maybe Trixie can introduce you to the woman who owns the co-op. She might have connections." Hope lit up Keisha's face.

"I doubt Trixie will talk to me after last night."

"You messed up big time, big bro. Call her and apologize."

The least he could do was try. He patted his pockets for his phone. Andre shook his head.

"My phone must have fallen out of my pocket at Xavier's last night. He dragged my sorry butt to his place."

His sister pulled out her phone and dialed Trixie. Keisha paced as she waited for Trixie to pick up. Even as a kid, his sister had boundless energy. Always moving, no matter what she was doing. The only time she stayed still was when Mama taught them to cook.

"No answer." Keisha frowned. "I'll text her."

She tapped on her phone. A moment later it buzzed.

"Was that her? What did she say?"

"Oh no." Keisha covered her mouth. "Trixie's dad had a heart attack this morning and was taken to the hospital. She's at Reagan waiting to board her plane home."

"It must be serious if she's flying home. Mr. Nguyen hasn't spoken to her since she left New Orleans. He's not a fan of Trixie's career."

"That's awful." Keisha's face lit up. "Go to New Orleans. She's going to need you."

"But what about this?" He gestured at the burned building.

"Andre, do you love Trixie?"

He thought about how she charmed everyone at family dinner, the way she easily shook off hecklers during her pop-ups, and how her face lit up when she talked about opening a store. She was the best thing that ever happened to him.

"Yes." He stood up. "Yes, I love Trixie and I need to go to New Orleans."

"I knew it!" Keisha clapped her hands.

"What about the fire and Mama Hazel's?" This had been his mess, and he should clean it up.

"Go. I'll be fine. Xavier and everyone else will help. I'll meet with Mike and keep you updated."

Keisha wanted to take the lead now. He liked the sound of it. His sister was resourceful, and she wouldn't have to clean up alone. She was right. Everything would work out somehow.

Hope swelled in his chest. It'd been too long since he felt this hopeful about anything.

"Can I borrow your phone to book my flight?"

"Yes, but—" Keisha wrinkled her nose. "You stink. Let's go home and get cleaned up before you beg Trixie for forgiveness. I'll book your flight while you shower."

"Good point." Andre was covered in soot and ash. He probably smelled even worse.

She hooked her arm through his and they began the walk back to their house. He followed her lead. For the first time in his life, he let his little sister take care of him.

CHAPTER 35

"Oh, Má." Trixie tiptoed into her dad's hospital room to find her mom asleep in a chair. She found a blanket and covered her up. Her dad was also asleep. Ba looked so fragile with so many machines hooked up to him.

She'd taken a Lyft from the airport straight to the hospital. And convinced the nurse to let her into the coronary care unit even though there was a limit of one visitor at a time.

"Trixie, is that you?" Her mom sat up and rubbed her eyes "You got here fast."

"How could I not?"

"I hope you didn't pay too much for the flight," said her mom.

To anyone else, it might have sounded like nagging. This was how her mom demonstrated her love, by worrying about Trixie's finances.

"Don't worry, I found a last-minute deal," she lied.

"Good. Did Lucy text you?"

Trixie nodded, her throat tight. She'd spent most of her flight demanding updates from her sister. They were monitoring Ba—as the next couple of days would be the most crucial—in case he had another heart attack. All they could do was wait.

"You have been a bad daughter. It's been a long time since you called." This time her mom was scolding her.

"Well, I'm here now." She wasn't ready to tell her about Andre and what a terrible mistake she'd made getting back with him.

"You look tired. Did you eat?"

She laughed. "Yes, Má. I grabbed some food at the airport."

"Expensive and bad-tasting. Text your sister and tell her to bring the leftover fried rice from home."

"I will."

They ran out of safe topics to talk about, and the silence between them grew, interrupted by small beeps and whirs from her dad's monitors.

"Are you back for good?" Her mom finally spoke but didn't look at Trixie.

"No, I signed a lease in DC. I'm opening a store." Even at twenty-five, she wanted her mother's approval. She wanted to hear her say *I'm proud of you*. But Viet parents didn't say that to their kids. "But I can postpone it and stay until Ba is better."

"Won't you lose money? You'll still have to pay rent." Her mom shook her head. "Stay for a few days and go back to your store."

"I wanted to tell Ba the good news." Trixie smoothed out his blanket. "I want you—him to be proud of me. I'm tired of not speaking with him."

"Ai-ya," her mother said, and sighed. "We are proud of you."

"You are?" Why did she have to pull teeth to hear her mom say those words? "Even though I'm not a lawyer like Lucy or an engineer like Binh?"

"From the moment you were born, I knew you would be different. When you were three, I brought you to an astrologist. She confirmed my beliefs and warned me that you had a long, hard journey before you'd find your way."

"She probably said that about everyone." It was vague enough to apply to almost anyone. Trixie didn't hold too much faith in Vietnamese astrologists.

"You have changed."

She motioned for Trixie to turn in a circle. After a couple of turns, her mom stopped her.

"I think you've finally found your way. This store makes you happy."

"It does, Má." Trixie nodded. Finally, her mom understood. "It's what I want to do. I wish Ba would understand that."

"He worries about you. As the youngest, you were more American than your brother and sister. It's harder for him to understand why you'd want a job that didn't guarantee to earn a good living. He doesn't want you to worry about money like we did. When we came to the United States, we didn't have the luxury of taking a job that made us happy. When we had the three of you, we worked harder to provide for you."

Trixie blinked the tears out of her eyes. This was the most intimate conversation she'd ever had with her mom.

"You and Ba sacrificed so much for us—for me. I want to make you proud, but I'm not book smart like Binh or Lucy. I'm not cut out to be a pharmacist."

Her mother clicked her tongue. "Who said you are not smart? You are."

"But I flunked out of school and—"

"How could you not be smart? You're my daughter." Her mother patted her chest and grinned. "Most important, you want to help people, like your father."

Trixie nodded. Her father was generous with his time and energy. What he lacked in money, he gave in his skills. After Katrina hit, he helped neighbors and friends rebuild their homes.

"I do want to help people," whispered Trixie. Then more confidently, "I am helping people right now."

"What you're doing is important. Sex makes people happy and helps them stay married." A girlish giggle escaped her mom's lips.

"Má!" Trixie couldn't believe her mom was talking about sex. "That's oversimplifying it, but yes. That's what I do."

But it was a start. That's all she needed to talk to her mom about the work she was doing at Bedroom Frenzy. What she wanted to do when Happy Endings opened. Her mom reluctantly accepted a hug from Trixie.

"What about Ba?"

"I have given your father more than enough time to come around. It's time to make some changes. If he doesn't try to understand what you want, I'll stop cooking, and he'll have to eat ramen every day." Her mother laughed at her own joke. Her father hated packaged ramen, because it reminded him how little he'd had when he came to the United States.

"You talk about me like I'm already dead."

"Ba!" Trixie grabbed his hand. "How are you feeling?"

"My chest hurts," he whispered.

"Because you had a heart attack—now you know why you need to eat brown rice instead of white rice." Má softened her tone. "You're not allowed to die on me yet, old man."

"Have to tell you something." Her dad tried to squeeze her hand.

"You should rest. I'm not going anywhere."

"You're a good daughter, Trixie."

"Ba." Trixie was at a loss for words. He was talking to her again! "I've been a terrible daughter. I should have come home sooner."

"No, you needed to find your own way." Ba squeezed her hand. His grip was weak, but he didn't let go. "You are so much like me. That's why I'm harder on you."

"How?" Trixie looked at his weathered face, dark from his years working odd construction and fishing jobs until he found a permanent position managing a seafood processor.

"My parents didn't want me to come here. They knew if I left Vietnam, they might never see me again."

"But you came anyway." This was all new to Trixie. Ba didn't talk about his family very often.

"I wanted to make my own life. Not the life they wanted for me."

"You and Mom were brave to come here with hardly anything."

"You are brave, too."

Trixie nodded, blinking rapidly to keep the tears at bay.

"You need to make your own life, not do what is expected. But this road is hard. I wanted you to do something else that had more security."

"I'm doing okay, Ba. It's not engineering or lawyer income, but I'm making enough to take care of myself."

"I know. Your mom told me."

So he was keeping up with her through her weekly calls with Má. Deep down Trixie knew that he wouldn't give up on her.

"I love you," Trixie whispered.

"Humph" was his only reply, but she could see the love in his eyes.

Those three words, *I love you,* were not words her parents ever said to her. As a kid she got upset when her dad never said it back.

As an adult, she realized how hard it was for her parents to express their love in that way.

"I'm glad you're home. I missed you." Ba squeezed her hand again.

With that simple declaration, the tears she'd been holding back slipped out. Everything would be right between them. She and her dad still had a lot to figure out, but they'd gotten over the biggest hurdle.

There was a commotion outside her dad's room. Suddenly the door flew open.

"Andre, what are you doing in New Orleans?"

"Sir, you cannot be in here." A Black nurse wearing scrubs with cats stepped behind him. "Only family can visit CCU patients."

"Trixie. Mr. and Mrs. Nguyen." He nodded at her parents. "I'm sorry to—"

"Sir, if you do not leave, I will call security." The nurse was fuming. "You're disturbing *heart* patients."

"I'll wait for you outside. Please give me a few minutes to talk to you," he pleaded as the nurse dragged him out.

"Was that your old boyfriend?" Her mom was bewildered. "Are you back together?"

"Yes. No. I mean, we were, but—it's complicated." Trixie held on to her father's hand. She didn't want to talk to Andre. Her parents needed her.

"Your dad needs to rest," her mom said after a few moments.

"Of course." Trixie bit her lip.

"I'm hungry. Can you buy me something from the cafeteria?"

"Okay, Má." Trixie nodded and hid a smile as she accepted the excuse her mom offered her. She'd give Andre five minutes to talk and send him back to DC.

CHAPTER 36

"Trixie!"

Andre ran across the waiting room, ignoring the *sssh* from the other people seated there.

"Keep your voice down," she whispered. "Please don't make a scene."

He looked out and found many faces glaring at him.

"I'm sorry," he said quietly. They seemed to accept his apology and returned to their magazines and phones.

"Can we talk?" When she hesitated, he added, "Please, Trixie. Hear me out."

"Five minutes. That's all you get." She sat down next to a gray-haired woman knitting a bright green heart.

"Don't you want some privacy?" He pointed to some empty chairs in a corner.

"Not after the way you kicked me out of your restaurant. These people don't know who you are, so why should it matter." She tapped on her phone and showed him a running timer. "You're wasting time."

"You tell him, girl!" a woman behind him called out.

Focus on Trixie, he told himself. Ignore everyone else.

"Look, I've never been good about sharing my feelings. I—"

"Maybe you start with 'I'm sorry,'" the woman knitting whispered loudly.

"Are you sure we can't move—"

Trixie pointed to her phone. He was running out of time—and fast. Andre took a deep breath. Now or never.

"I was an asshole and I'm sorry."

"Was that so hard?" He gritted his teeth at the knitting lady's commentary.

"I was arrogant and couldn't see past myself to accept help from the people who loved me the most. Especially you." He paused but thankfully no one else interrupted him.

"I used your family as an excuse to break up with you the first time—"

"He dumped me with a Post-it," Trixie told the woman next to her, who had put away her knitting for a better distraction.

"No!" Half the room gasped.

Andre waved his hand to quiet the waiting room.

"I pushed you away when you needed me the most. Twice. Last night at the bar, I said a lot of things I shouldn't have. You only wanted to help me, but I couldn't let you. My ego got in the way because I wanted to be the one that saved the restaurant. I thought if I was the one who saved our corner of Northeast, then it would make up for leaving when Mama needed me the most."

"Tell her you love her." The knitter nudged him with her elbow.

"I do love you, Trixie. But I didn't treat you right. I made your dream of opening your store less important than saving the restaurant. I wanted to be the top priority in your life, but I didn't do the same for you.

"I love you, Trixie, with all my heart. You make me a better man and I don't deserve you. You are so smart, incredibly brave,

and compassionate. I admire how you take an awkward topic like
sex and have taught so many women how to embrace their bodies.
You are brave and strong.

"You bring so much joy and love into everything you do. I
know you don't need me to be successful. But I can't imagine life
without you. If you'll have me back, I promise to always share my
feelings with you and treat you like the goddess you are. And un-
limited rum and Diet Cokes."

He glanced at her phone. The timer had run out, and he'd gone
over.

"Trixie? Please say something."

"You're such an idiot." A tear fell down her cheek. "You just
shared your deepest feelings with me and all these strangers."

"Yeah, I did. So, what do you say?"

"You're a hard man to love, but I love you, too. I'll give us one
more try."

"Don't fuck it up, man," said a burly white guy.

"I'm going to do my best not to," Andre replied.

"Kiss! Kiss! Kiss!" the room chanted.

Trixie giggled and put her arms on his shoulders. Andre waited
until she was ready. He knew now that he couldn't control every
aspect of their relationship.

"Kiss him! Kiss him!"

"I guess we better give them a good show," Trixie whispered,
and pulled him in for a deep kiss.

Cheers erupted around him. He heard the knitter sniffle. "This
is so beautiful."

"I can't believe you followed me to New Orleans," she said when
they finally broke apart.

"I couldn't lose you again, Trixie. I had no other option."

"But how did you know I was here?"

"I called every hospital in a thirty-mile radius to see if they'd admitted your dad. Do you know how many Kevin Nguyens live in New Orleans?"

But all those calls had been worth it. He'd found Trixie and got back the woman he loved.

EPILOGUE

Three months later, January

W elcome to Hazel's Kitchen, where food is love." Keisha raised her champagne glass. "Andre, we did it!"

"I can't believe it," replied Andre as he raised his old-fashioned to meet her drink. "This was all you, Keisha. Cheers."

There was so much to be grateful for with tonight's grand opening. Keisha's meeting with Mike Chen went better than anyone expected. His mom's stories of their childhood neighborhood had made him nostalgic. When he'd learned how gentrification was pushing out his friends and neighbors, he had to do something. His work in Silicon Valley had earned him plenty of money but not enough time to enjoy it.

Mike's mother convinced him to invest his money into their old Northeast neighborhood. Instead of turning the building into condos, he proposed creating a co-op. He offered a rent-to-own agreement to any tenant who wanted to return after the fire damage was fixed. Once they worked out any hiccups with this building, Mike wanted to do the same with the rest of the neighborhood.

Keisha handled most of the restaurant redesign. For one of her business class assignments, she'd designed the concept for a new restaurant. When she presented her ideas to Andre, he had been blown away. His sister had studied the current market and trends to combine them with their mother's vision. She'd created a more modern menu served around a communal table to encourage people to put away their phones and talk to their neighbors. Her professor was so impressed, she'd introduced Keisha to a local culinary incubator, which had offered them a grant and helped them reboot Mama's restaurant.

Three months later, they stood inside Hazel's Kitchen. The two of them had grown up in this restaurant kitchen. The original recipes would always be Mama's, but Keisha and Andre added their mark to the restaurant. Keisha's was the new design and vision for the restaurant, while Andre continued to experiment with new dishes and introduced southern-style craft cocktails to the menu.

The grant they received from the incubator covered several months' rent. Winning the grant and Mike's "disruption" of the neighborhood had given the restaurant plenty of publicity. Combined with their agreement with Mike, they would be able to continue their mother's legacy of free community dinners every Monday night. Once a month, the dinners would be turned into an open forum to bridge the gap between the long-established community and the newcomers.

"Thanks for finally listening to me." She winked at him. "I knew you'd come around sooner or later. Sisters are always smarter."

"I'm not going to argue with you about it, because tonight is a celebration," he joked, "but brothers are definitely smarter!"

"You wish." Keisha waved at a group of people who entered

Hazel's Kitchen. "It's my professor! She's walked me through the pros and cons of switching majors."

"Go, I'll keep an eye on everything."

Keisha left him at the bar to go greet her professor and guests in their newly opened restaurant. Hazel's Kitchen was a true collaboration between the two siblings. He'd finally realized how wrong he'd been to leave Keisha out of their family legacy.

"Andre Walker, this place is beautiful. Your greens better be good!" Mrs. Harris leaned on her cane as she approached, cackling. "I suppose I should give up the rivalry now that your mother has passed, but she's probably yelling at me from up there."

"Mrs. Harris, you called me Andre." He was shocked.

"Well, that's your name, isn't it?" She gave him an exasperated look, but her eyes were teasing.

"I'm glad you made it." Andre kissed her cheek. "Thank you for coming."

"Of course I'd come to your grand reopening. You're like a son to me, Andre."

He beamed. Andre couldn't think of a better way to celebrate his mother than with Mrs. Harris and the entire neighborhood— the extended family he'd perhaps never deeply appreciated until after the fire.

Her eyes darted around the room, taking it all in. "This reminds me of my family dinners growing up. It's a bit more bougie than our tiny table with barely enough room for my parents and us six kids, but it was full of love." The insurance company had declared the entire building a total loss, but they'd been able to salvage a few tabletops and the front door. Those pieces had been refinished to make their new family table.

Xavier had dug through the wreckage to recover the MAMA HAZEL'S DINER sign. It was mostly intact, except for burnt edges and half the *r* in *Diner* had broken off. Before the soft open, the three of them hung the sign over the bar as a reminder of their roots.

Best of all, Trixie's co-op was around the corner. He brought her lunch every day and tried to help tend the store while she ate. He would never be as good as Trixie when it came to selling vibrators, but he'd made some pretty big sales.

Mrs. Harris placed a hand on his shoulder. "Hazel would be so proud of you and Keisha."

Andre nodded, his throat suddenly tight. He blinked quickly to rid the wetness from his eyes. When did it become so dusty in here?

"Where's that gal of yours?"

"Mrs. Harris, you look great!" Trixie walked up right on cue, having detached herself from the Boss Babes gaggle across the room, and hugged the elderly woman.

"What's this I hear about you going off to San Francisco?"

Trixie laughed. "Not for a while yet. I want to get the boutique off to a solid start, but I'll be starting a program there in the summer."

This time when Trixie had decided she wanted to go back to school, Andre had helped her make a pros and cons list instead of pushing her into it. She'd applied and been accepted to a program out there to become a certified sex therapist.

"Well, we'll miss seeing you here. Especially your Andre. I knew you two were meant to be. With a little help, of course." Mrs. Harris winked.

"Of course you did." Trixie grinned at Andre. "You know, the food scene there is amazing. The chefs there are doing some innovative things. I might have to convince you to take some time off and come with me."

The promise in her eyes had his heart beating faster already. A vacation with Trixie sounded like heaven.

"Now, where can a woman get some food around *here*?"

Laughing, he escorted Mrs. Harris to the new restaurant's centerpiece, the long wooden table loaded with large plates. There was a tower made from squares of yellow cornbread, plates piled high with fried chicken, ceramic baking dishes stuffed with macaroni and cheese, plus a Dutch oven filled his now popular collard greens braised with kimchi. Half the seats were already taken by neighbors and new friends.

Andre drank in the sight. A year ago, he never could have imagined so much happiness in his life. He was a lucky man.

TRIXIE WAS STILL watching Andre navigate Mrs. Harris around the table as the older woman pointed to the greens and no doubt started claiming her own recipe's superiority again.

"Wow, she keeps on moving," said Keisha as she approached and handed Trixie a Diet Coke. "You know our family community dinners have never been the same since your private class. Mrs. Harris has been talking about her vibrator nonstop!"

Trixie laughed. Of course she did.

"You outdid yourself here, Keisha. Restaurant and hospitality management won't know what hit them!"

Keisha was thriving in her new major. The college had even given her class credit for her real-life experience running Hazel's Kitchen.

"Thank you for helping us launch the very first DMV Dialogues night. And recruiting the Boss Babes to help."

Each month a community expert would be brought in to open a discussion about various topics. Tonight's topic—to Andre's dismay—was safe sex for the senior community. Sexually transmitted infections were rising for that demographic, Trixie had learned during her classes. No one wanted to talk about it, but with Mrs. Harris's help, they had a good crowd tonight. The delicious food was a big draw, too.

"How could I say no? Everyone here has helped me with so much, I want to do my part for the community, too."

"Next month Zoe is coming to teach basic hand-sewing skills. Can you believe that my friend and I can't even sew on a button?" Keisha scanned the notes on her phone. "I just need to line up speakers for the rest of the year."

"You're a natural at this. I talked to the Babes and we'd like to officially invite you to become a Boss Babe."

"Really?" Keisha squealed. "Yes, I am in!"

"Good. I'll text you details about our next meeting." The two women hugged. Keisha had blossomed the past few months. She would be an asset to the Boss Babes.

Keisha's phone rang. "I have to take this. Start without me?"

Trixie took a deep breath and inhaled all the mouthwatering scents floating in the air. As expected, the guests were milling around the buffet, set on the restaurant's giant reclaimed table. She was too nervous about her presentation to eat.

"Hungry?" Andre said behind her.

"Maybe after." She shook her head. "This is my first time speaking as a sex-educator-in-training. I hope I don't forget anything important."

"Are you sure? I had Zoe pick up some gỏi cuốn for you." He

handed Trixie a cardboard takeout container. "From her parents' restaurant."

Summer rolls were one of her favorite Vietnamese foods. The hand-rolled rice wrappers were filled with rice noodles, cucumber, shredded lettuce, pork, and shrimp. They were light enough not to upset her stomach.

"Thank you for thinking about me." Trixie turned to kiss him. "You're the best."

"I expect payment via sexual favors later," he whispered.

"You got it." She kissed him again. "Now go back to the bar and make me one of your new fancy cocktails before DMV Dialogues starts."

"As you wish."

"Wait, one more kiss for the biggest celebrity chef in the Northeast. I'm so proud of you." He was happy to comply.

"I couldn't have done it without you, Trixie. I love you."

"I love you, too, Andre."

Trixie looked around the room. She was surrounded by new friends and neighbors. Her Boss Babes were here to support her. Almost three years ago, she had come to DC with barely anything. Now she had found something she never thought she could.

Happiness.

A NOTE FROM THE AUTHOR

No matter what time of day or how many times a week my mom calls, she always asks, "Ăn cơm chưa?" When I left for college, her question annoyed me, because of course I'd eaten. Between her care packages and the campus cafeteria, I was in no danger of starving. The freshman fifteen I gained was proof.

Eventually I realized this simple question, which bookended our long-distance conversations—yes, she asked multiple times during each phone call—was my mom's way of telling me she loved me. Food is how my mom showed love, much like how Andre's mother fed her neighbors' stomachs and souls. The giant pot of phở my mother simmered on the weekends or the watermelon she cut into giant cubes were physical declarations of her love. As my kids tell me when they visit our family in Louisiana, the bowls of freshly sliced fruit are always filled to the brim.

So when my mom asks, "Ăn cơm chưa?" it's a reminder that she wants my belly to be as full as her heart.

I didn't set out to write a foodie romance, even though food plays a vital role in my heritage. I wanted to write characters that reflected my life and not those stereotypical Asian characters we often see in mainstream media. I wanted no virginal lotus blossoms or evil dragon ladies in any of my stories. (Even if I have a soft spot for Lucy Liu's ruthless character in *Ally McBeal*. Every time I hear the opening bars of "Wicked Witch" from *The Wizard of Oz,* I fondly think of badass Ling Woo.)

What more dramatic way of smashing a stereotype than writing Trixie, a Vietnamese American woman who educates women on pleasure and sells sex toys? As tough as it is for Viet families to say *I love you*, it's even harder for us to talk about sex, never mind pleasure. As in we only hint at the first and never, ever, discuss the latter. Well, I'm talking about it with as many people who will listen!

I hope this book changes how you talk about sex and pleasure. I'm probably preaching to the choir here, but let's normalize talking to our friends about it. Believe me, they want to know when you've discovered a vibrator that rocks your world as much as they want to hear about the café that makes the best bánh mi you've ever tasted. Both are pleasures we need more of.

Now that I've made you hungry all over again, try out the recipes I've included in the next section. Then join my newsletter at thienkimlam.com for even more food and sex toy talk.

RECIPES FROM *HAPPY ENDINGS*

COLD BREWED VIETNAMESE ICED COFFEE (CÀ PHÊ SỮA ĐÁ)

Traditionally, Vietnamese coffee (hot or iced) is made with a special filter, called a phin. I was never patient enough with those, except when I watched it drip, drip, drip next to me while I slurped a hot bowl of restaurant phở. My cold brew method is much easier. With a little bit of preparation, you can cold brew enough coffee to get you through 4 or 5 hot afternoons. I dare you not to drink more than one a day.

Ground New Orleans–style coffee, such as Café du Monde or
    Community Coffee New Orleans Blend
Filtered or bottled water
Sweetened condensed milk
Ice

SUPPLIES
A large jar or pitcher that holds at least 16 fluid ounces (I reuse spaghetti
    sauce or applesauce jars)
Paper coffee filter and funnel

1. Make the cold brewed coffee: Fill a clean jar about a quarter full of coffee grounds. The measurements will be different depending on the jar you've chosen. Using a ratio of 3 parts water to 1 part coffee grounds, slowly add filtered or bottled water. This is going to make a very concentrated coffee, so you'll want to use good-tasting water.

2. Place the jar in the refrigerator and allow the coffee to brew for at least 4 hours. Overnight is recommended.

3. When you're ready, strain the coffee using a funnel lined with a coffee filter (or similar). Because the brew is ultraconcentrated, it should be very dark. If you're not making iced coffee right away, the strained cold brew can be stored in the fridge for up to a week.

4. Make the iced coffee: Add sweetened condensed milk to a tall glass until the bottom is coated. Now add a little bit more. (Isn't that scientific?) If you want to measure, start with 1 to 2 tablespoons. Add more if you like it sweeter.

5. Fill the glass two-thirds full of cold brewed coffee. Stir to dissolve the sweetened condensed milk, until it's no longer visible in the glass.

6. The coffee will still be fairly dark. Taste and add more condensed milk to taste. Add ice (or coffee ice cubes). Stick in a straw and pretend you're at your favorite Vietnamese restaurant. Enjoy the buzz!

PANTS-ON-FIRE APPLETINI

Andre was smart to create cocktail pairings for Trixie's toys. Pants-on-Fire is inspired by two very popular flavors of Blow Me massage oil. Warning: this drink is delicious but potent.

Ice
1.5 oz apple-flavored vodka
1.5 oz sour apple liqueur
.75 oz Goldschläger
Sliced green apple, for garnish (optional)

1. Add ice to a cocktail shaker. Combine the ingredients and shake until well mixed.

2. Strain into a martini glass and garnish with a sliced green apple if desired.

3. Drink up!

Tip: One shot glass holds 1.5 oz.

Thien-Kim Lam writes stories about Vietnamese characters who smash stereotypes and find their happy endings. A recovering Type-Asian, she guzzles cà phê sữa đá, makes art, and bakes her feelings to stay sane. Thien-Kim is also the founder of Bawdy Bookworms, a subscription box that pairs sexy romances with erotic toys. She's been featured on NPR, BBC America, and NBC. Connect with her at thienkimlam.com.